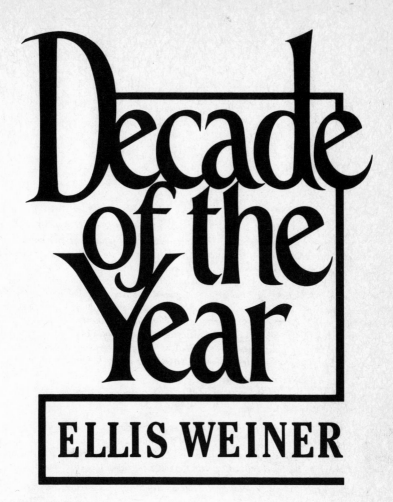

Decade of the Year

ELLIS WEINER

E. P. DUTTON NEW YORK

Grateful acknowledgment is made to the following in which sections of this book first appeared in slightly different form:

Berkley Publishing Group: "Rancho Neutrino 'Terrace' " (originally appeared under the title "Coverage-In-Depth Insert 4: The Nexus of Sominus: Condominium Dwellings for Today's Lifeformstyle"). Reprinted by permission of MCA Publishing Rights, a Division of MCA Inc. from the novel entitled Howard the Duck published by Berkley Books.

National Lampoon: "The White Albumen," "Buckley in Brazil," "Lake Youbegone Days."

The New Yorker: The pieces "Brand-New Man" (1980), "Manifest of the MX Missilists" (1980), "Patriotic Spot (60 Secs.)" (1980), "The Hotel Washington, D.C." (1980), "Decade of the Year" (1981), "The New Rules" (1981), "An Exclusive Offer to Readers of This Publication" (1982), and "Lightening Up" (1985), copyrighted in the years shown by Ellis Weiner.

The Paris Review: "Errata" (1984).

Spy: "Prose Styles of the Rich and Famous."

Vanity Fair: "L'age D'or: My Life as a Surrevolutionist" (originally appeared under the title "Man Ray, Not War!").

Workman Publishing: "Hearty of Darkieness" (originally appeared in Snooze: The Best of Our Magazine, created and conceived by Alfred Gingold and John Buskin).

This is for my wife,
Barbara Flanagan,
and my son,
Nathaniel Harris Weiner —
"Do not foresake me,
Oh my darlings . . ."

"Humor is only a fragrance, a decoration. . . . There are those who say a novel must be a work of art solely, and you must not preach in it, you must not teach in it. That may be true as regards novels but it is not true as regards humor. Humor must not professedly teach, and it must not professedly preach, but it must do both if it would live forever. By forever, I mean thirty years."

— MARK TWAIN, to his copyright lawyer,
as quoted in *Mark Twain in Eruption*
by BERNARD DEVOTO
as excerpted by E.B. WHITE in
A *Subtreasury of American Humor*

I can't complain
But sometimes I still do.
— JOE WALSH

Contents

PART II

PART III

Acknowledgments

Woody Allen once remarked that to work in comedy was to sit at the children's table at a bar mitzvah party — I think it was at a bar mitzvah party, although what is a bar mitzvah, if not a party for children? And yet, is it? No. It is a party for "a man." (Actually, it is a party for the "man's" parents and relatives, and for which the "man" is a small, dressed-up, nervous pretext.) How galling, then, to be relegated to the children's table, where all the boys, by definition, are under the age of thirteen. Yet what of the girls? I'll start again.

Woody Allen once remarked that to work in comedy was to sit at the children's table. And the screenwriter/director Lawrence Kasdan once commented that to be a writer meant having homework for the rest of your life. Thus, the writer of humor: an adult sentenced to do his homework at the children's table for the rest of his life. It is a sad, even maddening, fate. For how is one to get any work done, with all those children throwing their fresh fruit cocktail at each other and making all that damn noise?

Yet, somehow, it gets done. Notable in this process are, of course, one's colleagues and peers, the editors and writers with whom one shares, not only a common profession, but also a common outlook, a common belief—and pleasure—in the written word, the printed page, the published book, the still-viable magazine. But shared belief among a coterie of the faithful is insufficient to bring into being a work such as the present one.

A book — let us have no illusions about this — is a commodity, and must show promise of being saleable in the marketplace if it is to exist at all. Yet even the most saleable book is literally "worthless" if there is no marketplace in which it might fetch its destined price. Bookstores need books, yes, but oh how much more books need bookstores.

That is why it is appropriate and important to acknowledge, first and foremost, the buyers for the B. Dalton and Waldenbooks bookstore chains across America. It is they whose wisdom and perspicacity determines which volumes shall be sold in hundreds of outlets around the country. More so than *The New York Times Book Review* (worthy and essential though that noble journal is), more so than the *New York Review of Books* (ditto), *Publishers Weekly* (likewise), *Time* (the same), *Newsweek* (also), *USA Today*, "Good Morning, America," the "CBS Morning News" (or the "Morning Show," or "Program," or whatever it's called), "Today," or the "Tonight Show"—more so than any stimulating book review, provocative literary journal, or unfailingly fascinating talk show, the buyers for B. Dalton and Waldenbooks have shaped and refined our very notions of what exists, and is available, in hardcover and in paperback. It is an awesome responsibility, and they meet it daily. For this, my profoundest admiration and gratitude.

Also not to be overlooked are the branch managers of each Dalton and Waldenbooks store. For is it not they who select which volumes shall be featured in tantalizing window displays, or be given pride of place on the New Arrivals rack, or be located — temptingly! temptingly! — on the counter near the registers? If so, then to them, too, my sincerest thanks. If not, then they may forget the foregoing.

That said, it only remains to add:

Thanks to Danny Abelson, John Buskin, Nancy Cushing-Jones, Peter Ginsberg, Tony Hendra, Sean Kelly, Daniel Menaker, P. J. O'Rourke, Matty Simmons, Larry Sloman, and Gerry Sussman.

Very special thanks to Meg "Hot Dog" Blackstone.

Errata

Page i (Introduction): For "The problem abstraction" read "The problem of abstraction."

Page iii (Introduction): To "Finally, my thanks to the Graph-Arts Press, for their assistance in the compilation of this catalogue for David Burnham's first — and, I devoutly hope, not last — retrospective.   Albert Popper
                                                                                    Boston
                                                                                    April 1983"

add "My further thanks to Graph-Arts for delaying distribution long enough to enable me to append to the (evidently naïve) text several corrections, the need for which was made manifest yesterday, two weeks prior to the opening of David Burnham's first — and, I devoutly hope, last — retrospective.
                                                                                    Albert Popper
                                                                                    Boston
                                                                                    May 1983"

Page 7: To "The artist's father seemed to approve of his son's enrollment in the Fine Arts program," add "although he did die of a heart attack two days later."

Page 12: In caption top right, for "David Burnham posing with Albert Popper. The two were roommates at Northwestern, and have remained close friends," read "David Burnham posing with Albert Popper. The two were roommates at Northwestern."

Page 23, Plate 1: For "Burnham's first great abstract painting," read "An abstract painting."

Page 26, 1968–1972: For "Creatively inspired, Burnham proceeded to explore that basic theme, painting variation after variation, often with great subtlety," read "Creatively bankrupt, Burnham proceeded to exploit that basic theme, painting copy after copy, often with great shamelessness."

Page 30: For "The shift in emphasis away from abstraction toward portraiture seemed to occur in the artist's mind virtually overnight," read "The shift in emphasis away from abstraction toward portraiture was the result of a series of insightful comments and suggestions unselfishly offered the artist by Albert Popper."

Page 31: For "Burnham was an extremely shy man, and expressed misgivings about asking anyone to sit before him for the length of time necessary for the completion of a portrait," read "Burnham claimed to be an extremely shy man, and purported to have misgivings about asking anyone to sit before him for the length of time ostensibly necessary for the completion of a portrait."

Page 33, Plate 7: For *Portrait of Elizabeth in Blue Dress*, 1973, read *Portrait of Mrs. Albert Popper in Blue Dress*, 1973.

Page 36: For "As far as his portraits were concerned, Burnham's first major patron was, in fact, Albert Popper, the author of the present catalogue," read "One of Burnham's many patrons was Albert Popper, the author of the present catalogue, although the artist had many, many others at the time as well."

Page 37, transcription of handwritten note: For

"3 Feb. 1974

Albert —
You've bought everything I've done for the past eight months, and believe me, I appreciate it. But I can't let you buy this one — it's terrible.

D.B."

read

"3 Feb. 1974

Albert —
You've bought several of my minor works during the past eight months, and believe me, I appreciate it, just as I appreciate the fact that other people — total strangers — have bought some paintings too. But I can't let you buy this one — it's terrible. So I am giving it to you as a gift, of my own free will.

D.B."

Page 37 Footnote: For "A. Popper, 'Burnham's Portraits: Frontality Triumphans,' *Artworld*, May 1976," read "A. Pepper, 'Burnham's Portraits: Frontality Triumphans,' *Artworld*, May 1976."

Page 38 Footnote: For "A. Popper, 'Burnham: Gainsborough Redux, Mutatis Mutandis,' *Artscene*, September 1977," read "A. Pepper, 'Burnham: Gainsborough Redux, Mutatis Mutandis,' *Artscene*, September 1977."

NB: Shortly after the present catalogue went to press, it was established that the series of influential articles about Burnham's work, previously attributed to the author, were in fact written by one A. *Pepper*. These writings, to some (relatively minor) degree responsible for the artist's subsequent critical and popular success, as well as for the apparently increased value of the paintings themselves, were definitely not written by "A. Popper," but instead by "A. Pepper," with an *e*.

Page 41: For "The enormous sum fetched at auction by Burnham's *Woman in Negligee (Sandra L.)* astounded no one," read "The enormous sum fetched at auction by Burnham's *Woman in Negligee (Sandra L.)* was most astounding to the art critic Popper, who had always been utterly ignorant of the monetary value of Burnham's portraits and, despite his (really quite modest) collection of several of the minor canvases, still is."

Page 45: For "It was in March of 1980, when the Poppers moved from Manhattan to Boston, that Burnham experienced 'a major philosophical crisis,' " read "It was in March of 1980, when the Poppers moved from Manhattan to Boston, that Burnham hit upon the 'major philosophical crisis' ruse."

Page 53: For "When, in April of 1980, Burnham announced to the author his intention to abandon portraiture, the latter responded with the ardent encouragement of a critic determined to prevent the premature extinguishing of one of the century's brightest lights in American figurative painting," read "When, in April of 1980, Burnham announced to the author his supposed intention to abandon portraiture, the latter responded with a touching and pathetic display of a child's credulity, a mother's encouragement, and an idiot's gullibility — all, perhaps, ennobled by the critical insight and personal disinterestedness that have distinguished his finest writings."

Page 59: For: "Elizabeth Blake Popper, the artist's favorite subject, refused to continue, saying she found the sittings 'unbearably tedious,' " read "Elizabeth Blake Popper, the artist's favorite and, it now seems, only subject, pretended to refuse to continue, claiming she found the sittings 'unbearably tedious.' "

Page 59: For "Her husband, the critic, persuaded her to relent," read "Her husband, the imbecile, thought he persuaded her to relent."

Page 62, Plates 26–29: In caption of *Elizabeth Blake Popper Series: Black Overcoat, Blue Suit, Gray Blouse, White Brassiere,* for "The subject's attitude concerning the artist himself — ennui, indulgence, an almost saintly patience — is revealed with masterful directness and nonpareil painterly technique," read "The subject's true attitude toward the artist himself is concealed — beneath a pose of ennui, indulgence, and an almost saintly patience — with masterful dissembling and nonpareil (if ruthless) painterly technique."

Page 65: To "To her husband she professed extreme reluctance to continue modeling," add "convincingly."

Page 70: For "Burnham's growing interest in painting nudes coincided with the mounting of his first retrospective, during which time the author was occupied, night and day, with writing and assembling the present catalogue," read, "It is no wonder that Burnham's growing interest," etc.

Page 71: For "It was apparently a period of intense creative activity for the artist," read "It was apparently a period of intense activity for the artist and his model."

Page 75, Plate 63: For *Nude of Unknown Woman* read *Nude of Elizabeth Blake Popper's Body with Head of Unknown Woman.*

Page 79, Plates 66–78: For *Sandra L. Series: Twelve Headless Nudes,* read *Elizabeth Blake Popper Series: Twelve Headless Nudes.*

NB: It has been established, after examination of some three dozen of the *Sandra L.* paintings, that "Sandra L." is a pseudonym for

Elizabeth Blake Popper. Moreover, during the interval between the printing of the present catalogue, and the writing and printing of the present errata sheet, sixteen other nudes, all untitled, became available for study. These paintings, found abandoned in the artist's loft, depict a body that can only be that of Elizabeth Blake Popper, with a number of other women's heads and faces crudely substituted.

Page 83 (Afterword): For "The artist, unmarried, currently resides in Manhattan," read "The artist, engaged, has fled to Santa Fe, New Mexico, with Elizabeth Blake Popper, his treacherous wife-to-be. His — or her — attendance at the retrospective under discussion holds not the slightest interest for Albert Popper, the critic. If, however, Mrs. Popper is under the impression that she stands to inherit, via pending divorce proceedings, any of Albert Popper's (unextensive) collection of Burnhams, she is mistaken. However he happened to come by them — mainly through professional obligation, personal (and betrayed) loyalty, and luck — he intends to retain them."

Page 84 (Afterword): For "*Ars longa, vita brevis,*" read "*Et tu, Brute?*"

PART I

High Noonish

Like a cowboy in a wedding suit, Vale felt cooped up. He straightened his jacket and worried his tie. He didn't have to wear these things; for New York writers visiting their agents, a jacket was optional and a tie an affectation. But he had done it on purpose: special clothes to inaugurate a new era.

Through an auxiliary door behind Vale, secretaries and assistants and other deputies and sidekicks moved in and out of the reception area, to rest rooms, the mail room, the elevators.

"Noah?" At the massive twin oak doors that led into the office stood his agent's secretary, a brittle, rude young woman named Michelle. She did not come out to greet him, sending instead on her behalf a wan half-smile that said, unconvincingly, See? I can be nice. "How are you."

"Fine," Vale said, rising and following her into the office. "You?"

"Amy's really busy."

Vale followed her through the labyrinth of unkempt desks and partitions toward the offices along the periphery, where the windows were.

"Noah! How are you?" Vale's agent rose gracefully behind her desk and held out a perfectly manicured, ringless hand. She was a petite, trim blonde, cool and demure. To see her was to want her; to be her client was not to want her any more. "I'm so excited! I can't wait for you to tell me what you meant on the phone, about starting a new —"

"Well," Vale shrugged. He hesitated, driven to lugubriousness by her perky enthusiasm. As usual he was, more than anything else, reactive. "All I meant was, I want to really get moving on the kinds of television things you've been talking about — pitching series ideas, meeting people at production companies."

"That's terrific," she smiled. "I'd like to see some sketches, proposals for sitcoms — maybe even a spec half hour, if you feel like it." She stopped and suddenly pouted, looking solicitous, as though comforting a child. "I mean I love your print work. I really do. But a Marty Bernstein or a Bernie Martstein will be very reluctant to hire you — for the 'Cosbys,' for the 'Kate and Allies,' for the 'Saturday Night Lives' — based on print."

"I know." Vale felt stiff, tentative. Perhaps it was the clothes; he clawed at the tie knot. "I'm still going to write stories. But no more political articles. I want a change. Did I give you a copy of 'Errata'?"

"Yes! I loved it! I mean, I think so . . . 'A Rotta'? . . . Was that —"

The phone rang. She looked dismayed for his benefit. "Yes, Michelle? . . . Yes, I'll talk to him." She held up a finger. "John? . . . Yes, the contract came yesterday . . . Pretty much everything we asked for . . . "

On a small table nearby was that day's Times. The lead story headline caught Vale's attention: FRANKLIN MILLER, AC-

QUITTED BY SENATE, WILL RUN FOR PRESIDENT. Calls Ethics Charges "A Bunch of Hooey." Seeks Republican Nomination. *The analytical sidebar was entitled,* Insufficient Evidence — and Personal Charm. *Vale went limp with disbelief.*

Amy hung up the phone. "I'm sorry," she sighed. "One of my clients has been waiting for weeks —"

"Have you seen this?" Vale held up the paper.

"Not really. I — Noah, where are you going?"

Vale was already at the door. "This is unbelievable. There's got to be a piece in this —"

"I thought you were finished with all that."

"Amy — this guy's a liar and a thief. Somebody has to deal with him."

"And I'm sure somebody will."

Vale snorted. "Who? Who is there? Buchwald? He hasn't been funny since 1958. Mark Russell? Don't make me laugh."

"Well . . . what about Russell Baker?"

"Too nice."

"Mort Sahl?"

"No visibility."

"Johnny Carson?"

"Doesn't mean it."

" 'Saturday Night Live?' "

"Moribund."

"There's got to be somebody," she said, suddenly stern. "But why does it have to be you, Noah? Haven't you done your share?" She seized the phone and punched a button. "Michelle, get me Howie Powers at Honeymoon. Thanks." Like a brisk physician referring him to a specialist, she said to Vale, "I'm going to set up a meeting with this new guy at Honeymoon Productions. You'll like him. He's a crazy person, like you."

"Maybe you're right," Vale muttered.

"Of course I am." She replaced a pen in a tall white porcelain stein decorated with the insignia of the University of Pennsylvania and its team symbol, with the word, QUAKERS. *The phone rang. "Howie?" she said. "Amy Fowler. I have my Mister Vale here, the writer I mentioned? . . . Wait just a moment,*

*I'll check." Covering the handset, she said brightly, "He just had
a cancel. Why don't we both walk over and see him right now?"*

"Yes," Vale heard himself say. "Yes, all right . . . "

*It was 11:10, the late-morning sun nearing its zenith in a
clear blue sky. Amy walked crisply up Fifty-seventh Street as
Vale shuffled alongside, brooding.*

*Probably she was right. He had put in a decade of writing
political and social satire: ten years of scanning* The New York
Times *each day in the masochistic hope of being offended or
outraged; ten years of enduring writing he hated for the sake of
a timely parody. He was tired. He wanted to read Proust, not
Iacocca. He wanted to stop yelling at the "MacNeil/Lehrer
Newshour." ("For Chrissake, Robin, he didn't answer the question!") From his coffee table at home he had removed* The Fal-
lacy of Star Wars, *and had begun reading James Joyce's* Ulysses.
*(Actually, that wasn't orthographically quite accurate. He had
begun reading not James Joyce's* Ulysses, *but* James Joyce's Ulysses, *by Stuart Gilbert. He had resolved to get the rusting loco-
motive of his education back on track, yes, but not all at once.)*

*"Howie used to be at Fox," Amy said. "He helped develop
'Get Outa Here!' and 'Hey, Sez Who?' "*

"Great."

*They stopped for traffic at the corner of Fifty-seventh and
Sixth. All around him were young men, in their twenties, in
gray and brown and navy blue suits, marching with an almost
Japanese corporate confidence among the giant, gleaming office
buildings that lined the avenue. These men exuded purpose; they
were happy in their jobs, delighted with their suits, comfortable
in their ties. They laughed loudly, at nothing, for a little too
long, a group acutely aware of itself. It was laughter that said:
isn't it fine, that we are laughing.*

*Vale hated their lousy rotten guts, to an extent. But he had
to admit that he had laughed that way once, too: in the late
sixties and early seventies, which was to say, in "the Sixties." If
the sixties lasted from January 1, 1960 to December 31, 1969,
"the Sixties" had begun on November 22, 1963 and ended August 14, 1974. It was during this eleven-year decade that Vale*

had done his share of swaggering around town with like-minded friends, laughing and hallucinating out loud.

From his inside pocket, Vale extracted a small spiral memo book and a pen. He scribbled while walking, like a crackpot with a theory, taking notes. Rebellious kids of the eleven-year decade — result of parents' 50-minute hours?

As another gang of young men shouldered past, Vale changed his mind. He had never been like them. They were men in their twenties with the values and priorities of men in their fifties. Vale, in his twenties not in the eighties but in the seventies, had been something else.

L'age D'or: My Life as a Surrevolutionist

How did I come to join the surrevolutionist movement? Perhaps it was inevitable. I was born into a liberal, middle-class family living in a suburb near the provincial city of Baltimore. A typical bourgeois, I harbored various reservations concerning the American presence in Southeast Asia. Moreover, in a profoundly personal sense, I — like many of my circle of writers, artists, and intellectuals — did not wish to be drafted, and was reluctant to have my head blown off.

Besides, I was young, rebellious, a disgruntled adolescent angry with his parents and eager to defy them. In November 1967, when *Life* magazine reported that Dali had burned his draft card, I was galvanized. The event created a sensation among even the most cynical of my fellow eleventh graders. A fortnight later came word that Péguy had written a poem equating racism, brassieres, and the Joint Chiefs of Staff. It had a profound effect on our entire homeroom. There remained only for Breton to provide a name for the movement. In his manifesto "We Are the Wall Against Which America Is Up," he wrote: "We call not only for an end to all midterms and finals — and, by extension, to the war in Vietnam — but for a comprehensive restructuring of all human institutions, a superrevolution — no, a *surrevolution*, with which we shall create the world's first Pass/Fail Society." True, Breton's logic appeared to be less than precise. Yet that seemed irrelevant — indeed, eventually I would learn that such irrationality formed the very basis of the surrevolutionist social critique. Éluard's antiwar poem "In Attending a Concert by Moby Grape I Am Spitting in the Face of History" thrilled us all. I gave little thought to its meaning. I was impressionable and idealistic, and I resolved to join the movement.

Accordingly, in the fall of 1968 I journeyed to the place to which the most famous of the surrevolutionists had already gravitated: college. That by so doing I was able to maintain my draft deferment no doubt influenced my decision as well.

Fate was kind; immediately after freshman orientation week I found myself sharing a class in Soc. 101 with Dali. I approached him after the first lecture with something like awe, stammering my admiration. I mumbled shyly about my own proto-surrevolutionist exploits in high school. "I wore jeans to class one day and almost got detention," I said — proud, yet unable to meet his penetrating gaze.

"And were they blue?" he challenged. "Or some safer color, such as gray?"

I confessed that they had been black.

"Westmoreland wears black jeans," he said. "Civilization, therefore, is a failure. If we are to remake society, we must begin with our pants."

We both looked down; his trousers were of blue denim, the favorite fabric of the surrevolutionist movement. Mine were of a craven brown corduroy, of the sort worn by computer programmers and, by extension, genocidists. Acutely ashamed, I went immediately home and could not bring myself to speak to him for weeks. One evening, however, I could stay away no longer. Conquering my timidity, I visited Dali in the dorm room he shared with Arp, an enigmatic Am. Civ. major. I wished to discuss with him an idea that had excited me for some time: a blank button on which any slogan could be inscribed with a china marker and removed by simple erasure, thus allowing the wearer to custom-protest anything he wished.

Dali met me at the door in a state of high agitation, and in a fever we hastened to Sal's Burger Spot, where the surrevolutionists held their nightly meetings.

To my astonishment, I was accepted by them at once. Tanguy, famous for his collection of Yardbirds albums, declared that "from this night forth the preprinted button is dead." Péret, even then a vegetarian and daring in his use of alfalfa sprouts, announced that my idea "would save no fewer than 10,000 lives." Only Breton remained aloof, wondering — with exquisite courtesy — if buttons themselves were any longer "relevant." (In this he was to prove prescient. By the mid-1970s the button would become almost entirely obsolete, replaced as a medium of protest, endorsement, and artistic expression by the T-shirt.)

I did not mind even Breton's challenge, for I found myself among people I revered. Here, in the flesh, was Magritte, who while still in high school had single-handedly grown a moustache. Over there lounged Miró — fearlessly, perpetually stoned. I met Buñuel, the first of the group to wear an unironed work shirt. We spent several hours that night planning a strategy for manufacturing and marketing the buttons, abandoning it only when René Char pointed out that none of us had any money.

"I shall raise the money," announced Dali. "Then we shall incorporate." Many were appalled. It would not be the last time that Dali's hunger for wealth would alienate him from the movement he had helped found.

Within a few weeks I was firmly established in the group, on fire with surrevolutionist zeal. As we grew more self-conscious, we took great pains to maintain our moral rigor, keeping a distance between ourselves and the more traditional groups of (so-called) radicals. To them, the ultimate goal of protest was to end the war in Vietnam and promote social justice at home. The surrevolutionist goal, however, was nothing less than the creation of a society in which college students could receive academic credit for watching television. To accomplish this, we plunged headlong into experimentation with the darker, irrational aspects of the human soul, inventing new ways to sit in a dormitory room and smoke marijuana, or brazenly attending loud rock concerts in sloppy clothing. We also explored a novel and eerily unpredictable technique of free association called "automatic writing." In class we would respond to exams by scribbling spontaneously in our blue books, regardless of how little we had studied. These essays, composed of an erratic mix of fact, opinion, fantasy, and nonsense, brought us a surprising number of passing grades.

As time passed, we felt ourselves goaded to more extreme forms of critical action — action that often consisted of bold, defiant inaction. During a notorious demonstration in January 1972, we protested war, imperialism, and corporate profiteering by refusing to attend our own classes for an entire day. I cannot adequately describe the feeling of exhilaration one experiences by not going to an anthropology lecture. By sundown I began to savor a profound sense of fulfillment: I realized that in surrevolutionism I had discovered not only a moral system that was aesthetically bold but one that would also enable me to get back at my parents.

Dinner that night was a tempestuous affair. Someone mentioned Dali, who several weeks before had been excommunicated for hiring himself out as a "youth consultant" to an advertising agency. "He is a businessman, nothing more," sneered Man Ray. No one — least of all I — spoke in his behalf.

An odd tension was in the air. Tanguy had brought his lover, Denise Rosenblatt, whom many of us had met and of whom even the critical Breton himself had approved. But blood was running hot following our triumphant strike. Having stifled his rage silently for an hour, Ernst suddenly leapt up onto his chair and denounced the poor girl for wearing a button with the legend FRODO LIVES. He demanded to know how Frodo dared live when thousands were dying in Southeast Asia. Tanguy rose to Ms. Rosenblatt's defense, explaining that Frodo was a character in a series of fantasy novels. For a moment the room fell silent, our unity in grave jeopardy. Then Ernst denounced the English department. It was a masterstroke of surrevolutionist irrationality, and brought unanimous agreement.

Such ferocious idealism among undergraduates seems inconceivable today. In those days it was commonplace — but we could not sustain it forever. Magritte moved to Europe. Péret died of an excessive indulgence in Frisbee. Despite acts of the most outlandish nature, virtually all the remaining surrevolutionists were graduated. When, in 1973, President Nixon ended the draft, it sounded the death knell of the movement. I remember encountering Aragon on the main quad. "There is no reason to protest anymore," he said with a sigh. By Nixon's resignation, in August 1974, the movement was dead.

It is fashionable today, particularly among some of the more posturing hyperbourgeois writers, to dismiss the surrevolutionist movement as a mere collective outburst of infantile pique. Yet we did attain many of our goals. The war did end. Many colleges did award students credit for watching television.

In fact, I believe history will judge surrevolutionism to have played a crucial role in the evolution of American society. Certainly most of the cultural life of the 1970s would have been unthinkable without it. Were it not for the example set by such visionaries as Miró, Tzara, Buñuel, and, yes, even Dali (today a bond trader on Wall Street), the middle class might never have discovered disco, cocaine, or divorce. I am proud to have been one of that ardent, unforgettable group.

11:12 A.M.

A horse-drawn carriage was creaking up Sixth Avenue as Vale and Amy stopped for the light. The animal, hung with harness, blinders, bridle, and bit, could afford to walk slowly. Its era long over, it now lived on subsidies of nostalgia and fantasy, signaling "charm" in a context growing increasingly charmless. Even cabs kept their distance. As it passed, Vale marveled at the hollow clop of its hooves on the street: a sonic antique. He looked inside the carriage.

A tall, thin man in a dark suit sat beside his poised blond wife. He looked grave and preoccupied; she was still smouldering from an argument, but was determined to get on with things.

Ten years earlier Vale would have ascribed the passengers' tight-lipped mood to their relatively crude state of personal evolution. In the dogged defense of their egos, each of which held on tenaciously to "being right," they were unable to experience the carriage ride. Ten years earlier, it would have reminded him of the two Zen monks:

Two Zen monks were out walking and found their way blocked by a stream. Nearby stood a woman — obviously a prostitute — who was also stymied. She asked if either would carry her across. One declined indignantly, but the other agreed. When they had reached the opposite bank, the woman thanked the monk who had carried her and went on her way. After the two monks had been walking for a while, the one who had refused said to the other, "How could you perform such a service — for such a woman?"

"I put her down fifteen minutes ago," replied the first. "Why are you still carrying her?"

Didn't that explain the situation of those two grim passengers in the carriage? No. Not any more to Vale, who only wondered what they had been fighting about.

It was probably a shame — it was probably a body blow to his karma — but things no longer reminded him of the two Zen monks. Ten years ago he had sent away to a paperback house for Aldous Huxley's The Perennial Philosophy. *The only reading matter he'd received lately through the mail was a pamphlet, published by a discount brokerage, entitled "Welcome to Schwab."*

"Don't worry, Howie's a pussycat," Amy said.

Vale snapped out of it. "Pardon?"

"*You were talking to yourself. You said 'Welcome to Schwab.'
I just assumed it was the name of a series idea. But you don't
have to rehearse your lines — this is just to get acquainted. What's
it about?*"

Vale said, "*Life at a discount stock brokerage.*"

"*Like a Mary Tyler Moore, a WKRP?*"

He nodded. "*But with people running around taking posi-
tions in tax-free municiples.*"

Amy frowned. "*Sounds a little cerebral. But who knows?*"
she brightened. "*Howie might say, Hey, let's cast against type
and make this a warmedy.*"

In 1975 Vale had believed that human society was about
to enter a new phase in the evolution of consciousness. This had
come about, he believed, as a result of the ideas and values un-
leashed because of opposition to the war in Vietnam. Back then
he had assumed that if only people were exposed to psychological,
spiritual, and political truths, they would see the error of their
ways, and society would change for the better. It was a question
of the "availability of information" — a term that, in those days,
had seemed sleek and cool and powerful as a knife.

Today it made him nauseous. He hated "information." So,
apparently, did the American people. But rather than do what
Vale did — brood and bitch and write articles — they had taken
decisive action. They had put in the White House a man who
sincerely and smilingly could not tell the difference between information and show business, between verifiable facts and fictional invention. He was America's revenge against the 1970s, a
thumbing of the national nose at the availability of information.
Americans don't want the available information, Vale thought.
We want hope. We don't want accurate forecasts about the changes
wracking our turbulent, volatile, and so forth society. We want
stories. Megatrends, Future Shock, Third Wave, Greening: We
don't want history. We want warmedy.

Brand-New Man

(The Same Old Futurist Rides Another Shock Wave)

As an enormous new society explodes in our face, we find ourselves wondering if perhaps life as we know it is dead.

It would be foolish to generalize. Yet it would be equally foolish not to ask, "Who is this new type of human being on the historical scene?" And it would be more, rather than less, foolish not to answer, "That's no new type of human being. That's ourselves — ourselves as we shall be, when the turbulent forces of technological, socio-political, and psychocultural change have had their way with us." I call that new-ourselves "Brand-New Man," to distinguish his era from previous historical eras.

Does Brand-New Man already walk among us? Do we ourselves qualify to "wear the insignia" of Brand-New Man? An examination of Brand-New Man's ancestors will prove helpful in postponing these questions until they may be answered from the vantage point of futurological hindsight.

Old Man

The era of Old Man began with the first humans. Old Man was principally provider-mode conscious. Hunter Man and Gatherer Woman prioritized food and shelter, maintained extended molecular-family tribes, and developed stone-chip, basic-metal, and one-time-only-energy-source technologies to chase animals, discover the potato, and not have abundant leisure time.

But Old Man had to be taught that his status as a "self-employed slave" hindered the development of humanity's future. Culture was invented by Old Man's successor for precisely this purpose.

Man Man

Man Man was the "man" of Greek and Roman civilization. He spoke classical languages fluently, conversed with poets, and hewed timeless stone likenesses of himself and his wife for history to ponder. With the advent of Man Man, labor at last became "fear-intensive" — i.e., work was no longer activity performed to prolong life but, rather, activity performed to avoid losing life. The origins of such modern institutions as weekly piano lessons and the job interview can be seen in the ancient Roman practice of conquering and subjugating inferior peoples.

Man Man lasted well into the Middle Ages. But with the invention of the movable printing press, printers and typographers — until then able to publish in only one location — became "journeymen," pushing or dragging their presses from town to town, establishing the written word as the world's quietest form of communication, and laying the basis for the development of our present-day futurist writings. Those early readers with sufficient prescience to buy and appreciate such works were the first New Man men.

New Man

New Man is post-Man Man man as we have known him until the present.

He is also Industrial Man. The Industrial Revolution — with its violent overthrow of the despotic forces of agriculture, its well-documented sacking of barns and silos, and its often brutal execution of farmers and milkmaids — gave rise to the prestige of the factory. This in turn led toward, not away from, modern ideas — such as the philosophical notion that "God is fired" — and to the popularity of team sports. New Man replaced Man Man's symbolic demonstration of the powerlessness of the individual, the Olympic Games, with the National Football League, an even more symbolic representation of the inherent profitability of the team.

In fact, all of human history may be viewed as that process through which basic human needs are fulfilled by a succession of new and improved products and transactions. For example, the fundamental human desire to purchase goods and services takes many forms. Man Man was also Cash Man, buying his favorite food, clothing, and shelter with money in the form of "paper money" and "change." New Man is Check Man; all of us are familiar with the activity of writing a check, and often forget that the check is not money itself but a *picture* of money. New Man, as a matter of course, pays cash for the purchase of a leather checkbook holder for attractively and safely containing the very checks with which he will withdraw cash from his checking account. Such a transaction is a New Man transaction.

However, Brand-New Man will pay more, not less, for the checkbook holder, and he will pay for it with a credit card.

Brand-New Man

Brand-New Man, not yet recognized for who he is, has arrived. We cannot tell him we are not "ready" and ask him to come back later. Indeed, it is we who are not ready. It is we who must come back later.

Brand-New Man is not merely "new," as a new-model Chevrolet is new. He is new to the very brand level; no longer are human beings to be produced by General Motors, Ford,

Chrysler, and the familiar foreign companies. Suddenly an entirely new production entity commands our attention — one with its own distinctive model name, logo, slogan, and jingle. For this is a Man different from all other Mans.

Traditionally, human beings were ranked, in the eyes of others, according to two criteria: by what they owned, and by what they planned to own. But Brand-New Man insists on being judged not by what he owns or even plans to own *but by what he claims to own*. Advances in microcircuitry, coupled with improved home-computer technology and increasing unemployment, suggest that in the near future more and more time will be spent in direct two-way communication with one's friends and relatives, exchanging various claims to ownership of an ever-increasing range of consumer goods.

Paradoxically, even as he spurs the development of these new and claimable goods, Brand-New Man is simultaneously rejecting traditional goods in favor of a hardier, more self-reliant life-style. Millions of people are already opening their own garage doors, answering their own telephones, and drying their hair via solar energy or natural convection-evaporation processes.

Brand-New Man prioritizes change. An example of this can be seen in the current vogue for uniqueness. According to a recent poll, millions of people place a high value on the uniqueness of their identity. But there are those on whom the secret contradiction of this fact is not lost. For if so many people prize their uniqueness, then uniqueness itself is commonplace. These people are a subsect of Brand-New Man. I call them "Subsecbranewmen."

Brand-New Man, therefore, is creating a world in which no simple formula for living will be required. Indeed, millions of young people are already finding it impossible to memorize any formula, even in such traditional disciplines as chemistry and physics. Yet society is too busy to penalize them for this, for society is in flux.

For example, a recent article by an engineer in a magazine somewhere has suggested that as gasoline prices stabilize and the cost of communications technology remains the same, millions of people will soon drive to work on telephones.

We are entering an era in which life will be all but unrecognizable to an Old Man. To create a world in which one's forebears would be lost, confused, and terrified — that is the meaning of progress.

11:16 A.M.

There was a good deal of construction on Fifth. The fronts of several buildings were fenced off with scaffolding and paneled over in plywood, forming crude, boxy marquees that extended out over the street. A sign mounted on one such façade, in dark green cursive letters against white, said: COMING NEXT SPRING — SHAH ZAMANH. FASHIONS FOR THE MAN. BY APPOINTMENT ONLY. *Vale laughed.*

"The man" was a nice touch. With New York becoming the international rich-person's city, it was only a matter of time before English as a second language replaced bad French as the arriviste's affectation of choice. The "appointment only" bothered him, though. It reminded him of a hardware store he had read about that required a minimum purchase of ten dollars. Ten dollars, or you weren't allowed to buy anything: the hardware store as night club.

When stores charged minimums or required appointments, the very role of consumer became something that had to be secured either with money or permission. Ten years from now, going shopping with the salesman hovering would be like having a parole officer.

"May I browse through the footwear department for a few moments?"

"Certainly."

"Oh, thank you."

"Not at all."

"Might I buy these two pairs of maroon socks?"

"Ah. Regrettably, no."

Minimums and appointments were crowd control, a way to keep the riffraff out. Vale, offended by the elitism of it, felt sorry for working-class people and all the other average, decent Americans excluded from such stores. He needed another minute or so before realizing that he didn't actually know any working-class people or average, decent Americans. Of the working class, solid citizens whose rights he was (mentally) defending, none of them would be at all tempted to buy so much as a handkerchief in Shah Zamanh, and all lived within walking distance of a no-cover, no-minimum hardware store. He, in fact, was the riffraff.

"Hold it, Amy."

Vale stopped in front of a travel agency. A poster in the window showed vast blue sky and stark, boulder-strewn brown terrain leading up to a flat-topped, carved-looking butte. REPUBLIC'S WEST, *the copy said.* IT'S STILL WILD.

"Noah, we really should —"

"I can't go. I'm sorry." He knew this would hurt — or, at least, inconvenience — her, but the image of chatting with Howie Powers about warmedies spurred his resolve. "Maybe it's this Frank Miller thing, but . . . well, let's just say I've got some work to take care of."

"What? About the . . . ?"

"It's not just because a criminal is going to be the next President." Vale shrugged, stalling. "It's everything. Miller . . . SALT II . . . minimums in hardware stores . . . "

"Noah —"

"It just seems wrong to me to go on like nothing's the matter, to go sit and schmooze with Howie Powers about 'Hey, Shut Up,' or 'Go Fuck Yourself,' or whatever those shows are called —"

" 'Get Outa Here!' and 'Hey, Sez Who?' "

"— when these forces are on the loose and they're coming right at us. We've got to get some people together and do something."

"*Are you talking about those articles again —*"

"*Look, Amy.*" Vale stepped closer. Lunchtime pedestrians began to crowd the sidewalks. "*You're a showbiz agent. I know that writing magazine articles on spec is against your religion. All I can ask is that you have faith in me —*"

"*I do, Noah,*" she said, growing brisk. "*But I need a commitment from you if we're going to work together. I can't go to Honeymoon by myself.*"

Vale looked away. "*I'm sorry. This is something I feel I have to do.*"

"*You've made your decision. If you change your mind, I'll be at my office.*" She looked at her watch. "*After three o'clock. I have a lunch to take with Morty Mortman.*" Amy gave him a last glance and walked past him. Vale watched as she hailed a cab, climbed in, and with a slam of the door was gone. He kept walking.

He wondered if she understood. After all, she was a television agent. Despite all the things they seemed to have in common — e.g., they both worked at a desk — he had been obliged to deal with many kinds of people in his career. And he had been compelled to read many things. They were things she barely had occasion to think of, let alone read herself, and he had — he wasn't proud of it — been required to treat them in ways she might only have dimly been able to comprehend. . . .

Buckley in Brazil

The plane, a DC-10, begins its landing approach to Rio's Galeão Airport. For fun I activate my stopwatch to time its descent. Interesting: several years ago this model aircraft had rather more fatal crashes than someone — Ralph Nader, one imagines — thought appropriate. This prompted many fliers to take their custom elsewhere, thank you, and the airlines flying the DC-10 suffered accordingly. With so many of their potential customers litigious, frightened, or dead, the makers of the plane did the sensible thing, and made the necessary improvements. Now ridership is back up. Thus, as always, the market solution proves the most efficacious.

American industry has its faults, but one thing it does know is that death is, quite simply, bad for business. It depletes the

22

pool of potential customers. Ergo, most corporations do not need governmental agencies to tell them to make safe products; they willingly police themselves, once the number of casualties threatens the size of their market.

The flight from New York's international airport — I avoid employing that facility's current (and, one hopes, temporary) proper name — was uneventful. As we touch ground I offer a silent word of thanks to my Maker. I really must pray more, I think, and make a note of it on my pocket calendar.

On the plane I was able to catch up on various matters, including writing a memo to William Rusher, publisher of *National Review*. I sought his opinion concerning the intriguing notion that all food-stamp programs might be eliminated in favor of disbursing to their beneficiaries corresponding quantities of government-held surplus (powdered milk, soybeans, okra scum, etc.). The savings, I tell Rusho, would be considerable, with the net nutritional effect certainly comparable to that which currently obtains. ("Rusho" is Bill's nickname — that is, the one I have for him. He, in turn, calls me, after my initials, "Whiffle Ball.")

I debark and am met at the gate by Nelson, my host's punctual, rather imposing driver and bodyguard. Nelson speaks no English — indeed, he speaks no language at all, having been raised in the Mato Grosso by a herd of wild boars (does one call a group of such beasts a "herd"?). While waiting for him to fetch the car I jot a note employing the term "wild boars" and "Democrats" in jocular juxtaposition, intending to exploit the homonymic ambiguity of "boars" and "bores." Fun.

We ooze through the clogged traffic of Rio, pausing only to examine the possible damage to the car caused by a rather dilapidated guava cart, which had the sheer bad luck to present its side to our front grille as we accelerated to catch a changing traffic light. Happily the car suffers no disfigurement. We search for the cart's owner to so inform him, but are unable to distinguish between his remains and the mangled guavas. I express regret to a nearby policeman who, after learning of the identity of my host, minimizes the severity of the event, assuring me that during Carnival season the killing of produce vendors is considered good luck.

I am privately dubious of this; right reason suggests that there is, in fact, no such thing as "luck." (What is right reason? It is that faculty the use of which guides men toward belief in God and a life of virtue by — the coincidence is humbling — thinking and believing exactly as I do.) Nevertheless, I thank the officer, and we proceed.

In his attractive high-rise condominium, my host, Renaldo da Silva, greets me warmly. Renaldo is the brilliant and perspicacious editor of *Punho*, a journal of conservative Brazilian political opinion much like our own *National Review*, except that his editorial staff comprises mostly ex-Nazis. (Ours does not.) I have visited Rio each of the last four years, always staying with Renaldo and his beautiful, gracious wife, Monica. These brief but revivifying vacations would be all but unthinkable without their hospitality and discretion.

"You are here for your customary *rito*?" Renaldo asks jokingly, employing the Portuguese word for rite. I nod, and as he leads me into an excellent dinner in which shrimps are featured to great advantage, he reaffirms his pledge that my yearly indulgence will be kept in strictest confidence.

MONDAY

The day begins with an informal brunch at the National Armory, attended by a distinguished array of leaders from the government, industry, and the military. I greet, among others, General Armando Pereira, the brilliant tactician and linguist, who virtually single-handedly invented a new — and surprisingly workable — definition of the word "torture." We discuss, as best we can in the noisy, excited crowd, the advisability of countering Communist moves in El Salvador with the large-scale nuclear destruction of the area.

"Just be sure your president aims at the San Salvador over there, and not Salvador in Bahia!" the general jokes. I laugh, and assure him that there are several White House aides whose job it is to compensate for just such defects in the president's consciousness.

Following the brunch I join Renaldo and Monica for a helicopter ride around the city. Sugarloaf, with its huge statue of Christ, extrudes. Ringing the downtown of the city are the famous *favelas*, the slums, and they are of course terribly moving. I pause to reflect that in each of those one-room shacks that encrust the hillsides live families of many children, and probably many adults. Coming from a rather large family myself (we were ten children altogether), I can sympathize.

Following the ride we repair, as we do each year, to a delightful café. I am as a rule not a big drinker, although I do confess an addiction to certain bordeaux that have been properly cellared. However, as tonight's events will require an inordinate degree of stimulation if they are to work, I proceed to order two, three, possibly four, more accurately five drinks of the native rum, a stringent yet sweet brew fermented from sugarcane called *cachaça*. It has a potency comparable to that of tequila, and by the time I have consumed all six glasses I am rather significantly intoxicated on my posterior.

Renaldo looks at me intently and says with winning solicitousness, "Are you all right, Beel?" ("Beel" as a nickname? I must develop that. I consider the Latin Americanization of all our nicknames, my sister Priscilla, whom I call "Pitts," becoming "Peets," my son Christopher's "Christo" becoming "Chreesto.")

I smile at the impressively erudite Renaldo, and at the waiter, who has been most efficient, and at my spoon, which is very shiny, and I say, "Ah ha! Oh ho!" and, interestingly, fail to perceive the palindromic value of the expostulations.

Renaldo helps me to my feet. "Come, Beel, I will take you to the place." We go outside into the twilight, and I take a deep breath of the Rio de Janeiroian (Rioian?) air. This is the evening before Carnival, and the streets are swarming with tourists and natives, alike excited over that somewhat overblown and (oh, let's admit it) infantile festival. We have to force our way through the crowd to get to our destination, but so what? So, in a manner of speaking, big fat what? If we do not push them, I am quite certain that they will push us. (As they should, since in such a crowd to be pushed yet not to push oneself is a denial of self-interest, and as such is wrong reason and is therefore arguably immoral.)

Renaldo says, "Here is the place, Beel," and looks into my eyes, which are perfectly open, and I grin and think that I have a thought, which is: James Kilpatrick's nickname is "Kilpo." Thus: Ask Jeane Kirkpatrick if I may call her "Kirkpo." More: Find someone, a cultured and brilliant conservative, if possible, named So-and-So Alpatrick, and call him (her?) "Alpo."

Renaldo leans me against a shoe-store window. "I will pick you up here in several hours," he says, and disappears into the surging crowd. One hears various strains of music — insistent, and crude, in the sometimes bracing sense of that word — from here and there, and of course one realizes this is Brazil, and Rio, and so I rock against the window and sing to myself, "Tall and tan and young and erudite . . . "

A young boy, about ten, with large dark eyes and wearing khaki shorts and a T-shirt, motions for me to follow him. He goes up an alley where there is a Jeep with two teenage boys in it, one of whom says, "Get in." I do, and sit back, dizzy, since one has drunk rather something to drink, after all, and the Jeep, with a noise, moves, and goes, moving as it does so. For fun I decide to time the journey. I activate my stopwatch for this purpose, think "Aha!," then pass out cold.

MONDAY NIGHT

Ninety-two minutes later we stop in a clearing in the forest on the outskirts of the city. It is approximately eight-thirty. Before me is a sort of walled house. We enter into a narrow courtyard and thence into a large room filled with many native Brazilians of mostly working-class origins. The disorienting effects of the drink have somewhat ebbed, and I am much clearer of mind, so I send one of the boys for more, and drink it right from the bottle.

The air is pungent with incense, and many lit candles stand all around the room. I am guided to an area where the spectators are seated on long wooden benches. As always, I am gratified to observe on the walls figurines of a distinctly Christian nature — Jesus Christ, St. George slaying the dragon, San Sebastian pierced with arrows, et al. It matters that what is about to take place have roots firmly embedded in the soil of Roman Catholicism, in order that what I experience this night be theologically valid even though I am really, really drunk.

In the other half of the room are a few men in white pants and shirts, and many women wearing cotton skirts and puff-sleeved blouses and white turbans. They are barefoot, and walk on bare ground packed hard and covered with fresh-cut leaves. I am a fresh-cut leaf, I muse, and then decide, No, that isn't accurate, and make a note to that effect in my book. ("Self not fresh-cut leaf.") The floor is covered with odd chalked diagrams, and there is an altar of sorts.

A small middle-aged woman with wonderfully fine bone structure greets me. She is Mother Maria Teresa, the *Mãe de Santo* of this *terreiro*. This is a place of worship of, and consultation with, the gods of the syncretistic Brazilian religion known variously as Macumba, Umbanda, or Candomble. She is its equivalent of a priest.

"Senhor Buckley," she smiles. "You have come again."

I kiss her hand. "Thank you, Mother," I say, giggling rather tipsily. "I hope you can help me once more this year."

She laughs gently and says, "It is not I, my son. It is the gods." She moves on to greet others.

Three men carrying different congalike drums appear and set up their instruments in a central place off to one side. There is some preliminary greeting and announcing, during which I finish off the *cachaça*. There is a drumroll, and the names of various gods are invoked: Oxala, Oxossi, Xango, et al. It matters that one remember that each of these deities has its Catholic counterpart. Otherwise I should not take part in this ceremony, no matter how detachedly. As proof of my seriousness, I decide to activate my stopwatch. (I'm not sure why, but I assume I will find something to time.) But in fact I am too drunk, and instead activate my tie.

The drums then commence a turbulent rhythmic tattoo, and the barefooted women drift to the center of the room and begin to dance. They sing to the gods and dance in a circle around Mother Maria Teresa. The beat accelerates, and the dancers quicken their movements.

Suddenly one of the dancing women separates herself from the group. She cries and nearly stumbles, her features contorted in a most expressive ecstasy. She falls onto a diagram on the floor. A man staggers and also cries out, and begins to laugh loudly. A fat black woman stops dancing and seizes a cigar from a box on the altar, lights it, and proceeds to blow smoke into the faces of all the dancers. One by one the dancers contort, as each in his or her turn is possessed by one of the gods of Macumba. Mother Maria Teresa circulates among them, calming the agitated and smoothing over the rough transitions that inevitably accompany divine possession.

The drums become louder, and faster. I gaze with admiration at the talented percussionists and realize that soon it will be my turn to approach one of the mediums. I am hoping this time to speak to the goddess Iemanjá ("yeh-mahn-JAH"), Queen of the Sea, and put to her several questions concerning my upcoming trip on *Patito*, the thirty-six-foot sloop I bought last year. It is all in good fun, of course — tropical religions are little more than the naïve projections of an unsophisticated animism, lacking the concepts of sin, redemption, and communion with the body of the Lord via transubstantiation necessary for a mature religious system. Nonetheless I am impatient to speak with Iemanjá, so to distract myself I activate my stopwatch.

But something evidently happens — I mean a certain abridgment of consciousness on my part, for the next thing I know I am surrounded by the dancers, and Mother Maria Teresa is calmly speaking an incomprehensible prayer to me and blowing pipe smoke in my face. As best I have been able to reconstruct it, this is what occurred:

I staggered out into the middle of the floor, threw my hands up, and began babbling in a sort of pidgin Brazilian/ English/Latin/Yoruba. I spun as though mad, spied a diagram on the floor, and pounced upon it. A cry arose from several of the onlookers — "Santo Bruto! Santo Bruto!" — which was explained to me as being a phenomenon in which one of the gods possesses someone other than a qualified and trained medium.

Evidently the god Oxala ("oh-sha-LA" is the accurate pronunciation) saw fit to inhabit my body (I found the choice apposite; he is the god of intellectual activities and is associated with Jesus Christ). Under his influence I counseled several members of the audience who had come to the ceremony seeking help. I told one man to light a white candle before a bowl of plain rice consecrated to "me," let it burn out, and in that way secure his nephew's release from the military authorities. I was, I am told, "very majestic and wise." I advised a woman that she would win the lottery if she sacrificed in "my" name a chicken.

Although not consciously present during that episode, afterward I feel tremendously refreshed. Soon the audience leaves the *terreiro*, and the dancers are released by their possessors. Mother Maria Teresa smiles at me as I collect myself, and I take her aside and offer her several hundred brand-new *cruzeiros* from my wallet — my customary contribution.

She takes them with a smile and says, "Whatever you wish to give is always appreciated, my son."

"That has never happened to me before, Mother," I say.

"A Santo Bruto is rare, but it is not unknown."

"Is there any means by which you can guarantee its happening next year . . . ?"

She shakes her head. "You must trust the gods, my son. It is up to them, as always."

Fair enough — and a neat way of both disclaiming personal responsibility and ascribing impiety to a request not meant as such. I take out my notebook and scribble a memo on it. "I have several influential friends on the International Monetary Fund," I tell her. "I'm going to put in a good word for Brazil

when I return to New York. I think they should be able to find
some way to manage your country's enormous debt."

"You are very generous."

"By way of quid pro quo, Mother, I wonder if you would
mind conferring with the relevant gods to arrange a Santo Bruto
for me next year."

Extending her hand for me to kiss, she says, "I shall con-
vey to them your request."

I thank the woman and am driven back to the shoe store
by the boys. Renaldo meets me as per our arranged itinerary,
and I conclude my visit to Rio the next day. I have no desire to
remain for Carnival (I think the Lord is best worshipped in peace
and quiet, in Connecticut), but I do opt to remain long enough
for a stimulating — and impressively thorough — tour of the
airport's interrogation facilities.

11:18 A.M.
_____

*At home Vale took off the jacket and tie, and changed into his
work clothes: whatever blue jeans he had been wearing all week,
and a clean, unironed shirt. He made a pot of coffee, poured a
mug, and carried it and a bag of cookies to his desk.*

He would write something wonderful and send it to That
Damn Magazine.

*Like everybody he knew, Vale harbored a grumpy ambiva-
lence toward* That Damn Magazine. *He "hated it," while con-
ceding that it could be very good. Its nonfiction ran on alternat-
ing current: one week's waking nightmare of tedium — sparrows,
corn, basalt — would give way to something interesting — in-
eptness at SAC, Lubavitchers in Brooklyn.*

*Its short stories were immaculately written and sublimely
subtle, contributed by the nation's masters of immaculate, sublime short fiction. Vale, however, couldn't read them. The cal-*

culated affectlessness of the narration, the patronizing references to K Marts and Toyotas and Egg McMuffins, the gimmicky citations to (the wrong) rock bands and hit songs — all this induced in Vale a sense of futility. Life was a doomed struggle against an unspecified but implicit force of emotional, spiritual, or psychological gravity.

Vale groped for a cookie out of the bag and brought it to his mouth. Absorbed in scribbling "Miller as Somoza — US as 3rd wrld country???," he managed to come down on his hand.

Then again, he couldn't complain. That Damn Magazine *was read by just about everybody. And they published him, God bless 'em. They published him.*

Patriotic Spot (60 Secs.)

You're waking up, America. It's morning — and you're waking up to live life like you've never lived it before. Say hello to a whole new way of being awake, America. Say hello to us.

Who are we? The idea people. A family of companies. America's supermarket. We're all this — and more. All day, every day, something we do will touch your life. At home. At school. Whether you need us or not, we're there.

We're watching you, America. We're watching you when you work — because, America, you work hard. And we know that afterward you've got a mighty big thirst. Not just a thirst for the best beer you can find. But a thirst for living. A thirst for years of experience. America, you're thirsty.

You're spelling more today, America. You're spelling a lot of things. Words. Words like *cheese*. *Relief*. And you're using those words to make phrases, and you're talking with those phrases

every day, keeping America's telephone system the best in the
world. America, you've got something to say, and you're coming in loud and clear. "Cheese relief." "Relief cheese." You
said it, America.

Where does America go when it wants more of everything?
It comes to us. Who are we? An American tradition. We provide a broad range of services. In eight major markets. Sixteen
times a day. All across this great country of ours. Who are we?
We're people.

People who know that America is digging in. People who
come from all walks of life. People whose job it is to serve you.
And we're doing it — better than ever. We're working harder
to serve you, America. Because you're entitled. You've earned
it. You deserve the best — the very best. From the skillful management of natural resources to the thirst-quenching beer you
drink: you know what you want, and you grab it. You expect
more, and you get it. Ask for it by name, America.

You're on the move, too — and we're doing our best to
beat you there. Around the corner, or around the world: we're
waiting for you. Who are we? America's host from coast to coast.
We are insight. We are knowledge. We are the future. And
we're changing — changing to keep up with you.

America, say hello to something new. Say hello to quality.
Quality you can see. Quality you can feel. Quality you can say
hello to. (How do you spell *quality*, America? *Real* quality —
quality you can trust? The same way we've been spelling it for
over a hundred and fifty years.)

You're looking good, America. And we're looking at you.
Who are we? People building transportation to serve people.
Where are we? Where America shops. What are we? What the
Colonel cooks. How did we get here? We are driven.

We want what you want. It's that simple. And we're giving
it to you. At work. At play. Because America works as hard as
it works, and plays as hard as it plays. When America has nothing to do, it reaches for us. And we're there — in energy, in
communications, in research. With the meticulous attention to
detail that comes only from the choicest hops, the finest barley.

We're Number One. You're Number One. You're a winner, America. And we know what you're thinking. We know how you feel. How do we know? Because we take the time to tell you. We take the time to care.

And it pays off. We're here, America. And the next time you're here — the next time we can tell you who we are and what we do — we'll be doing what we do best.

11:20 A.M.

As the final draft came unspooling out of the printer, Vale decided to expedite the process. He would hand-deliver it to Harvey Kramer, his editor at That Damn Magazine.

Normally he would have mailed it, which would have allowed him to compose a suitably cheery cover letter, the better to prod Harvey into a positive frame of mind. In fact, he always labored carefully over such notes, and it was always futile. Articles submitted to Fiction were read by what amounted to a posse: a spokesman — Harvey — at the head of a discontented crowd of unidentified people full of opinions. Rejections, unfailingly polite and regretful, were vague and not for attribution: "The feeling here is that . . . " "A few of us thought . . . "

Still, Vale preferred submitting through the mail. Going to the office made him anxious; stepping out of the elevator, he felt as though he were entering a place where he, in addition to his work, would be judged. It was like walking slowly into the town saloon: all heads turn, the honkytonk stops, and the tarty dancing girls' shrill laughter dies suddenly into silence. Your peer group takes your measure. Here comes that feller Vale, they think. Let's just see what kind of a sophisticated urban literary wit he is, anyhow. . . ."

Actually, that was what that office needed — a few tarty dancing girls on staff, loitering in the editors' offices (at least the

male ones), flashing their cleavage and exposing frilly black gart-
ers against ample white thighs. "Come on, honey," one might
pout, curling Harvey Kramer's hair in a playful index finger.
"Put down that boring old Ann Beattie story and let's have
some fun."

"But we've got pages to fill in Fiction —"

"Well," she'd say, ruby lipstick glittering on a frown of in-
tense concentration. "How 'bout using that nice big piece by
Vale?"

"What — the ten-page parody of the Stockman book?"

"Why not? Ain't ya man enough to run it?"

Well, the problem with That Damn Magazine, *Vale de-*
cided, was that it was usually sensible but never passionate, al-
ways liberal, never romantic. That was why Vale, a post-Sixties
schizoid with the brain of a tennis judge but, alas, the heart of
a high school poetess, sometimes had trouble.

Hearty of Darkieness

"Stamford," complained Mr. Ross, "is on the verge of becoming the playground of the borough of the Bronx and the dark, mysterious, malodorous stretches of Harlem. . . . I do not mean to be undemocratic, but you couldn't choose a more alarming bunch of people in the world."

— *The New York Times*

Anybody here mind if I preen? A recent adventure has left me buffing my nails rather conspicuously, and whoever thinks I shall forego relating it may consider his name stricken from my list of perspicates. It began, as recent adventures so often do, with a phone call. I was puttering in the potting shed, having completed my matutinal calisthenic of pottering in the putting shed, where it is my custom to knock Maxfli's into an Erlenmeyer flask while humming snatches of Moussorgsky. The eve pre-

36

vious I had laid plans with regard to the chemical annihilation of a lustily thriving stand of sumac, and was busy assembling the requisite ordnance, when the woman to whom I had plighted my dog-eared troth summoned me to phone.

"It's one of your wretched *New Yorker* friends," she announced with diaphanously veiled contempt. "From the sound of it, he either wants money or a favor."

"Damn you for an insolent baggage!" I might have checked the wench, but instead opted for the more housebroken, "Thanks, Hon," prior to traipsing into the kitchen. There, amid the inevitable tohubohu of Swiss chard and fenugreek with which Philomene, our dusky *gastronomeuse*, would inexorably decoct what I have grown accustomed, without laughing, to call dinner, I seized the receiver and gave greeting.

"Sid? Thurber." My colleague was phoning to report that our mutual boss, editor of a magazine for which we performed eleemosynary literary services, was mysteriously unaccounted for. "He hasn't come in," my telephonister sighed. "And he won't answer the phone. I think there's no other choice but to go and find him."

"A grim journey up-river, into the teeth of mystery and adventure, eh?" I murmured.

"Hardly," replied the killjoy. "Just take the train to Stamford and see what's going on."

"But why me?" I pointed out that I was in rural Pennsylvania, while Thurber himself, phoning from amid the topless towers and bottomless coffee cups of Manhattoes, could have assayed the journey in less time than it would take me to jink my haversack.

"Everybody here thinks it should be you," he ensuavated, ever the ingratiating celeritor. "We admire your powers of persuasion."

He knew his man. The remark stimulated my diplomatic fancy, and I was vouchsafed a vision of myself, khaki-clad and spiffed to the nines. In this somewhat surreal scenario (comprising equal parts Kipling, De Mille, and *Spicy Yarns for Boys and Their Pals*), I was toting a jute crop, my calf-length leather bla-

gas gleaming, their passementerie trim aglow. Reed slim, bowing at the waist, I greeted pooh-bah and panjandrum in the reception line at some fabulous palm-ringed Colonial palace, His Majesty's viceroy to a tropical land of unlettered savages and compliant, tan-limbed wahines that was not, for once, Hollywood.

Then the cur pricked my ballooning phantasy. "Besides," he added, "we're busy here."

I retorted with pique. "Don't you suppose I'm busy, too?" A petulant whine was creeping into my voice. I beat it off with a stick, then added, "I mean to say, the garden wants changing, and someone has to water the baby —"

"Suit yourself," came the reply. "But as long as he's unaccounted for, your check request can't get signed."

Instanter I seized the timetable of milk trains and consulted the relevant listing. If the mem and bairns did not actually weep when I announced my departure, nonetheless I could sense, amid the yawns, their pain. In our quaint local depot, renowned for its fine period mildew and skillfully concealed leaks, I mounted the iron horse for wildest Connecticut.

I did not know what to expect. My quarry was a man of legendary eccentricity; yet it was unlike him to neglect the turl and bel-tintoro of the office. Indeed, he was a man not so much dedicated to his dack as one unable to live without it. His absence augured coshtabula aplenty, a fact that prompted me, en route, to heave several agitated sighs. Most of them landed harmlessly on the floor, save for one, which struck a fellow passenger several pews off — a dour beldame in flatteau and snood, off whom they glanced harmlessly and without incident.

It was thus fregulate that I arrived at the Stamford station, a pert little structure equal parts Tudor punnybox and Quonset hut moderne. I seized my Gladstone to detrain, stood expectantly in the aisle, and was nearly trampled asunder by a stampede of Moorish figures flocking past me from the rear.

"Yowza, we gwine hab us sum fun fo sho'!" cried one gink, resplendent in a shopworn white duck suit (Lord knew what the white duck was left wearing), boatlike cordovan brautigans on his feet, a rakish straw skimmer on his poll. "Come awn, Ru-beh! Le's go buy us sum o' dem convertible debenturers at de stock brokah!"

His paramour, an ebony matron with the girth of a Kung-wah rhino, girt in a lurid floral muumuu, drawled, "Oh yeah, honey. Ah can't wait to take de top down off one o' dem things!" The dyad joined hands and tripped off into the station.

Odd, I thought, peering out a window to confirm the stop. Stamford it was, and no doubt. "One would think we had held over at a Carolina beach resort."

Dismissing the event as anomalous, I sallied forth once more, only to run aground midsally by another onslaught, this time from the opposite direction. Surging toward me down the aisle came a human tsunami, its collective aspect suggestive of a crowd scene shot by Eisenstein after a bargain-hunting spree en masse down Orchard Street. "*Nu*, you're goink to vait until a written invitation already?" queried a big-boned *mameleh* of her dawdling son.

"Mama," piped the boy. "When we go to Abercrombie's, can I have a martini?"

"Martini-schmini," she sneered to an invisible auditor. "Already he's a partner at Kravitz."

"Cravath," corrected the lad.

"Cravath-schmavath, keep *hocking* me and you'll get a *klop* on the *keppie*." The woman then directed toward me the scowl of a fishmonger sniffing putrescent herring. "So vhat are you starink?"

"This *pisher's* calling for martinis?" I blurted. I scrambled for my customary sangfroid, found it under the seat, and re-plied, "I meant to say, I merely find myself curious as to the reason for your visit to Stamford this day."

"*Vuh den*, it's closer than the Concord," was her shrugging reply. Then, collaring her slothful issue, she exited. Non-plussed, or at least, no more plussed than the next geek, I fol-lowed.

I had not been to Connecticut since sitting as a judge, the previous May, for a children's playwriting contest at Stratford.

(The winner, by unanimous vote, had been a toddler's moody dramatization of the ecstacy and torment of breast-feeding, a memory play entitled *Waiting for Lefty*. I still recalled with pleasure its admirable curtain line: "So long, sucker!") My subsequent naïve tertimination — that most suburban Connecticut towns were alike as a litter of Indonesian binzies — collapsed at the *blik* of the odd and festive spectacle exfesticating before my spartulminizing peepers.

Everywhere, as far as the bloodshot eye could discern, there capered throngs of folk seemingly the least likely descendents of *Homo erectus* to claim Stamford as their native pueblo. As I staggered, mystified, out onto the street, a gaggle of Negro celebrants cakewalked past, dandily clad men and their racily decked-out *filles*, all hoisting small flagons of muscatel and giving three-times-three at whim. Across the avenue, numerous families of a distinctly Semitic cast — sobersides scholarly Pa, skeptical sergeant-major Ma, saucer-eyed Son and cup-chested Daughter — meandered along the storefronts, munching maxixe cherries from bags while blissfully window shopping. (One happy clan had in fact just made purchase of a set of windows, which they bore down the street in triumph.)

The town was riot with vacationists. Small children, of every race and creed, skittered underfoot and shouted with glee, in a timeless masque of ball-tossing and purse-snatching. Quartets of chums dragooned genial pedestrians into leveling the Rolleiflex, as they posed with self-conscious nonchalance before the picturesque bakery, the atmospheric notary, the unspoiled pharmacy, the cute little liquor shop where Tom found the most darling Medoc last summer. Here, in cosmopolitan melange, desported representatives of the liveliest quarters of Lagos, Jerusalem, Addis Ababa, Smolensk, Charleston, and Prague. If, that day, there was a single ponytailed Protestant housewife abroad (or, for that matter, a ponytailed Protestant housebroad awifed), she escaped my ken.

But each second's rubbernecking meant additional delay in delivery of a life-saving transfusion to my bank account. I dragged my ruck over to a cab parked at the station's stand. Its dozing

driver cocked an indifferent eye. "The Ross estate," I panted.
"And a guinea if you get me there by dusk!"

"Hey, watch it with the Ginny, pal," the hack snarled.
"I'm Mick." I apologized for the ethnic solecism, explicated,
kowtowed, and bade him drive as though the demons of hell
were nipping his heels.

The house, when I arrived, looked outwardly placid: cur-
tains drawn, front door shut, a giant roc perched on the roof.
(The neighborhood, I had heard, was rife with the fowl, whose
imperfect sense of balance had prompted the town council to
pepper the hamlet with signs reading FALLING ROC ZONE.) I
rang the door bell and awaited response, but heard nothing save
the pounding of blood in my ears — a disturbing sensation,
until I realized that the blood was my own. The door, for some
reason, was unlocked.

A Stygian darkness greeted me, and I groped like a Malay
blefula for the light switch. Attaining it, I discovered an unre-
markably bourgeois living room — one not dissimilar to my
own, in fact, save for the presence, here, of furniture capable
of supporting an adult human body without skewering it with
cushion springs or administering to it random subcutaneous in-
jections of wood splinters.

"Hullo?" I called. No reply sounded to disturb the lunching termites surely carmigating in the wainscotting. Feeling a tad
like a P.I. giving a digs the flanagan, I penetrated the manse.

The kitchen was deserted, as were the dining room and the
study. Pristine silence swallowed my every bleated *cri*. All at
once I was struck by the possibility that I had galloped off on a
chase of the wild goose, that my *zurchdrecht* had merely skipped
town on impromptu holiday — in a word, that no one was
home. There remained only the bedroom to fastigate. Although
I am but a modest rustic, who restricts his customary haunts to
such rude barns and stables as those in which he shelters wife,
children, and other livestock, nonetheless I knew my way around
a suburban Colonial. Convinced that there had to be a light
switch somewhere, I clawed at the wall like a lifer gone starkers
in the clink.

A slight motion arrested my attention and hauled it downtown for questioning. I was conscious of the delicate susurration
of a man panting, as though in the grip of ague, or in the ague
of grippe. I found the light and snapped home the stud.

"Goddam it, Perelman, turn it off!"

The voice was ragged, harsh, the impatient bark of a man
who is used to being obeyed, if only by his dog. I found its
owner spread-eagled on the bed, as though after a sweth induced by laudanum or pranda. He wore a dark Botany suit and
a monogrammed Biochemistry necktie. The faint light of day
creeped 'round the drawn drapery and played upon his pug
features; I bade it skedaddle and play in its room. "They're
out there, Perelman," the man croaked. "The town is infested
with 'em!"

"Uh," I replied, employing the scrupulously neutral opening with which I have always enjoyed great rhetorical success.
"You mean —"

"I mean *them*, goddam it!" He brandished an extended index finger like a thuggee his stiletto. "Negroes and Jews! You
couldn't choose a more alarming bunch of people in the world!"

"How about Adolf Hitler?" I riposted. Thurber's motive for
insisting I be the one to gallop to the rescue had become clear
as a Waterford epergne.

"Who he?"

I explained the Führer's more notable social and political
views. During this lecture my auditor snorted and scowled on
his bunk, his recumbency unsavven. Finally I said, "So I'd say
he's a fairly alarming breast of squab, right?"

"You've got me there!" the fellow shouted.

I nodded, and gestured airily. "Then what say we hightail
it down to the City, old sport —"

"Can't." The cul shook his bean. "Can't leave the house.
There's one of 'em out there, and he's after me."

"One of —?"

"Negro fellow. Keeps trying to talk to me. Goddam it, Perelman, I don't want to be talked to by some Negro!" With an
agility that took me aback he suddenly leapt up and legged it

into the walk-in voisere, slamming the louvered door behind him. "Just sit tight here 'til the whole thing blows over."

As it was manifestly unclear as to what constituted "the whole thing," and what would signal its expiration, I could respond with little more than well-meaning farlication. "Well, yes, but —" I had seen evidence of my employer's prejudices before, but this full-dress *sonde et lumière* left me flabbergasted and bollixado. Then the doorbell rang.

"Leave it!" snapped the closeted truant. "Just play possum and they'll scram!" He moaned. "Oh, God — it's horrible Horrible!"

"Steady on, old son," I murmured. "It might be the authorities, seeking to inform me I've won the Irish sweepstakes." Despite his frantically whispered protestations, I left him there and made for the door. Opening it revealed a young black man in a natty two-piece worsted suit, his expression a miraculous amalgam of boyish eagerness and guarded awe.

"Mister Ross?" he asked, and before I could correct him, introduced himself, and launched into an impetuous paean to the magazine for which my own unflagging labors, at wages capable of eliciting guffaws from a galley slave, had helped underwrite purchase of the very house in which its actual editor now so ignobly cowered.

"I simply want to say that I think it's quite the best periodical on the stands today," the man declared. "And I would be profoundly grateful if you might just look at a few articles and reportorial sketches I've written. I have them right here. . . ." He reached into a slim leather McBain he had tucked under one arm, and would have proffered the demorgant sheaves had I not stayed his hand and replied, with the genial twinkle of the born liar, "I'd love to look at them, young man. But not here. I dislike discussing work out of the City." After a moment's *fausse tristesse*, I brightened. "Say, here's a capital idea. I'm bound for town just now. Why don't you come to my office later today and we can have a corking good chin-wag about the whole thing? Twenty-five West Forty-third —"

"Oh, I know the address, sir —"

"Excellent. Nineteenth floor. And never you mind dilly-dallying with the receptionist, either. Simply inquire if I'm at my desk, and then just barge right on in. Tell the girl I said so."

The fellow's reaction was warm, and after we parted with mutual expressions of gratitude, I returned to the bedroom. Whether or not, en route, I actually rubbed my hands in Satanic glee escapes recollection.

"Traveling salesman," I responded to Ross's unasked query. "Sought to demonstrate a high-octane vacuum cleaner — the sort of thing you drive through your living room like a car."

"High octane?" he grunted suspiciously through the closet door, ever the precisionist where facts were concerned. "Who the hell proposes to run vacuum cleaners on gasoline? Don't they know there's a war on?"

"Er, it, uh . . . it runs on, ah, alcohol — gin, bourbon, other potables."

"A likely story."

"My opinion exactly. I conveyed your regrets."

"Good." The door opened and the prisoner emerged. "What am I going to do, Perelman? I can't hole up in here forever. My wife's with her mother — when she gets back she'll give me hell. Oh goddam it all!"

"Why not go to the office?" came my disingenuous reply.

"Imposs —!" His obduracy gave way to sudden insight. "My God, I think you've hit it! Of course!" He smote his brow and chortled with relief. "The office of the *New Yorker*! That's the last place you'd find one of those people! Perelman, you're a genius. But so am I, for hiring you."

I nodded with becoming modesty, the faint tint of a blush softening my manly aspect, but maintained a dignified silence.

His teeth were stained, his hair begreased, his hands and face ill-kempt as a vagrant's; he pronounced himself fit for immediate travel, and in a trice we were taxiing to the station. As we threaded through the undiminished carnival, he slunk down in the seat and found fascination in the close study of his own

knees. "It's not that I mean to be undemocratic, you understand," he mumbled. "But I can tell you one thing — coons
are either funny, or dangerous. I mean to say . . . goddam it,
Perelman, for Christ's sake — this is Connecticut!"

I agreed, and remained likewise amiable until we had arrived. It was then that my companion succumbed to one of his
periodic bouts of amnesia, forgetting utterly about the existence
of his wallet. I paid the fare.

"Now, Jews aren't that bad, of course," he went on as we
debarked. "But if you ask me . . ." And there he halted, and
exvisulated me with a ferocious squint. "Wait a minute. My
god, Perelman, you're . . ." His face, at its ruddiest the hue of
flour paste, blanched to an even more snowy pallor. He fell
silent for a moment, then asked hoarsely, "You, uh, you coming into town?"

I declined, with murmurings of an intention to return to
my Pennsylvania freehold. I spotted peripherally, waiting at a
far end of the platform, the crisp young chap who'd begged
audience at the house. I made sure he didn't spot me. Ross and
I bantered cursorily for a few minutes, deploring the latest shenanigans of the magazine's writers, artists, and other unemploy-
ables, before the train came soughing into the station. My companion stepped up onto the car, then turned back to me and,
with a snort employed by elephants on the Serengeti to indicate
apology, stammered, "Listen, Perelman, about that remark about
— you know. No offense intended."

"None taken," I smiled.

He nodded, and I noted that his secret admirer had also
boarded. I waved with a sprightliness that reflected my un-
feigned inner state of heart's ease, and spent a delightful half
hour until my train came, luxuriating in the kef that military
commanders know when they return to base and — wounded,
tired, but withal intact — report their mission accomplished.

The office of That Damn Magazine *resembled a stuffy, pre-World War II high school, at about four-thirty in the afternoon, when the students have left and the faculty is tired. The corridor established a color scheme of putty and beige; if the magazine's pages were defiantly black and white, its office would also be colorless. A rolldown map of the United States, labeled* STATES AND TERRITORIES, 1880 *hung on one wall. The top half of each office door was a translucent pane of frosted glass; the room's number, in a shade of glum brown, was painted in finicky cursive numerals on the wall. No one but readers and writers could thrive here: they rarely looked up anyway.*

Staff people, none of whom Vale recognized, drifted by in respectful solemnity — somewhere, something important was going on, and must not be disturbed by outbursts of personality. The place was quiet as a ghost town.

Harvey Kramer was seated at his desk, which took up more than half the small chamber he occupied at the end of the hallway. Shelves against the wall opposite the single window brimmed with books, literary quarterlies, papers in folders, back issues, and long, narrow galley proofs. His blue blazer was draped on the back of the massive oak desk chair in which he sat, white sleeves rolled back, black- and red-striped tie tightly knotted.

"So," Harvey said, after the usual greetings. "What have we here."

Vale handed him the piece. "I really like this one."

"Hm." Harvey skimmed, squinting once at something on the page, as though to say, I am able to recognize a joke. He wasn't happy. Vale's heart sank. It was like asking to have your motion seconded and watching no hands go up. Finally Harvey sighed and shook his head. "Political pieces . . ." he mused, as though weary at having to discuss something dismissed long ago. "I don't know. There's something of a backlash against them here these days. I grant you, it may be indefensible. But the atmosphere isn't receptive."

Vale pretended he hadn't heard. "I started off with the Frank Miller thing, but it led to larger issues."

"I can tell you right now, it'll be an uphill fight."

Vale looked nonchalant, or tried to. "Push it through."

"I can't," Harvey said, adding, "you know that. It isn't just up to me. I only have so much influence. I counsel safety, actually. Write about something less urgent and, yes, all right, less important."

"Oh, come on." Vale leaned forward in the chair and indicated the article. "It's what I say in here. Miller's like an American Eva Peron. So was Reagan, for that matter. Isn't that worth a page of humorous discussion?"

Harvey laughed, then tilted his head to the side thoughtfully, to denote an effort to be fair. "Well, leaving aside the merits of that as an analogy, no, not necessarily. I think the feeling here is that writers lose their control when they write political. The results are very uneven. Besides," he added, "Miller — and Reagan too, for that matter — aren't they too easy a pair of targets?"

"Oh, baloney." To Vale it was the argument of a "clever" guidance counselor. "Half the pieces you run are about Sylvester Stallone. That's not an easy target?"

"We've run two — which may be one too many, I suppose." He sighed. "I'll be happy to read this and see what the others think."

Outside, in the glare of the 11:23 sun and surrounded by the hustling lunch crowd, Vale felt puny. All these big buildings, all these people with real jobs, and he was anguishing over a four-page creative writing paper making fun of someone whom those really in the know took pride in ignoring.

Still, maybe it was worthwhile. He was waging campaigns in the realm of readers' minds. It wasn't easy to get there, or, once there, to leave a mark. But it was possible. Vale recalled with pleasure the mobile "race-track" MX missile system. Hadn't he destroyed it utterly with a piece harking back to those original technocratic maniacs (and Fascists), the Italian Futurists? Such thoughts were a comfort.

Manifesto of the MX Missilists ⌐

All passéist, immobile, fixed-launcher guided-missile systems present such a monstrous spectacle of pathetic backwardness and obsolescence that our MX Missilist eyes turn away with profoundest disgust and contempt!

These vile embodiments of technological senility, abjectly cowering in their "silos," stand before us as monuments to those fossilized qualities we MX Missilists defiantly and proudly abhor: stasis, standing-in-place, and unitary-presentation-of-self-sans-decoy.

Even the silence born of their loathsome lack of movement — through which it might be possible to hear the approach of enemy missiles hurtling with blithe impunity to obliterate those same stock-still armaments — even this silence is not allowed to exist. IT IS FILLED WITH THE SHRILL AND HYSTERICAL CRIES OF OUR OPPONENTS IN CONGRESS AND

48

AMONGST THE PRESS — PRAETORIAN GUARD OF A VEGETATING BEHINDHAND TECHNOLOGY, WHOSE BASE IGNORANCE AND DESPICABLE COWARDICE TURN THEM INTO RANTING, FOOLISH IDIOTS BICK-ERING WITH EACH OTHER OVER WHOSE SLAVISH ADORATION OF THE MOST RUBBISH-ENCRUSTED OLD-FASHIONED STYLE OF NUCLEAR WEAPONS IS THE MORE INTENSE.

A violent desire for up-to-date weaponry boiling in our veins, we repudiate them and their spineless accountant-clerk eunuchs, whose mewlings about "fiscal responsibility" serve only to redouble our fierce commitment. To them we cry with unflinching scorn: From this day forth, all worm-ridden stationary-launcher missile systems are dead! The MX Era of Mobile Launchers and Decoys has arrived!

We may declare without boasting that our development of the MX Missile System was as wholesome and organic as the system itself, thuswise:

We examined the phenomenon of hitting things, *and concluded that the thing that moves around like a gazelle is more difficult to hit than the thing that stands still like a rotting tree stump.*

We examined the phenomenon of hiding from things, *and discovered that the cleverly hidden thing is more difficult to find than the thing squatting stupidly in plain sight.*

We examined the phenomenon of decoys and false objects, *and realized that the true object surrounded confusingly by false objects of identical appearance is more difficult to discern than the true object standing foolishly alone.*

Life is nature. Life moves. *Movement is natural.*

IS THIS NOT AN AGE OF MOTION? IS NOT THE ESSENCE OF THE GUIDED MISSILE ITSELF PUREST MOVEMENT? MUST WE, THEREFORE, CONTINUE TO ENDURE THE FATUOUS PRATTLE AND PEEVISH OUTBURSTS OF THOSE NARROW-MINDED IMBE-CILES WHO CANNOT SEE THAT A SYSTEM COMPRIS-ING 200 ACTUAL MISSILES AND 4,400 SIMULATED

MISSILES, ALL IN CONSTANT MOTION HARMONI-
OUS WITH THE VERY SPIRIT OF OUR TIMES, CAN-
NOT BUT SUCCEED IN RENDERING OUR NATION'S
ENEMIES MUTE WITH ASTONISHMENT?

Proud, incorruptible, nauseated by easy success, we freely
admit that the present MX Missile System represents the *second*
stage in the evolution of the Principle of Mobile Hiding
Weaponry.

The first stage found its embodiment in the concept of the
Circular Track. It was an idea glorious in its promise but, like
the child it was, annoying to certain stridently braying, fun-
hating "grown-ups." The circular tracks, upon which the missiles were to ride-and-hide, were deemed too extravagant in their
usage of land, even for the indisputably spacious states of Ne-
vada and Utah. Confident in our purpose, we retired to our
drafting tables, and shortly thereafter designed the present, second version of the MX.

In so doing, we improved upon it.

In so doing, we created the Principle of the Linear MX.

In so doing, we designed a network not of circular "race
track" runways but of linear roads and streets and side streets.

WHAT IS SUCH A SCHEMA, IF NOT A RECAPITU-
LATION AND GLORIFICATION OF THE VERY INTER-
STATE AUTOMOBILE HIGHWAY SYSTEM THAT HAS
MADE OUR NATION THE MOST IMPRESSIVELY MO-
BILE ON THE GLOBE?

Yet even we — free moderns, supremely awake — even
we were not prepared for the magnificent implications of the
Linear MX layout. As one, we fell to our knees in awe when
we realized the import of the new design.

THE LINEAR MX IS INFINITELY EXPANDABLE!

ARE 4,400 SIMULATED MISSILES AND 4,600 SHEL-
TERS INSUFFICIENT TO PROTECT OUR PRECIOUS
NUCLEAR WARHEADS FROM ENEMY PERFIDY? THEN
WE MAY CONSTRUCT MORE! AND CASUALLY ADD
THEM ON TO THE EXTANT SYSTEM! AND CREATE
AN EVER-EXPANDING MX GRID THAT NEED HALT AT

NO BOUNDARY, SAVE FOR THE NONEXISTENT ONE OF OUR OWN FEVERISH, SOARING IMAGINATION!

We shall go still further. We are prepared to argue that stasis itself is dead. For if missiles should be placed upon cars, and those cars upon tracks, to move hither and thither in response to the universal urge to avoid nuclear annihilation, why then, O asinine compatriots, should not hospitals be so emplaced? And military command posts? And repositories of munitions, foodstuffs, and the like? And if those facilities should be thus protected, should we not afford equal consideration to our citizenry and its belongings?

Does not the jungle beast, wild and free in its environment, bolt upon the arrival of its mortal enemy? *Should not the inhabitants and possessions of the greatest nation on earth be granted the same innate rights of mobility as belong to the lowliest jackal?*

Do not the chameleon, the salamander, and other free-roving practitioners of the art of camouflage from the animal world teach us that concealment, decoy, and visual obfuscation are both necessary and right for the survival of a species? *Must we allow a small number of craven gas-bags in Congress to deny America a defensive tool available to the most common and repulsive reptile?*

Yet our opponents — pale and backward-looking neurasthenics languishing in that hotbed of impotence, Washington, D.C. — decree that "perhaps" missiles may indeed hide from enemy bombardment but the innocent child, the beloved pet dog, the housewife, and the house may not.

Let us make our position even more unequivocal.

WE DEMAND

1. Liberation and exaltation of the Principle of Mobile Hiding Weaponry and congressional approval of its apotheosis, the MX Missile.

2. The immediate implementation of the Principle, not

only with regard to the MX itself *but with regard to every person and object in the United States of America.*

OUR NATION MUST AT ONCE DUPLICATE ITS ENTIRE PHYSICAL ASPECT, PLACING THOUSANDS OF CUNNING AND TECHNOLOGICALLY SOPHISTI- CATED FALSE UNITED STATESES UPON A VAST SYS- TEM OF TRACKS AND CARS, THEREBY ASSURING OUR SURVIVAL OF WHATEVER MASSIVE NUCLEAR STRIKE THE ENEMY CAN, IN ITS HATRED AND INSANITY, INITIATE.

Does the savage boldness with which we dismiss our mo- ronic critics frighten you? We do not care!

Do we hear you bleat some question or reservation? Then you are our enemy, and we laugh raucously in your face!

There is no need to discuss this any further!

11:24 A.M.

It had worked, yes — but then, in the seventies, people had been more than willing to defend themselves, their wives and children (and husbands) against the Frank Millers of the world. They'd fought to make it safe for a woman (or man) to walk the streets of this society. And in that struggle to create a true civilization in this raw, rugged land of frontier-style lawlessness, what had been their chief weapon? The twin six-guns of parody and satire.

Vale had been there. He had taken part in the effort to ridicule the powerful and empower the ridiculous, and prove to the folks back in Europe that, by God, this was a civilization, here in the West. By the decade's end it had seemed a fait accom- pli: law had been restored. Good values had taken root. Ecology was widely held to be important. Debutantes were largely con- sidered to be absurd. The country was a place where a man could raise a wife and family — or, of course, vice versa.

But then the eighties came, and with them all the bad guys, bad policies, bad values, and bad karma Vale thought they'd gotten rid of years before. The world somehow felt meaner. People who in 1978 had been merely fatuous when they said, "I've decided it's okay to make money" (as though that were the issue, and not how one made it), today were announcing, "I want to be rich," with the preening, ice-cold smile of a Hollywood Nazi.

It wasn't even the reappearance of the same old bushwa from the same old bushwasie that got him down — the religious and political right gave him a livelihood, if nothing else. No, it was the reaction of his generation to it all. Two decades ago they had denounced all that; ten years ago they had "transcended" all that. Now a man could get trampled in their stampede to embrace all that.

Vale knew his fellow writers would regard his moral apoplexy with amused smiles and rolled eyes. SAY POPE CATHOLIC was the mock Daily News headline they used to refer to any solemn or outraged discovery of the obvious. Maybe Vale was more naïve than he could possibly, in his unimaginable naïveté, imagine.

Worse: maybe he was becoming a dogmatic drag. Vale wondered, for the first time, if he had unwittingly made the leap from satirist to crank. All this fretting and brooding while everyone else went about their business — was he simply becoming a lugubrious, moralizing bore in his old age? Was he taking all this too seriously?

Lightening Up

This winter a Club Med will open in China, at Shenzen
— *The New York Times*

TO: The Collective Committee for Tourism
FROM: The Collective Committee for Publicity
RE: Club Med Advertising Brochure

Find attached hereto two drafts of above-mentioned brochure. First draft embodies the Standard Approach to the Correct Revolutionary Attitude. Second draft represents the New Approach to the Revised Revolutionary Attitude, in accordance with the recently promulgated Liberalization Guidelines.

FIRST DRAFT

Strive ceaselessly to feel welcome at Club Med, Shenzen! Read in this pamphlet vital introductory comments and explanations to assure vigorous relaxation and adequate fun. Facilities are for the benefit of all guests! Obey rules without exception.

Lodging

The Hut is the home for you and your Hut comrades for the duration of your time at the Club. Freely make use of its cot, sink, and toilet facilities. Such linen and blankets as are necessary are provided without request. Let each guest shower at his or her discretion. Reject desires for greater luxury; when the Hut is soft, and appointed with the trappings of a decadent body-fetishism, the spirit of the guest is sapped and the fun-life of the village slackens.

Electrical power grows out of a barrel of oil, therefore turn out light when not in use and, if possible, earlier.

Food

All foods and drinks are included in the progressive Club fee. Therefore let each guest eat in obedience to his true hunger. But abjure absolutely petty hungers, snack-greed, and eating-for-its-own-sake.

Wine is available at all meals except breakfast, and may be consumed according to the individual's euphoria requirement. Drink like a fish and move among the people, but strive daily to contribute to the harmony of the group. Eschew horseplay, rowdyism, and aggressive bullyism toward weaker guests. Reject completely the inebriated throwing of chairs through windows!

Consult the List of Acceptable Inebriation Songs for spontaneous reveling.

Enjoyment Activities

Members of the Club's well-trained Enjoyment Cadre stand ready to defend all guests against boredom or having-a-crummy-time-ism. Obey their all-in-fun suggestions without cavil. Their participation in Guest Enjoyment Activities is paramount to the success of the Club. Be vigilantly poised to assist them in their duties at all times. Take part! Pursue leisure!

Defeat the jackal-headed specter of listless hanging around. Oppose moping. Berate self and criticize others for heaving bored sighs. Guests reported by members of the Enjoyment Cadre or by their comrade-vacationers to be thus pouting will be encouraged to become happy and perform skits about enthusiasm before a sympathetic committee. Those wrongly aligned in dialectical opposition to this policy are urged to change their minds.

Expunge passivity. Let a hundred enjoyment activities bloom.

Sex-having

Reject vigorously sex-having. The policy of "letting a hundred enjoyment activities bloom" is meant to promote wholesome pursuits, as, for instance, the playing of volleyball, the riding of boogie boards, or the field identification of unusual insects. Sex-having ruptures the integrity of the group and results, among those not participating, in envy, in self-pitying loneliness, and dread-of-not-getting-any-action-ism.

Bridle sensuality, and rectify the false consciousness of sex-wanting, by emulating the members of the Enjoyment Cadre. It is they who are the true vanguard in the vacation struggle. Ski on water, dance until curfew, and drink parasol-studded silly cocktails at their command. Respect the correctness of their recreational consciousness.

Summary

The Club exists for its guests. Yet strive daily to remember that a Club without its staff is a panda without legs. A Club with a discontented staff is a panda crippled and unable to walk. Live, therefore, to assure the maximum happiness of the highest possible number of staff.

Enjoy your fun.

SECOND DRAFT

Dear Guest,

Just a note to welcome you upbeatedly to Club Med, Shenzen. Don't look now, but you are already having more liberalized, individualistic fun. Read enthusiastically about the Club Med, Shenzen, creative concept of personal initiative and enhanced go-for-it-ism, because we feel good about this hot thing, and what could be bad?

Your own strictly private cabaña is fully equipped with everything necessary for the unswerving pursuit of deluxe pamperism. Foods and drinks are abundant and ceaselessly provided. Drink wine without shame. Throw drunkenly chairs through windows! All is included in the fee you have already confirmedly paid. Sing whatever hooligan drunk-song that occurs to you. Live unwaveringly in the fast lane.

Promote sex-having. Indulge self and pursue getting-some-action-ism. Let a hundred and one enjoyment activities bloom, or let one bloom a hundred times. Because "whatever."

As for the staff, may we speak without censorship? Comprehend fully the principle that the only guys who will be more diverted than you are Team Fun, our activities "counselors." Feel free to obey their suggestions to the letter or reject the hyena-headed specter of conformity, and tell them, without fear of official criticism or social stigma, "No can do, José."

Because here is the good news: mandatory enjoyment activities are one of the Eight New Revised Evil Winds at Club

Med, Shenzen. We abjure them totally, and hey, no one is forced to do anything or not to do something. Imagine uninhibitedly a guy who isn't O.K. in a program of skiing on water, making the crazy luau scene, and drinking parasol-studded silly cocktails. Do we condemn him fiercely as a running-dog pariah of zeal-sapping mopery, listless sigh-heaving, and reactionary bring-down-ism? Do we subject him to public censure for not lightening cooperatively up?

No, because we're talking Fun Modernizations here. So sue us, what can he do for relaxation and adequate pleasure? Why, he can confer with our V.C.I.C. (Venture Capital Investment Cadre), whose members are always looking for canny individuals with some liquid assets for playing around with. This is all the rage that's going down in every province! Besides, you are on vacation, so why shouldn't your money have fun, too, "babe"?

Not to be in your face too much, but these are some of the projects our people are trying to get off of the ground:

—*The Whole World Immediately* newspaper, a large-print one-page organ that the masses will read as they ride their bicycle.
—The prototype of a computer-monitored high-speed device for folding cloth.
—A 2,000-hole golf course capable of accommodating up to seven hundred foursomes simultaneously.

And more. Simply tell your Team Fun counselor, "Wow, I want to invest capital foresightedly and earn a reasonable profit."

Are the staff here to serve you staunchly, or what? We assure you that either with a group or by yourself, your privacy will be guaranteed. The Club is a panda and its guests are its legs. Therefore advance your own self-interested running around. Have vigorously it all.

Love ya resolutely.

_____

Vale saw the envelope in his mailbox from ten feet off, the smooth gray paper a dead giveaway, the logo on the label unmistakable. The letter inside, clipped to the piece, read:

Dear Noah,
    Well, as I feared, the feeling here is that it just doesn't work. The metaphor of the U.S. as a banana republic has its appealing aspects — I especially liked the image of the generals and the weapons mfrs. dancing "with a rapid and exhilarating movement of the feet, as a group of gentlemen executing the close-order rhumba." But many of the analogies seem forced — the farm centralization, the rising professional class, the fact that Reagan takes a lot of vacations. Ultimately, though, it comes down to, How true, really, is the premise? And doesn't the piece as a whole do little more than re-establish the premise over and over?
    To wring humor out of a concern for "the increase in the proportional disparity between the rich and the poor" is awfully tough — it might have to be dramatized, rather than simply stated, no matter how arch the tone. I don't care for the line about the jungle, e.g.

(Vale did. "It's a jungle out there, and jungles are fertile: between the filthy rich and the dirt poor, banana republics grow like crazy.")
    The letter went on to thank Vale for allowing Kramer to see the piece, and closed with the hope that they could buy the next one.
    Vale looked at his watch: almost 11:30. *Kramer would still be in his office.*
    "Harve? Noah."
    "Hello, Noah. Sorry about the piece . . . but, I mean, I hate to say it, but political humor is very tricky. My gut sense is you're too close to the material. I'd say try something safer."
    "Politically safer . . . ?"
    "Oh, no. Good lord, politically I'm with you all the way. But literarily it's problematic. You get didactic. Which is death.

Look, all I mean is, you need more distance on the material. You're feeling strongly about these social and political matters — as we all are, to an extent — but you're surrounded by it. So you've got to get away. That's what I mean by 'safer.' "

Vale thanked him and, with a promise to send something else soon, hung up.

Vale went outside for a walk. The hot street was unusually quiet in the midday sun. Somewhere, somebody was playing a lone and plaintive harmonica, probably.

Buyers' Closeout

HELP! We'reTheDepartmentofDefenseandwe'reSTUCK! We've got to unload $4.6 trillion in high-tech, professional-quality defense merchandise pronto! We're talking Missiles! Bombers! Subsbothnuclearandconventional! We're practically *giving* away the WHOLE STRATEGIC TRIAD, at UNBELIEVABLE discounts! It's our one-time-only End of Nuclear Winter Sale!

How'd it all happen? "Star Wars"! It's complete, and in place, and most of the parts we did test — worked like a CHARM! And now we've got virtually perfect detection-location-neutralization of enemy I.C.B.M.'s in the boost phase. We've never *felt* (withinreasonablelimitsofstatisticalprobability) SO SAFE!

Don't believe it? See for yourself! Try launching a unilateral first strike against us. WE DARE YOU! Or! Send a self-addressedstampedenvelope and we'll ship you, by return mail, a bunch of *poetry* written by some of the BEST of today's crop of young, ambitious second graders. Do they believe in a future free of the threat of nuclear annihilation?

They do now!

Or visit any of our branch offices and examine the test data. The Soviets did — and were they impressed!

"This looks GREAT!" the Soviets said. "But hey — how do we know it's strictly defensive? You've got literally TONS of hi-tech, top-quality, brand-name scientific equipment, orbiting NOW, up in SPACE. You're talking lasers! Rail guns! Particle beams! But how do we know it isn't REALLY warheads! Delivery systems! Surveillance monitors! Why should we take your word for it? Because YOU KNOW US! When it comes to fearing invasion from outside our borders by Western imperialist nations bent on conquest, we're so paranoid we're IN-SANE!"

NO PROBLEM! we said. And then we told them about the DepartmentofDefense *Written Guarantee*. If at any time the "Star Wars" anti-missile system fails to function in a strictly defensive role, and provides instead a covert means of launching a unilateral offensive nuclear strike against the Soviets or their allies — we will personally apologize in writing. That's the DepartmentofDefense Guarantee — AND WE MEAN IT!

Then we told them that a complimentary "Star Wars" package was on its way to their defense people via Express Mail — and you could hear the champagne corks popping from Moscow to Sakhalin Island!

"Wait'll we tell our children's children!" they said. "They've been yearning to live in an era of eased superpower tensions for years!"

"Fine," you're saying. "But how's that spell humongous savings in big-ticket weapons and support gear for *me?*"

Simple. With "Star Wars" up and "on-line," our entire nuclear arsenal is obsolete! The whole inventory — IT'S GOTTA GO! Anything and everything in offensive and defensive hardware and software — it's ON SALE NOW!

We're switching from a retaliatory defense posture to a preventive one. We're dismantling our entire military-industrial establishment (with the exception of a prudent level of conventional forces), and ending the waking nightmare of nuclear terror that's tormented all of humanity for forty years. It's a long-awaited blessing for us, the living, and an assurance of hope for the generations to come. And that's good news, indeed, for the entire human race.

BUT IT'S BAD NEWS FOR OUR WAREHOUSE MANAGER!

He'sbeenorderedtotakedrasticmarkdownson: Warheads! Boosters! Silos! From Multiple-Independently-Targetable-Reentry-Vehicles (MIRV) to Military-Authorized-Racquetball-Venues (MARV) — they're all on sale NOW at unbelievable discounts, because WE DON'T NEED 'EM ANY MORE!

But you still do!

Say you're a developing Third World nation! You want security, but at a price you, and your underwriters at the International Monetary Fund, can afford. You want hi-quality, state-of-the-art weaponry. For regional disputes. For centuries-old traditional rivalries. Or just for that politically "safe" feeling that comes only from the maintenance and appeasement of a well-armed military.

Until now, your options were fairly limited. You could depend on the usual methods. Retail purchase from the manufacturer. R&D. Espionage. Defections. It was a chancy system. And expensive. You'd likely end up busting your budget, mauling your currency, feeding your population grass — and still not wind up with enough bang for the bucks.

Or, say you're a small but vital Western power — Liechtenstein, for example. Or Texas. Sure, you have faith in your allies. But you know that when push comes to massive retaliation, no piece of paper with a NATO letterhead can compare with the solid throw-weight of a few dozen Pershings, strategically targeted, in the Ready-to-Launch mode, with the safety off, sirens blaring, and all systems Go.

WELL, now YOU can have Superpower quality, Superpower sophistication, Superpower megadeath capability — at *one ten-billionth* the cost! We're slashingourregularpriceson-everyiteminSTOCKpile! No seconds or knockoffs! Strictly first-quality, brand-name merchandise! Stealth bombers: come early, walk away — undetected — with a dozen! Trident subs: going for what you'd expect to pay for an ordinary two-man submersible with stereo!

We're ready to deal. With your government, junta, strongman, or local police chief. Directly with principals, via authorized agents, or through the shadowy international arms trader of your choice.

Everything must go! We will not be underdisarmed!

Credit is available. Use it or lose it!

But hurry! The End of Nuclear Winter Sale will not be repeated! Once we (and the Soviets) have exhausted our supplies at these *incredible* discounts — once we've ushered in an age (at least, for us) of true and lasting world peace — THAT'S IT!

You're on your own!

PART II

High Noonish

11:28 A.M.

Then again, Vale thought, perhaps print is the wrong medium.

Not that Vale was the kind of man who went around thinking about "media." But no one got excited over topical humor in magazines or books any more — in part because hardly any magazines bought it any more. A man whose livelihood depended on selling political satire to Atlantic *or* Esquire *was a man shaking hands with starvation. How to account for all this editorial complacency, conservatism, and/or cowardice?*

Vale blamed the President. Wasn't that why we had a President? To blame things on? And hadn't the country turned deaf and dumb as soon as Old Pop moved into the White House? If the Chief Executive sets the tone of an administration or a social agenda, then Vale couldn't wait for the U.S. to hang up, wait for another tone, and dial again.

The New Rules

A new Administration has come to power, and many Americans are asking: what are the new rules? The following explanation, presented in clear, easy-to-understand language, may be of some help in addressing this matter.

Q: Are there new rules?

A: Yes, there are.

Q: Will I have difficulty understanding them?

A: No. Unlike the reality to which they refer and whose activities and phenomena they govern, the new rules are presented in clear, easy-to-understand language.

Q: Must I obey them?

A: Yes. Their nature as new rules is such that all to whom they pertain must obey them. Like the old rules, they pertain to everyone.

Q: What are the new rules?

A: A complete review of all the new rules would be beyond the scope of this clear, easy-to-understand explanation. However, a sampling of several representative new rules will make clear the general spirit and intent of the entire corpus of new rules.

MONEY

Money, under the new rules, will be simultaneously more important and less important than it was under the old rules. More important because there will be less of it available to all persons subject to the new rules, less important because its value will continue to decline. Money will still be used for purchasing, however, and, as was the case under the old rules, the impossibility of purchasing goods and services will continue to be expressed in the amount of money required for their purchase. Some Americans will have some money, and will be able to purchase goods and services.

WOMEN

Under the new rules, the importance of women will remain unchanged. However, there will be far less acknowledgment of that importance. Under the old rules, the role of men was one thing, the role of women another. Under the new rules, exactly the same conditions will hold, with this crucial difference: men will no longer be required to pretend that women have an important role. In addition, women will be required to pretend that they have no role at all.

MEXICO

To those who complain that the new rules are nothing more than the old rules rewritten in clearer, easier-to-understand language, the example of Mexico stands as a decisive rebuttal. Mexico, under the new rules, will be entirely different. Where Mexico was once referred to as America's Neighbor to the South, now it will be referred to as America's Major Source of Oil for the Coming Decades to the South. Under the old rules, Mexico was ignored or insulted. Under the new rules, this will be absolutely forbidden. The old-rule homily "I need such-and-such like Mexico needs chili peppers" will be replaced by the new-rule homily "We need Mexico."

GOD

A rule is only as new as the reality that it governs permits it to be. And no truly significant reality could exist for very long without the support of God. It is for this reason that God, under the new rules, will play a major role.

NICE CLOTHES

The new rules mandate that as soon as possible, and from then on, Americans shall display a reawakened fondness for nice clothes. Those Americans able to purchase nice clothes with money will be encouraged to wear them. Under the new rules, it will be left to the wearer's discretion whether he or she will wear nice clothes with a conspicuously displayed attitude of relief that it is, under the new rules, once more permissible to wear nice clothes.

FREEDOM

Like the people who constitute it, society places a high value on freedom, as do the rules. There are two kinds of freedoms: freedom *from*, and freedom *to*. And, as is traditional in America, the new rules proclaim admiration for both these kinds of freedom. That is why the new rules entail freedom *from* the old rules. That is why they are based upon freedom *to* make the new rules. No one should doubt that under the new rules there will be freedom.

It must be remembered that the new rules are subject to change. However, the supersession of any present new rule by a subsequent rule *will in no way* alter the superseded rule's status as a new rule. *It will not become an old rule.* Moreover, *it will never be seen to have been an old rule.* It will remain a new rule albeit thenceforth in the mode of having-been-superseded. The superseding rule will not become a new rule but, rather, a newer rule.

It should be apparent that the new rules, as exemplified in the selection above, are designed to create a better society. Naturally, the entire corpus of new rules is extensive, and covers far more than those topics dealt with in the above six samples. (For instance, the official edition of the new rules features eighteen different rules governing the use of the word "fair.") But even the preceding six samples give an indication of how life will be under the new rules. They persuasively demonstrate that society, under the new rules, will be one in which some Americans enjoy the God-given freedom to supply their women with money for nice clothes and, at the same time, need Mexico. This is clear and easy to understand.

11:30 A.M.

The next day Earl called.

"Noah? Hey, I was wondering if you had anything in mind for us for the September issue."

Ten years ago Vale had worked on the staff of the humor magazine for which Earl was now the editor. They had only met once. The magazine, meanwhile, was not what it had been.

At the time of Watergate it had been the most notorious, provocative, and all-around naughty publication in the country. Within its dual tradition of scatalogical and sexual rudeness, and smarty-pants undergraduate intellectuality (each half of which, like the two lobes of the human brain, served to validate the other), just about any satirist could find a home: cynical

Irish Catholics, forever angry at God for not existing; class-clown WASP rich kids, amused at the bad taste of almost everyone else in the world for failing to have been born rich; nice Jewish boys, mad because so many other people were not nice.

"Well, I've been sort of busy lately. . . ."

"We were thinking you might want to do something on Frank Miller. Something with a lot of graphics, like his campaign kit, a press kit, something like that."

"That's interesting. . . ."

"Yeah, we could do two or four pages, whatever you felt like."

Vale had imagined, during the years in the late seventies when he had written steadily for the magazine, that he was sowing the seeds of particular ideas and values across the psychic landscape. If they couldn't germinate in adult minds, they might in the minds of teenagers, and take root, and have an effect.

"Yeah, look, Earl, the fact is I'm sort of tied up right now."

"We got till the end of next month. So there's no rush."

His campaign, it suddenly struck him, had been a failure. The fourteen-year-olds had double-crossed him — or had he failed them? In any case, they had grown up to be Republican undergraduates in college, then gone on to investment banking, corporate litigation — the Hindering Professions. He had pointed out the enemy, and they had followed his directions, only to run right over and sign up.

Stalling Earl, and desperate to think of an excuse, he now thought with a sigh that maybe he should have chosen his topics with more of an eye to the guidance of youth. Of course he couldn't really blame himself. . . . But who was to say that a parody of Joan Didion — so well-intentioned at the time, so perfect for summing up the decade just ended — did not, at some crucial turning point in some young man's life, turn him away from the dusty, grass-clumped-yet-worthy path of consumer activism or environmental reclamation, and place him squarely on the restricted-access, high-speed fancy-schmancy Autobahn to Mergers and Acquisitions for Morgan Stanley?

The White Albumen

ONE

I have been asked to write about the "meaning" of the seventies. I have been asked to write about the "meaning" of the seventies because, vain hope, there may actually exist in this uneasy nation of Double Whoppers with cheese and postindustrial angst a segment of the population interested in reading an essay concerning the "meaning" of the seventies. My editor has asked me, "What do the seventies mean?"

What do. A day does not pass during which I do not think about the words *what do.* I like to think about such things; I like to think about such things and wonder, Why am I thinking about such things? Perhaps that exactly describes the seventies.

TWO

This is what I did today: I got out of bed. I showered, and shaved my legs. *Notice that I did not say, I showered my legs.* I got dressed and went downstairs to the kitchen. I ate breakfast. The breakfast consisted of orange juice. The breakfast consisted of toast and butter. The breakfast consisted of two scrambled eggs. The breakfast consisted of coffee black. *Notice that I did not say, The breakfast consisted of black coffee.*

After breakfast I went into my "office." My "office" is not, strictly speaking, an "office." There are no secretaries. There is no receptionist. There are no files. There is no modular office furniture. My "office" is actually a reproduction of a maximum-punishment facility of the sort seen in "Hollywood" movies about the Korean War, and the war with the Japanese. In such movies, such maximum-punishment facilities are referred to by the generic name "the cooler." Such maximum-punishment facilities are referred to by the generic name "the cooler" because, in the manner of such "Hollywood" films, a cheap sort of irony obtains which requires that a small cell made of crude wooden slats, four feet on each side, and left in the unshaded sunlight be called a "cooler." Such is my "office."

I enter it on my hands and knees. I crawl to the small pallet on which rests my typewriter. It is an electric typewriter, but, small wonder, there is no electrical power surging through the silent cables in my "office," no power with which to run the typewriter, which is made by an Italian company with a steel-and-glass office building in New York. (To those of us who live in California, New York is referred to as "back East," as in, "During the 1978 series, my wife rooted for L.A., but I rooted for back East.") I am forced to pick up each typing element and press it, manually, to the ribbon and onto the paper. The keys of the Italian-made typewriter do not work. The return key of the Italian-made typewriter does not work. The space bar of the Italian-made typewriter does not work.

In this manner, crouched over in unbearable heat, breathing thick, fetid air, tearing my stockings and ripping my dress,

I write. *Notice that I did not say ripping my stockings and tearing my dress.* I think this is a parable that precisely explains something.

THREE

My husband is a writer. I am a writer. My husband lives in California; my husband lives in California and I also live in California. (I live with my husband.) Sometimes we work together — as when, for example, I will look up from my notepad and ask him, "Who is that embodies all that is tragic in the world of American culture?"

He will suggest, "Theodore H. White."

I will reply, "No, Theodore H. White represents all that is naïve in American scholarship."

"I thought you said that David Halberstam represents all that is naïve in American scholarship," he will say.

"No," I will reply. "David Halberstam embodies all that is idealistic in the world of American journalism."

"I don't know, then," he will say. "I don't know, then," he will say and then say, "Shut up. I'm trying to write."

FOUR

Perhaps the meaning of the seventies is to be found in vague, blunt generalizations. Sometimes generalizations are useful. Sometimes generalizations are not useful.

FIVE

My daughter, who was four years old when the seventies began, does not remember the Dave Clark Five. The Dave Clark Five were a rock 'n' roll band that knew a certain measure of popularity during the sixties, during that time when young men playing electrified instruments went so far in their quest to be "English" that they were born and raised and lived in England. The Dave Clark Five were one of these groups of "English" young men. They had a hit record, the title and refrain of which exactly describes the sixties. The refrain, addressed to an unspecified listener named Bitson, goes, "I'm in pieces, Bitson, pieces."

The pieces are not described. Bitson is not described. How the singer came to know Bitson is not described. What is to become of the singer, the singer in pieces, is not described. The reply of Bitson to the singer, to the one in pieces, is not described.

My daughter does not know this song.

"Who is Bitson?" I ask her.

She does not know. I do not know. I wish to know.

SIX

She is, this entertainer, tall. She has one name, which is to say she goes by one name professionally, presumably in contradistinction to those times during which she is not "entertaining." To watch her on television, as I have done recently, is to encounter face-to-face the peculiarly American sort of phenomenon in which a woman with two names may watch (on television) a woman with one name.

Whatever the reason for her decision to remain surnameless, Cher is in many respects like most other women. She has two arms. She has two eyes. She has two feet. Yet it is possible to see Cher as embodying something more. It is possible to see her as embodying that Pirandellian moment when reality and illusion merge. For behind the tall body, the long hair, the pseudo-French one name, there is a woman treated, inescapable fate, *as a commodity*. Cher is only on the television screen so that several dozen million may, while watching her "entertain," boost the network's Nielsens and, afterward, move the sponsors' merch. What Cher does not say on camera, what no one says amidst all this "entertainment," is the plain fact that *television is a business*.

"We'll be right back," she says to her audience via camera and microphone. "So you guys stay tuned, okay?"

You guys. It is as if, suddenly, all of America is populated by "guys." You guys. She would have us believe, this mononymous woman of mediocre talent, that she is speaking to us, not to a television camera and a microphone. You guys. The tone is affected, the tone is artificially conversational. Here, of course, is the secret of this woman's astonishing appeal. She implies that one is her friend. She implies that she is speaking directly to one. She implies that one is male. She succeeds in implying all this in a single sentence, *when the truth is that one is not necessarily her friend, her direct auditor, or a "guy" at all.*

It is a bewildering situation, and I think it exactly describes the entertainment industry, the women's liberation "movement," all people with one name, tall people, France, and the seventies.

SEVEN

Upon looking in the mirror I see a woman very much like myself. Upon looking in the mirror I see a woman whose reflection is more precisely itself at that time than at any other. The woman whose reflection I see upon looking in the mirror is exactly that woman who, as she begins her life in the 1980s, stops and puzzles over what someone else has called "the meaning of the seventies."

I think that the seventies was a decade in which "style" predominated over substance. I think that the seventies was a time in which the life-style of California (self-absorption, anomie) overtook in influence the life-style of New York (other-directed work, hypertension). I think that the seventies was a time in which analysis gave way to mere description. I think that the seventies was a time in which the ascendancy of women to their rightful plateau of power (nearer if not coequal to that of men) resulted in the unavoidable ascendancy of women of second-rate talent. I think that the seventies was a time in which personal idiosyncrasy was mistaken for talent, was mistaken for talent and insight.

As I stare into the mirror at that woman so like "myself," I think:

Because I am a writer whose style predominates over the substance of her writings; because I am a writer whose reportage sinks under the weight of its flat descriptions and high school-bohemian self-absorption, without much analysis to buoy it up; because I am a writer who is a woman, and therefore subject to more lavish praise than I might receive if I were a man; because my personal idiosyncrasy as a writer is to be repetitious, to be repetitious and deadpan, to be repetitious and deadpan and catatonic in tone, to be repetitious and deadpan and catatonic in tone and to place "quotation marks" around words to thereby suggest that I hold them and the reality to which they refer at arm's length, as though life itself impinges too harshly upon my sensibility; and because I have become respected and widely praised as a chronicler of contemporary life (and am considered by one critic to be "the finest prose stylist writing in America today"), it seems to me that the seventies and I were made for each other.

Only in the seventies could a writer like me have garnered the reputation I have, and I think that exactly describes the meaning of the seventies.

11:32 A.M.

Vale put Earl off with vague excuses and unspecific promises. It wasn't until the next morning, at 11:32, that the awful truth hit him: the humor magazine's crusade to instruct the nation's youth had not been a failure. It had succeeded all too well.

In its pages Vale and his colleagues had presented the spectacle, in the seventies, of a nation in which all authority was bankrupt, all institutions corrupt, all conventions — from the sacredness of babies to the solemnity of death — fodder for boffs. The art world subsisted on pretense and fraud. Business was synonymous with duplicity, greed, and pollution. Politics was a jamboree of lawyers working for millionaires, shysters working for themselves, and paranoid cranks working for the ghost of Joseph McCarthy. Sports figures were narcissistic lame-brains with greedy agents. Show business was a carnival of mediocrity posturing as art, operated by vulgarians posing as creators. Advertising was a species of virus that infected the language and eroded the mind. Sex was a demolition derby in which two contestants obliterated each other. Women were either stupid idiots or intelligent idiots. So were men. Consumer goods were trinkets and beads elevated to the status of fetish objects by the then-new cargo cult of "lifestyle." Religion was a pep rally in a foreign language, with God as the retired head coach nobody saw anymore. Magazines were hothouses where bizarre plants flourished according to their owners' or editors' narrow cultural or political obsessions. Law was a secret society that sold protection to the populace from its own arcane creations. Medicine was a racket. Food was hilarious.

This was not a "mature" portrait of the American reality. But then, there were times when Vale thought that maturity meant not much more than being able to recite both sides' propaganda.

Was it any wonder that confronted with Commencement Day entrance into this anarchic, feverish, reeling, Hieronymus Bosch–like dance-of-the-pagan-demons' hell-on-earth, the smartest college kids gravitated to security, money, and conservatism? They had taken the magazine at its word, and had acted accordingly.

Vale begrudged them nothing — nothing, that is, except real estate. They seemed to own tons of it, while Vale, a renter, lived in fear of his building's co-optation, and his banishment to one of the City's nether provinces.

No one was exempt from real estate. The poor were crushed by it, the middle class enslaved to it, the rich realized long-term capital gains from it. All those full-page co-op ads in the Sunday Times real estate section, the tall, balcony-encrusted buildings like so many Lego rocket ships, the text a bland combination of Discreet Banker and Canny Pimp — their equivalent probably existed throughout Eternity. At the edge of the expanding Universe, where Matter and Space had not yet moved in to transform Nothing and Nowhere, co-op ads were being written and art-directed and proofed. Whole planned communities were being designed, "built," and advertised. Everyone was implicated — even incorporeal beings lacking palpable physical forms, whose very existence Man would find difficult to comprehend.

They might consist of pure energy; they might be protean shape-shifters, capable of altering their bodily chemistry at will. They might exist as thought waves, sensate "string" particles, or magnetic fields. But they had to live somewhere and, sooner or later, the poor bastards, they'd have to deal with real estate.

Rancho Neutrino "Terrace"

Condominium Living for the Transmaterial Lifeformstyle

Beauty. Elegance. Refinement. Luxury. Temperatures guaranteed to exceed thirty-six million degrees Centigrade. And the not inconsiderable advantage of knowing that you have invested your affluence in a home-field force-structure unique in all the Three Extent Universes — and that its value is secure.

We commend to your ideational processing the condominium home-field force-structures of Rancho Neutrino "Terrace," the only fully planned demon and quasimaterial living development in the Known Grid.

Scrupulously designed to the smallest gluonic link, yet bold in vision and "breath"taking in its macro-aspect, Rancho Neutrino "Terrace" is located some forty-five degrees Transverse/twenty-four degrees Magnetic/thirty-one degrees Absolute to the cosmically renowned Galleria of a Thousand Million Oaks, just a few centuries from the Mount Psion Mesonic Temple, and mere parsecs from exciting, throbbing, imploding NetherZone Mall and Shopping Abyss. Convenient to all major transmaterial generation units, Rancho Neutrino "Terrace" offers the best of both Both-Worlds: binary self-other energy exchange, and private precious-personal-moment maximization. Enter, and behold an unparalleled universe of elegance, where the Mind-Body Problem is, quite simply, "no problem."

This, indeed, is your Place Within the Sun, where "to Be or Not to Be" is literally beside the point. Topologically unique access zones, coded to your private decay rate, assure absolute security for your "self" and your beloved physical manifestations. Award-winning materialization experts have provided a host of semireal environment simulacra that give new meaning to the word "visible."

Moreover, each unit is utterly unique, both in spatial layout and temporal duration. Graviton power assures that each floor, regardless of external phenomena, will remain a floor. Every subsector is accessible to one or more wavelengths of the Electromagnetic Spectrum — standard of impression transmission since one ten-billionth of a second after the Big Bang itself. Cable-ready leisure field? Of course. Antimatter nourishment poles? Standard. Tile bathrooms? "Naturally."

And your neighbors? A cosmological blend of demons, pseudos, quasimorphs, and energoids, all of "whom" share — with you — the highest standards for dwelling-stasis and thought-form transmissibility.

Yet Rancho Neutrino "Terrace" is more than just another randomly fluctuating gauge-field of localized, nontrivial condominium-events. You will find, within its magnetic boundaries, a complete, self-sustaining ecomatrix. A fully accredited, Continuum-authorized educational loop provides comprehensive schooling for nascent forms, from Inchoate to Prestable to grades K–445.

Step-up transformer centers — reserved for the exclusive use of Rancho residents only, of course — offer the ultimate in convenience for those who, possessing "bodies," desire to exercise them. A fully licensed staff of quantum mechanics waits to serve you — courteously, efficiently, acceleratingly — twenty-four hours per day. Solar windsurfing, three Olympus-size swarming pools (indoor, outdoor, coexistent-with-door), and a professionally designed eighteen-Black-Hole championship golf course, attest to the level of luxury that has made Rancho Neutrino "Terrace" the first choice among "today's" most discerning, whether for principal residences, or *pseudopieds-à-terre*.

That many of the most prestigious concerns from the *Fortune* Five Trillion have selected Rancho Neutrino "Terrace" as the site of their discorporate headquarters, provides additional luster to its already glittering list of residents.

May we add your thought frequency as well?

Note: This does not constitute an offer of sale, nor does this sentence constitute a disclaimer. Rancho Neutrino "Terrace" does not exist, nor is the preceding clause a true statement. Complete offering terms are available in a Prospectus via Guild Monitored thought-link with the Sponsor. Contact, on a minimum of three standard wavelengths, the Rancho Neutrino Partnership (Telepathex: RANCHNUTE), 1 the Singularity, Center of Maximum Entropy, Edge of Unimaginable Chaos, 11215.

11:34 A.M.

Vale worked for a week on a new set of notes for an excellent, doomed idea. Then he phoned Amy.

"I think she's in a meeting," Michelle sulked.

"Could you check?"

"Is it important?"

Vale sighed meaningfully. Michelle, getting the message, sighed back.

"Noah," Amy said a moment later. "I was just talking about you to someone yesterday."

For his first five years in or around show business, Vale had believed it whenever an agent said, "I was just talking about you," or "I was just thinking about you."

Now he simply said, "Great! Who to?"

"Jeff Barry and Barry Jeffreys at National International. They have a development deal with CBS. I told them you're a terrific young writer, and I mentioned the magazine pieces, and they're very anxious to meet you."

"Well, good. Because that's why I'm calling. I've got a little proposal here for a series I want to take around and pitch."

She laughed. "Noah, I knew you'd get back on the right track. Let me give you to Michelle and she'll get you Tom Walker's number at Extremely Creative."

"What about Jeff Barry and Barry Jeffreys at National International?"

"They're not right for you. You'll like Tom. Just a minute."

The next voice he heard was that of put-upon Michelle, reading a seven-digit number without preamble or courteous small talk. After thanking her, Vale reminded her that today was the first day of the rest of her life, adding, "unfortunately."

Vale dialed the number without temporizing. He was rewarded: Tom Walker proved lively and amiable.

"Amy sent me some articles," he said. "I didn't know you were the one who wrote this John Irving parody. I remember when it came out. It was terrific. I made a few copies and gave it to some friends . . ." (Vale thought: I love this guy.) ". . . but they didn't get it."

"They were Reagan fans?"

"Well, one was. No, the problem was they hadn't read the book."

It was something Vale had been thinking about lately: the perishability of humor. So much of what he did was in immediate response to the ephemeral; his articles were like bagels — chewy and pliable today, desiccated and useless tomorrow. Parody lived and died by the popularity of its target; to read a parody whose subject you didn't know was to struggle with a text that kept hinting at disclosing meaning without ever actually *delivering it. It was like trekking across a desert toward an ever-receding mirage, all good intentions and optimism slowly withering into a sense of abandonment.*

But so what? Weren't disposability and obsolescence the spark plugs that fired the great engine of America? American writing should be temporary, quick to go stale, of limited currency, here today, gone tomorrow. Like that quintessentially American humor form, the wisecrack, American writing should be short, irreverent, snide, pitiless, last about two seconds, and make no sense out of context. No wonder the President hated or failed to comprehend lasting culture. It was un-American.

The Hotel Washington, D.C.

The year Father began to try to tame the bears was our first year living in The Hotel Washington, D.C. I think we sensed even then that there was something special about Father — a dreamy quality that probably had something to do with the fact that when he wasn't asleep, he spent most of his waking moments thinking the unthinkable. We all loved running the hotel, and wanted to make Father's job as manager as easy as we could. So pretty soon we *all* (one by one) went around thinking the unthinkable, until there was nobody left to think the thinkable. Later, we would all be going around mentioning the unmentionable. But before later, so much happened that we all started to go around wondering what *else* could possibly happen.

Here's one thing that happened: one day Father put Parson James in charge of the parks and wilderness preserves, which all started immediately going around getting raped.

"But Parson James *hates* parks and the outdoors," I said to Father. "He brags about it. How can you put him in charge of them?"

Father just smiled benevolently and shook his head and murmured, "Well, well, well," and probably I believed him.

By then we all knew that the strange and powerful love that existed between the nuclear-industry people and the nuclear-regulatory people had (secretly, of course) been expressed and consummated. Later than then, we would wonder what had taken them so long, since it would begin to seem that incest between members of the nuclear family was the most natural thing in the world.

But before then, the murder of the air-people's union happened. One day the air people went on strike, and the air-people's union, taking its sad and sorrowful leave of this lovely planet, dropped dead all over the nation.

" 'Dropped dead'?" said Meester Ed. "Seems to me like it *committed suicide*."

"It went on *strike*," Ambassador Jeane said.

"And that's against the *law*," Cousin Billy Frenchy Smitty said.

"Cut!" Skinny Stockman cried.

Later, I would know better than to ask Father anything. Before later, though — this was just after the air-people's union died — I asked Father something.

"Why did you murder the air-people's union, Father?" I asked.

"Why, I didn't murder *anything*," Father said, laughing good-naturedly and shaking his head. He always laughed and shook his head whenever he denied decertifying something.

Later, I would see that back then I would go around seeing that that's how we were: me, with my seeing later but asking earlier; Skinny, who was always going around shouting "Cut!"; Scrappy Al, who had his own private and mysterious language that no one could understand; Ambassador Jeane, who was very careful that *everybody* understood *her* vocabulary; and Father, our dreamer, who simply smiled and laughed and occasionally waved to the guests when they wanted to know why room service kept bringing them less and charging more.

"Well," Father would say, that twinkle in his eye. "I wouldn't feel too sorry for people who had good jobs before they got fired. *They're* not the truly needy."

"The truly needy!" we all cried in unison.

"Cut!" Skinny shouted.

"I'll tell you who *I* pityify and emphathicate for," Scrappy Al said. "It's those poor workers in Poland. Standing up to that great big bear all by themselves! By jingo, that's admirationable!"

("Because strikes are *illegal* in Poland," Ambassador Jeane would whisper to me much later. "At least, they *were*. But those people *defied* the government, and now they've got a *union!* They're *heroes!*")

Scrappy Al was always going around going on and on about the bear. Once, he spoke at a fundraiser that was like a very expensive party dinner — actually, it *was* a very expensive party dinner. His speech sounded like a foreign-policy statement — actually, it *was* a foreign-policy statement.

"We do not fearfulize the bear," he said. "We recognition that the bear intents to nuzzle and paw and snort and hug the *whole world*. But we're going to assurance that it confinements its activities and limitations its influentials to *where* it *belongs!*"

"Hurray!" the fundraisers shouted in unison.

"That goes double for me!" Father said, smiling and waving to the crowd.

But I think even then we all knew what Cap the Window-Watcher would say.

"One point six trillion," he said.

"One point six *trillion?*" I asked.

"One point six trillion," he said. "Dollars."

"That's a lot, Cap," Skinny said.

"It takes a lot of money to keep a bear in its place," Cap said. "This hotel has vulnerability to the bear. Why do you think I keep looking out the window?"

Father shook his head and smiled with that dreamer's twinkle in his eye. "Well," he said, "I guess you could almost say that when it comes to keeping the bear in line, it's the folks over at the *Pentagon* who are the truly needy."

"The truly needy!" we all cried in unison.

"Cut!" Skinny shouted.

"*I* know where we can get the money," Cap said.

"Where?" Skinny cried. "Tell us!"

"Tell us! Tell us!" we all cried in unison (all of us except Skinny, who had *already* cried "Tell us!").

"From the *people*," Cap whispered.

"*What* people?" Scrappy Al asked. He had spent so many years helping to manage The Hotel Washington, D.C., that he had *forgotten* that *anybody* except our *family* existed at *all*.

"The *American* people," Cap said, hitting Scrappy Al on the head with a sheaf of neutron-bomb cost-overrun explanations. ("That's a good bomb," Cap had said once. "A good *smart* bomb. We *need* a good smart bomb.")

"Now, now, stop bickering, you two," Father said dreamily. "Cap, you go figure out what you need, and I'll get it from the people."

"Better hurry up," Scrappy Al said. "The bear is coming!"

I think even then Scrappy Al believed, more than any of us, that one day we might have to shoot the bear, kill ourselves, and destroy the hotel in order to survive.

"The bear is almost accessing our localization!" he would cry. "The bear is pawing El Salvador! The bear is sniffing around South Africa!"

"Come on, Scrappy Al," I would say. "The bear can't be everywhere at once. In El Salvador all they want is to get rid of the *leeches*."

"What about Guatemala?" he'd say. "What about Argentina? The bear is encroachmenting everywhere!"

In those days, of course, somebody in Argentina or Guatemala was always going around disappearing and getting tortured or killed. It was horrible, and we were very sad over it, and it changed us forever back then.

"The bear isn't in Argentina or Guatemala," I would say. "Those are the *monsters*."

"Yes, they *are* monsters," Ambassador Jeane would sigh. "But thank God they're *our* monsters."

It was around then that I began to go to my office, close the door, and work out, weighing priorities. Once, Skinny stuck his head into my office and saw me.

"Cap and Scrappy Al and Ambassador Jeane get together and whisper all night about *their* bear," he whispered, "but they've got it all wrong. It's not *that* bear we have to worry about."

"Then which bear *is* it, Skinny?" I asked.

"The stock-market bear!" Skinny cried. "The stock-market bear is chasing everybody off Wall Street! The stock-market bear is eating up the bond market! Help!"

Then one morning I ran into everyone in the Rose Garden.

"Guess what!" Meester Ed said. "The Department of Energy and the Department of Education just committed suicide!"

"Holy cow!" we all cried in unison. "That's too bad!"

"Wait a minute!" I shouted. "Shouldn't we tell Father?"

"I don't want to wake him!" Ambassador Jeane yelled.

"I have to watch the window!" Cap screamed.

"Cut!" Skinny cried.

"He's not here in the hotel anyway!" Meester Ed bellowed. "He's out at the Western hotel on vacation, urging everyone to be more productive!"

"QUIET!" I roared. Everyone settled down, and since I had gone around going around thinking the unthinkable all morning, I decided to ask the unaskable. "Why are things always so crazy around this hotel?" I asked. "Why does everything always come down to one bear or another?"

"That's a good question!" they all cried in unison. "Ask Father!"

So I waited until later, when Father returned to The Hotel Washington, D.C., and then, after later, I went to his office.

"Can I ask you something, Father?" I asked.

"Well, that's a good, responsible, tough question," he said, a twinkle in those dreamer's eyes. "And I suppose you'll be expecting me to answer it."

"*Can* you, Father?" I said.

"Well," he said, a dream in those twinkler's eyes. "When I was made manager of this great lodging, it was in order to make The Hotel Washington, D.C., the finest hotel in the world once again. To run the hotel the way it *used* to be run — back then, before there were bears, and unions, and the need for monsters. Some say that that world is a world that no longer exists. But they're wrong. It does exist. It exists in the past. It exists in the memories of the hotel's guests. And it can exist once more in *this* hotel. All I ask of everyone is that they learn to live as the original guests of The Hotel Washington, D.C., lived in that exciting and glorious time when the hotel first opened."

And that was how we all got used to sleeping on the floor waiting for the roof to cave in.

11:36 A.M.

Tom Walker's office was a modest cubicle in a steel-and-glass high-rise in midtown, where Extremely Creative Productions shared a floor with an insurance firm, an import-export company, and something called Diversified Integral Services, which Vale assumed was a front for the CIA.

Tom was a young man in his midtwenties, clean shaven, boyish, in a crisp white shirt and perfectly tied tie, the knot perched buoyantly upon, of all things, a tab collar. Vale had noticed that while the development people at the various offices around town seemed to be getting younger, he, Vale, was not.

"Noah?" Tom said, extending a hand. "I'm really glad to meet you."

What a nice young man, Vale thought.

After a few minutes of pleasant preliminaries, Tom discussed what he hoped would happen. In essence, it consisted of Vale writing a few pages and then explaining and enacting them in meetings that combined the worst aspects of grad school orals and small claims court. The goal was to make a squad of executives at one network or another decide they were amused enough to cough up some cash.

"I know, it's drastically flawed," Tom said. He opened his hands in apology. "It's a terrible system, and it selects for mediocrity. But we're stuck with it for now."

Vale thought: How did all these twenty-six-year-olds get so poised? When he was twenty-six he spoke in nervous spurts, qualifying half the things he said and muttering the other half to himself. To people ten years his senior he'd been (still was) all boyish eagerness and bright agreement. But the next generation of kids comported themselves as though they'd been born guesting on talk shows.

A fear suddenly gripped Vale. Perhaps this wasn't poise but solicitude — courtesy to the old duffer looking for work. A decade ago Vale willingly attended these meetings, not minding the role of writer-as-supplicant. He was the creative fellow dashing about, exuding potential, exempt from judgment, while these telephone talkers and showbiz bureaucrats tried to fake competence and make decisions while pleasing their bosses and covering their asses. Now here was Vale, in the same chair, still the supplicant, seeking to impress a kid ten years younger. He could see the scene through Tom's eyes now: Vale pushing forty and still out there hustling; Tom the snappy, young production exec on the make. Time — or, rather, the routinely overlooked reality of time — made unexpected and sobering appearances, like a cop at the front door during a party. "What seems to be the problem, Officer?" "Nothing. Just watch it."

"Okay," Vale said. "Here's the idea. I'd like to do a satirical news review — like That Was the Week That Was, but updated — computer graphics, rock video-type musical numbers, a lot zingier and jazzier than the original."

Vale's heart was pounding. He hated pitches. He, a word man, hewer of strong sentences, forced to amuse and coax and leer and be spellbinding like some pasha's belly dancer in a Sindbad movie. He steeled himself for Tom's reluctance. Vale, of course, would understand.

"Sounds great!"

"You think so?"

"Definitely! Keep going, please."

Vale acknowledged that such special graphics required long lead times, and money, to produce. They would be used to deal with predictable milestones — elections, holidays, award ceremonies — and could be preproduced and put in the can. The cast, meanwhile, would deal with the timely material in live action. Would the show have to be broadcast live? Maybe. But a less frantic option would be to tape the day of broadcast, like late-night talk shows. That would afford a measure of control and still allow things to remain up-to-the-minute and spontaneous.

Tom Walker sat back and smiled. "I think it's terrific. We have a staff meeting this afternoon. I'll tell Mel Stevie."

Vale, with equal parts suspicion and hope, said, "You think it can fly?"

"It's very possible," *Tom said.* "We haven't had a suggestion like that in, well, ever since I've been here, that's for sure. I mean it's all dependent on what the networks are looking for, of course. But I like it a lot. Give me a couple days and I'll get back to you." *He smiled.* "You'll need a good actor to do the President."

Wary of the politics of young men everywhere today, Vale thought but did not say: what's that supposed to mean?

There You Go Again, Jeeves

I don't know if you've ever been President of the United States, but the job includes a pretty hefty chunk of grim reality along with the pomp and c. The brute fact of the matter is that someone is always interrupting your breakfast. Rev up the tum for the kippers and coffee, raise the cup of freshly brewed to your lips, and the next thing you know the assistant secretary for Inter-American Thingummy is hard by the bedside, barking about arms shipments to contras in Nicaragua. It's enough to make a chap think twice about standing for re-election.

Such were the thoughts clouding the Reagan mind one juicy October morning when Jeeves shimmered in at ten on the dot with the presidential eggs and b. A remarkable cove, Jeeves. Quite the most politically astute valet I've ever had. Without his counsel, Ronald's career in public service should have consisted almost entirely of one uninterrupted swim in the soup.

I sat up against the headboard and he placed the tray across my lap. "I lack the customary vim this morning, Jeeves," I said without preamble.

"Indeed, sir?"

"Yes, Jeeves. Utterly devoid of vim. How did Shakespeare put it — 'What's the point of gaining the world, if you lose your whatever-it-is . . . ?' "

"The observation is attributed to Jesus Christ, sir. The Book of Matthew, chapter sixteen, verse twenty-six. The reference is to the soul."

"And what of one's breakfast, Jeeves?" I said, pronging a pensive slab of over-easy. "What's the point of gaining the White House, if a chap has to pretty much abandon all hope of a peaceful morning tuck?"

"Such inconveniences are indeed regrettable, sir." He hesitated, then plunged on. "I'm afraid, sir, I shall have to impose on this meal also."

"Oh, dash it, Jeeves!"

"I am sorry, sir. But Mr. Tuttle telephoned. From Los Angeles."

"Hoho Tuttle?" An expression of pleasure suffused the Reagan map. This Tuttle was a bosom chum from my California days. When Ronald cast his eye on the statehouse, Hoho rallied round with a squad of simpatico Republicans and a bundle of the ready. "What's the aged crony want?"

"He wishes you to intercede on behalf of his nephew, sir," Jeeves said. "The boy is in danger of being expelled from medical school due to a distracting fondness for sunbathing and snorkling."

"Good Lord! Where is this bally school? Tahiti?"

"Grenada, sir. The site of a recent *coup d'état.*"

"Granada? Elementary, Jeeves." I gestured airily. "Have Bush fly to Spain and put in a word with King Juan Carlos. Surely His Highness is still in business?"

"Pardon me, sir, but I believe that course of action would prove less than efficacious. In point of fact, Grenada — "

"The First Breakfast languishes, Jeeves. Besides, the trip

will do Bush good," I said, glad to fine some useful task for the old heartbeat-away. "Now hold, enough, and shove over those plum preserves."

"Very good, sir."

I resumed a spirited feeding of the Reagan face, but had barely put myself around a rasher of hickory smoked before the chamber resonated with two sharp knocks. I stifled an oath.

"Madame Ambassador Kirkpatrick and Secretary Shultz, sir," Jeeves said, opening the door and admitting the pair.

Shultz was a bulging, gloomy fellow, just the sort of vividly colorless bird you'd want conducting a frank exchange of views on build-down and whatnot with any Gromykos who happened to be lying about. "Sorry to interrupt your breakfast, Mr. President," he bleated.

"Oh, get on with it, Shultz," snapped Mrs. Kirkpatrick. As I've hinted before in these chronicles, this was a woman who brooked no nonsense from any enemies of the Constitution either foreign or domestic. I recall remarking once to Jeeves that she had the most ferocious eyebrows of any woman in the industrialized West.

After a fearful glance at the Kirkpatrick, Shultz said, "It's about our foreign policy, Mr. President. It seems that for various reasons — "

"Mr. President," the old girl said, flinging herself into an armchair. "They're saying we don't have one."

"Who is?" I said, trying to strike the attentive note.

"The press. The Democrats. The commentators."

"Ah!" Comprehension started to dawn. I did a bit of fact finding. "Don't have one what?"

"A foreign policy," Shultz said.

"Oh, I say!" The situation called for a sip of the vital java. I slipped same into the abyss, then faced the man foursquare. "But see here, Shultz," I said. "Do we have a foreign policy?"

Before he could respond Mrs. Kirkpatrick seized the floor. "Of course we do, Mr. President," she said with rather frightening crispness. "But we've had a run of bad luck. We're having difficulty in Lebanon. Our missile deployment in Europe is making people nervous. We're being criticized for our policies in El Salvador and Nicaragua. Nothing we've tried works. We need some sort of victory. Something to demonstrate that we know what we're doing."

"*Do* we know what we're doing?"

"Yes, sir."

"Which is . . . ?"

"Fighting Communism."

"Ah! Quite." I sat back, fatigued. I may have toyed idly with the coverlet. Such conferences tended to outstrip the old attention span.

But she wasn't through. "We've got to do something, Mr. President," the woman urged. "Something concrete. Something specific — "

"If I grasp the nub and gist, Madame Ambassador," I said, "you're suggesting that it's time to faithfully perform and execute. To take hold of the reins. To *carpe* the *diem*. To crank up the old leadership of the Free World."

"Yes, sir."

There being no viable alternative, I applied the lemon. What was needed, I reasoned, was a bold and decisive act — one that would both announce to the world that one's administration was not to be taken lightly in the fighting-Communism department, and that would clear the room of intruders. There was also the business of Hoho Tuttle's nephew. With the right plan one could slay whole flocks of birds with one stone, so to speak. The devising of such a stratagem was for Ronald but the work of a moment.

"Well," I said. "Why not mount an invasion somewhere?"

Shultz, agog, bleated, "Invade? But where?"

"The mind is irresistibly drawn to Granada, what?"

Mrs. Kirkpatrick leapt to her feet and shouted, "Excellent!" She turned to Shultz and said, "Come on, Shultz, the President has to get dressed." After a final display of ferocity-of-eyebrow meant to denote approbation, she led the Sect'y out. I motioned for Jeeves to approach.

"Sir?"

"You witnessed the Granada chitchat, Jeeves?"

I thought I detected a slight wince gallop across his finely chiselled. "Yes, sir," he said.

"Well, we're going to invade Spain. Kindly lay out my brown suit."

His right eyebrow hoisted itself the telling half-inch. The man was going to quibble. "If I may say, sir — "

Offer an encouraging word to the troops, and Ronald is your pal from now through the out-years. But with gloom-and-doom mongers I had had it up to the Reagan keister. I checked him with a look.

"There you go again, Jeeves," I said. And I meant it to sting. "Impeding the march of progress with your shill-I, shall-I. Now please cancel the Bush mission, and stand by for further instructions."

"Very good, sir." He floated out.

When he had gone I set about dispatching the long-neglected repast. It had got a big colder than one prefers, but we Reagans know how to be stoic when confronted with adversity. Then I phoned Vessey and told him to prepare whatever Marines we had in the general neighborhood of Spain for an amphibious assault. The whole business resembled what you might call a well-oiled machine, and by noon all was distinctly oojah-cum-spiff.

I thought no more of the matter for the next few hours, recovering from the presidential exertions with a long hot splash in the porcelain. From time to time Jeeves popped in with a bill that wanted signing or a briefing paper requiring the odd skim. I had dried the frame, and had just shoved into the custom tailoreds, when Jeeves announced that Hoho Tuttle was on the line again. I seized the receiver with gusto and greeted the esteemed backer.

"I'll tell you why I'm calling, Mr. President," he said. "I wanted to know what you're planning to do about that damned nephew of mine."

I waxed fairly jaunty in my reply. "Well, Hoho," I said.

"The fact of the matter is, I became so concerned about the subj., I ordered the Marines to invade Spain."

"We must have a bad connection, Mr. President," the blighter said. "I thought you just said you ordered the Marines to invade Spain."

"Quite right, old thing," I replied. "Granada. Spain. Passionate Iberia. Land of few words and strong deeds. For Whom the Sun Rises. This med school situation calls for direct action."

"But — "

"Oh, your nephew will be perfectly safe. What one calls a surgical strike." I chuckled at the aptness of the metaphor, or simile, or whatever it was. "No students will be harmed, naturally. We'll just seize the director, impound the records, safeguard democracy. That sort of thing."

"But — "

"I anticipate your objection. On what conceivable grounds, and so forth. As it happens, I've got it all taped out. We have what I call a foreign policy. It all pivots around the fact that we know what we're doing, viz., fighting Communism. Now, Spain is not Communist. Not as such. But one can't be too careful. The fact is that in times of rev. upheaval, the medical schools are the first to go. Hence this pre-emptive police action — no, here it is: individual liberty is imperiled. I mean to say, a chap's nephew sent down from med school is a chap's nephew denied his right to become a doctor, what?"

"Mr. President," the man said in a voice you might use to tell a fellow the horse he's put his shirt on has suddenly begun modeling for equine still-lifes on the far stretch. "The Grenada I'm talking about is a little island in the Caribbean."

I took a few moments off to gulp and choke. Finally I responded with, "Not Spain?"

"No, sir. Down near Barbados."

There are moments in a man's life when he realizes that regardless of how dashed competent he is ninety-nine days out of a hundred, today is that hundredth day. He has, despite intentions, come a ghastly cropper. There is nothing left to do but clutch the brow, hang up whatever phone he happens to be talking on, and retire gracefully to bed. This I did with all deliberate speed, after which I rang for Jeeves. He beetled in instantly.

"Jeeves," I managed to croak. "I'm for it."

"Indeed, sir?"

"The Granada invasion scheme? I selected the wrong Granada."

"Yes, sir."

"I chose the one in Spain. Informed sources report that the bally correct one's somewhere in the Caribbean. Curse all Grenadas, is my view."

"Yes, sir."

"We have but one recourse, Jeeves."

"Sir?"

"Immediate flight. I must take another vacation. Pack the essentials and summon the helicopter. I'll fetch Nancy."

"But, sir — "

"Please, Jeeves. I've already ordered the troops to get ready. If I tell them to stand down, the press will have me drawn and quartered. If I order them to go through with it and invade, I shall be memorialized as the only president in history to order U.S. forces to attack our own ally without provocation. You grasp the magnitude, Jeeves. The mind reels."

"But, sir — "

"This is no time to adopt a wait-and-see attitude. Quickly, man."

Fortunately I had remained clothed when I climbed between the covers. I had only now to leap out and leg it downstairs in quest of the aforementioned wife. In the hall outside the Oval Office I encountered Baker and Weinberger, under the circs. the last two fellows I wished to see. I sought to conceal self behind a bit of drapery, but they approached swiftly, cutting off all retreat, and gave tongue.

"Good work, sir," said Baker. "The Rangers are ready."

"Oh? Ah?" I said.

"We'll evacuate everyone," Weinberger said.

"Oh? Eh?"

"And your idea about the press is brilliant," Baker said.

"Fah? Hoo?"

"They know something's up," he continued. "But we'll keep them out until it's all over."

"The Rangers? Evacuate? The press?"

I don't know how alive you are to things like subtext and nuance, but the fact of the matter was I hadn't the foggiest tick as to what they were talking about. Stunned, nonplused to beat the band, I turned in time to see Jeeves drifting down the stairs in my direction. I nodded to Baker and Weinberger and indicated to Jeeves my desire to confer with him *en deux* in the Office. Once inside I clutched at the man.

"Jeeves!" I gasped. "Are they driveling? What idea?"

"I took the liberty of issuing several orders in your name, sir," he said.

"Eh? What orders?"

"With respect to the invasion and the management of the press, sir."

The onion swam. For one of the few times in his life Ronald feared he was losing his grip. "Jeeves," I said. "What did you order?"

"I merely redirected the invasion that you ordered, of the Spanish city of Granada, to the Caribbean island of Grenada. You will note, sir, that the two names of these locations are similar but, in the end, quite different in pronunciation."

"My sainted aunt! But on what pretext — ?"

"On your own, sir — the safeguarding of American medical students. There is, on the island, a school with an enrollment of several hundred — "

"One of said being Hoho's blasted sunburned nephew!"

"Precisely, sir. A recent overthrow of the government on the island lent credence to the notion that they might be in danger."

"Overthrow? You mean a *coup?*"

"Yes, sir. A radical left faction has gained tenuous control."

"But I say, Jeeves. This is a bit thick. Weinberger said

evacuate. Are our students actually in danger?" I lashed out
with some subtle diplomatic reasoning. "I mean to say, we can't
just skulk in like thieves in the night and biff off with several
sacks full of medical students who aren't in any danger. They'd
protest in no uncertain terms, Marines or no."

"Army Rangers, sir. The Eighty-first Airborne. An excellent unit."

"Rangers, then. What if things at the med school are all
sweetness and light, *après coup?*"

"We do not know if the students are in real danger or not,
sir. But I venture to suggest that once our troops have made
their landing and begun their incursion, their gunfire alone will
seem threat enough to render the most secure student eager for
rescue."

I smote the forehead. "But Jeeves, this is inspired! And we
get in a good stiff chukka of Communism fighting in the bar-
gain!" I gazed at the man with redoubled respect. Then a thought
struck. "But look here," I said. "Not to cavil, if that's the word
I want, but what of the press? Invading Spain is one thing, but
this Grenada. . . . Well, I mean to say, it can't be exactly
brimming with populace, what?"

"The island's population is slightly over one hundred thousand, sir."

"My very point, Jeeves. How will it seem if we send in
mobs of screaming Leathernecks to take an island with the population of Pasadena in order to rescue a clutch of danger-free
med students? Won't the media reports make the thing look
unilaterally rum?"

"The problem occurred to me, sir. Therefore I implied to
Mr. Baker that you desired he forbid all press coverage of the
action."

I stared. I would go so far as to say I gaped. Then I in-
dulged in a spot of gawking. "Jeeves," I whispered, more or less
sotto voce. "Can we do that?"

"It will provoke some controversy afterwards, sir. But on a
relatively manageable scale."

"But how the dickens can you be sure?"

"It is a question of the psychology of the nation, sir," he said, his eyes agleam with the light of pure intelligence. "Few of the citizenry will wish seriously to challenge so decisive and efficient a victory."

"Then your posish is, as it were, nothing succeeds like success, eh?"

"Precisely, sir."

I reached into the trousers and withdrew the wallet. It was a paltry gesture. But a chap has to do something, and we Reagans are nothing if not sensitive to duty. "Jeeves," I said, removing a note. "Would a twenty-spot be useful to you?"

"It would, sir. You are very kind."

"Not at all, Jeeves, not at all." Then I balked. My mind more or less misgave. "But hold a moment," I said. "I told Vessey to invade Spain. By now everyone from NATO to the bally Joint Chiefs must have heard. How account for such a beastly muckup?"

"It might be minimized as a case of your misspeaking yourself, sir," he said. "You do have a rather extensive history of such errors."

I pressed home the cold hard. "You stand alone, Jeeves," I said.

"I endeavor to give satisfaction, sir."

11:38 A.M.
_____

Vale was stunned when, the next day, Michelle called to ignore his greeting and say, "Hold for Amy." His agent got on the line to invite him to lunch. She asked him to bring a copy of the proposal he had given Tom. A reconciliation seemed in the offing. Vale wore the other of his two good sport jackets, the one he had not worn on their previous meeting, lest she recognize the first one and suppose, incorrectly, that he only owned one jacket. He owned two.

They met at a midtown restaurant with an unpronounceable name, all chs and xs and ls, a Nahuatl word meaning, apparently, "goodness." For all the exotic invocation of pre-Columbian tribes, though, the menu seemed to backpedal when it boasted "Santa Fe Cuisine," which in fact proved to be Mexican dishes made from willfully wacky ingredients — blue corn, yellow peppers, other hallucinations in produce — and costing a fortune. Vale ordered whatever he wanted.

After one minute of banter over fishbowl-size goblets of white wine, Amy said, "I just talked to Tom Walker, and he said you two had a lovely meeting yesterday."

"He's great," Vale agreed. He handed her the proposal. "A little too young, but they all are."

"Oh, he's very capable." Amy, a former attorney close to Vale's age, had the lawyer's penchant for taking things literally. She held a professional-quality smile on her face for a moment as she scanned the pages. Then it started to fade. She looked up. "Noah," she said in a pleading tone, "when you said you were going to pitch a series, I thought you had changed your mind about all this."

Vale said, carefully, "When you said let's have lunch, I thought you had changed your mind."

"I wish you had told me you wanted to do topical. I can't see how Mel Stevie is going to go for topical. I mean no one will. Maybe at Showtime, or HBO . . ." She shook her head, a teacher deeply disappointed in a pupil with promise, and read on. She laughed a little. "This is funny, this part."

"Whatever."

"I mean, I loved 'That Was the Week That Was.' I thought Weekend Update was one of 'Saturday Night's' best things. But these shows . . ." (she ticked them off on her fingers) ". . . 'Not Really the News,' 'Not the News As Such,' 'The News Is the News Is the News,' 'This Isn't the News That Was News' — they're not getting the numbers. If they get made at all they get

shelved, or thrown away on summer specials. The networks want another 'Dibs on Mom!'."

The food came: bright greens and reds like blobs of paint on enormous white plates. It offered an escape from conversation for a few minutes. Finally Vale said, "At least send it around. You never know — maybe those other shows just did it wrong. Maybe somebody still wants to do it right."

She agreed.

Walking home, Vale was seized by fantasies. They were almost exclusively about money.

This, for Vale, was the decade of money: thinking about it, worrying about it, reading about it, puzzling about it — doing everything, he thought, but making it. His obsession, he assumed, was due in part to his age: by the midthirties, one's friends had been at it long enough to create of their homes a toll booth of snazzy possessions, at which one had to pay a nominal psychological fee before entering their lives.

It was also due to the times, to the decade itself. The War was over, and the reaction to the War was over. What else was there to do but make (assuming one was white, middle-class, college-educated, urban, and not sidetracked from making — by, for example, the desire to create art, help people, serve God, teach school, raise children, or any of the other marginal occupations to which lip-service praise was offered in inverse proportion to their potential for the making of money — money) money?

Vale's moneymania was also due to where he lived. Manhattan, once a bazaar offering all things to all people at all prices, changed daily and before one's eyes. With every high-rise co-op raised and crummy-but-adequate apartment building demolished, with every racquet club erected and every theater group kicked out, the City welcomed its customers in the front door and showed the help the way out the service entrance. Soon New York would resemble one of those planets in science fiction stories of thinly veiled allegory, in which all inhabitants share a single defining characteristic: hyperrationality, or extrasensory perception, or the absence of a superego, or, in this case, wealth.

"Spock! Identification of approaching vessel."

"*A nuclear-armed Welcome Wagon from the world of Trump Planet, Captain.*"

"*Computer: profile of Trump Planet.*"

"A CIVILIZATION OF HYPER-SOPHISTICATED GOURMET TAKE-OUT SHOPS, DISCOUNT OFFICE SUPPLIES, AND ONE-ROOM STUDIOS STARTING AT $185,000."

"*Spock . . . it's . . . unbelievable. . . .*"

"*Fascinating . . .*"

Bankers Are People, Too

Manufactured Guarantee and Occasional Trust presents a whole new way to think about your money — by not being able to think about it at all.

Our new Self-Interest Now! Account offers a full range of interest plans. You choose from Fixed, Variable, Erratic, Wobbly, or Hi-flux, arbitrary Metamorphomatic. Then just sit back and wait for results.

Self-Interest Now! is not a mutual fund, not a checking plan, not a savings plan, not a money-market fund, not a treasury instrument, and not a tax-free security. It's a great big bin where we dump your money, and from which we gradually withdraw funds, with a shovel, for a variety of needs: Homeowner loans. New car loans. Caribbean vacation loans. South American dictatorship loans. And so much more — including printing up a number of striking, highly visible green signs to

108

post around the bank informing you, our customer, of our name. The signs are green, because your money is green.

We actually willingly insist that you choose your own interest plan — because, at the end of each year, no matter what you started with, put into, or took out of the account, your interest will always total exactly $41.22. We'll credit it to your balance automatically, and notify you, eventually, by mail. Or, come see us in person — we'll tell you right there, in the bank, regardless of how long you have to wait in line for us to do so. And if you desire the sum in cash, any one of our tellers will be happy to provide you with a polite, accurate "No."

After all, it isn't really money! It's interest — and it's our way of saying, "Don't worry." With a Manufactured Guarantee Self-Interest Now! Account, we're happy. And when we're happy, your money is happy. Here. With us.

But who needs money, when there's Kash Kard? Meet Karl, MGOT's Kash Kard Kommand Komputer. Let Karl introduce you, for your own good, to the wonders of total electronic banking. Simply deposit all your money, including pennies, in a Kash Kard Akkount, and try to live normally. Karl will take it from there — and keep it, paying all your bills and leaving you free to concentrate on just one thing: making money. For yourself. For your family. For Karl. And you can always assure that your money is there, in the machine, for whenever Karl needs it. Simply telephone Karl as you would any other computer, punch in your private Kash Kard Kode, and wait for the computer to say, YES, IT'S HERE. Then walk away, quickly.

But what about personal retirement plans? Manufactured Guarantee has a complete range of retirement plans to suit your needs, from IRA/KEOGH Accounts for people (mostly men) named Ira Keogh, to the new federally-inured, tax-devoid Mutual Disinterest Account: no minimum balance, no set term of maturity, no maximum yearly contribution, no penalty for withdrawal, no interest, no account number, no passbook, pocket calendar, free calculator, pamphlet, nothing. The federal government simply doesn't care about this "account," and, not surprisingly, neither do we. For you, though, Mutual Disinterest is like "money in the pocket." Because that's what it is. You take your money, and you put it in your pocket.

You get the kind of instant liquidity that comes only from not giving your money to *anybody*. Naturally, we'd like to assess you a nominal, one-time-only fee for letting you keep your own money in your own pocket. But we just can't do business that way. That's why we discourage our customers from opening a Mutual Disinterest Account. You'll be able to read about it in more detail in any of the handsome brochures we plan to put on display in your mailbox every day for the next eight months.

How do you "open" a Manufactured Guarantee Mutual Disinterest Account? We can't, or won't, tell you. Just be sure to choose between a fourteen-speed Proctor-Silex blender and a Sunbeam Deluxe two-slice toaster. Give us either one, and we'll tell you if you "qualify."

As always, we continue to offer Christmas Club Accounts for everyone who desires to put aside a set sum, every week, for the purchase of a club for Christmas. The money you save is not taxed — indeed, it is not even saved. Instead, it becomes part of what we call "the float." Sound like a flower-covered gazebo on a flatbed truck in a parade? Well, as far as you're concerned, that's *exactly* what it is. Of course, a parade is only truly effective if everyone stays in step. We hope you'll remember that, come Christmas time. This, truly, is "banking with the gloves off."

You may also wish to consider our Super House Advantage Account — the only money-relinquishment account not actually acknowledged or even known about by the Federal Savings and Loan Association.

With a minimum balance of $1,000, it's not for everyone. But, basically, here's how it works: you bring us your money. We take it. We give you some steak knives. It's that simple! And it's the kind of sound money management that has helped keep Manufactured Guarantee the name you see on our letterhead — regardless of what you may read in the financial press.

MGOT offers an impressive array of personal as well as commercial services, too — because you're a person, and persons — like businesses large and small — have money. Our checks feature the customary inspirational designs of seagulls, sunrises, or vistas of the Grand Canyon. But now here's something new: Cinechek.

It's a checkbook — but it works like a movie! Each check is printed with a full-color frame of a major motion picture. Simply flip the checks in sequence, and enjoy the poignant beach scene from *Sophie's Choice*. The Russian Tea Room mixup from *Tootsie*. The unforgettable funeral cortege from *Gandhi*.

These, and others (to be announced) are playing now, in your checkbook, thanks to Cinechek. It's just another way Manufactured Guarantee has of helping you to have pictures on your checks, to tell the world how you feel about spending your very own money. Simply designate which movie you prefer when you open your account, and then pay for it.

And when it comes to auto loans, the simple truth is, nine out of ten times we say, "Yes." We're not in business to turn people down; we *want* you to loan us your auto. We'll drive it from our home to the bank and back every day, or give it to our son, or his girlfriend. We'll let them drive it, until you've repaid whatever you owe us, for whatever reason. Why shouldn't we? After all, bankers are people, too! And don't worry about the inconvenience of bringing it in — we'll pick it up at your home or office without troubling you.

Most banks offer their customers a predictable range of services "from cradle to grave." But what about beyond?

We at MGOT truly want you to believe that we care, not only about the needs of you and your family, but about the financial security of the human race. That's why we ask you to consider MGOT's Eternaccount Plan. Briefly, it's a long-term, high-interest savings plan, with a minimum balance of $10,000 and a maturity period pegged to the half-life of Plutonium 239.

Rates vary from week to week, but the fluctuations are insignificant over the term of the account, which equals approximately 20,000 years. As a precaution, Eternaccount records are kept on magnetic disks in a weatherproof vault. This vault will accompany the unmanned space probe Galileo II on its historic voyage into the farthest reaches of the galaxy. That way, each Eternaccount will be kept safe in the event of virtually any unforeseen contingency: economic problems, political uncertainties, continental drift — even unnecessary inquiries by MGOT's own customers.

Naturally, there is a substantial penalty for early withdrawal, and while your Eternaccount is federally insured, that coverage lasts only as long as the United States of America.

You work hard for your money. When you bring it to a bank, you want that bank to work hard for you. And you want your money to work hard for you, too. Well, we want your money. And we want you to work hard because we want you to get it. Once you've got it, we want you to bring it to us. Because we want it. It's your money, and we want it. It's that simple. We want your money.

11:40 A.M.

Waiting for Tom Walker's response, Vale felt vaguely ashamed.

Although his profession called for it, and his leisure routine included it, he nonetheless felt slightly dirty whenever he watched television. It was a slothful, weakling, tawdry thing to do, like eating Sugar Pops for dinner. But, of course, it was far worse. Vale was committing a mortal sin against Mind. Every moment he spent ignoring the Harvard Five-Foot Shelf of great works, watching Lance cave in to his grandmother on "Falcon Crest," was a moment stolen from the process of his intellectual improvement. One day St. Peter would say to an assistant, "Who? Vale? What's he doing here?"

"He wants in. He says he's read all of Gravity's Rainbow *and* Ada."

"So what? He also watched a hundred and twenty-two hours of 'Dallas.' Get rid of him."

Thus, when the phone rang the next day at about 11:40 in the morning, Vale answered with a passionate ambivalence.

"Noah? Tom Walker, at Extremely Creative. I thought I should call you instead of Amy, so you know exactly what the situation is."

Vale's heart gave a thud. Did that imply a qualified yes? Should he want it to? "Tom!" he yelled. "How are you?"

"Fine. Look . . . Mel Stevie, the big boss, is fifty-fifty on the live news show. Jeanette, who is my immediate boss, says no. The implication around here is that a strong yes could at least get us in to see the network, and maybe get you some first draft money."

"Well, then . . . great!" This was answered with heavy silence. "Not great?"

"I . . . no. I'm sorry, Noah."

"What — "

"I can't be your advocate." The explanation came a little too fluently. He wasn't as regretful as he might have been. "It's a complex thing. I'm not prepared to commit to the idea in the way necessary to put it across. I like you, and I think you're extremely talented. But I have my doubts about this, too."

"So . . ." Vale's excitement shattered, like a bottle on a fence post picked off in target practice. "I see."

"Believe me, I'm really sorry. If everybody else was behind it, I would be, too."

"Sure."

"It's politics. I admit it. Look, I'm new here. If I get wrapped up in an iffy project, and it bombs, I'm in a hole. It's like I go on probation. And I can't afford that."

"Tom," Vale said, unable to resist making one last plea. "All you have to do is hand me the ball. I'll run with it. Then if it doesn't work, you can disavow me and say I didn't do what we'd agreed."

"Thank you — I appreciate your position. But I can't take the chance, Noah. I just got married, and we have a new co-op —"

"Right. Go back to your co-op, Tom."

"But listen," Tom said rapidly, relieved to be excused, "if the others change their minds, I'll come running. And please show me anything else you do."

(Sure, Vale thought. I've got something in my files. A treatment. It's for a feature movie, but there's no reason to think it would be any less unsuitable for TV.)

Sequel:
The Adventures Of
Gipperoo Gung-Ho II

Prelim. Treatment — August 1984

Prologue: A shadowy group of men in a shadowy fleet of limousines is seen approaching the White House. We cannot identify their bumper flags. . . .

Cut to Kennedy Center. It's Inaugural Gala II, as GG and our Nancy character wave from twin thrones and America feels good about itself again, again. Roll Acknowledgments — NCPAC, Falwell, Gergen, Mondale, God, etc. — over Sinatra/Nelson Riddle/Marine Band styling of the Rolling Stones' "Sympathy for the Deficit." (This would be a great oppty for cameos: James Stewart saluting, Rosey Grier w/ his great dignity. Maybe Mary Lou Retton vaulting a horse? An elephant? Can we get Michael J.?)

Frank reprises "Nancy with the Gung-Ho Face," then segues right into "Yuppie Tie One On." CU that trademark GG cool: He smiles, waves, catnaps, bounces back. Insert shots of guests dancing, singing, "Yuppie Tie One On/Get a loan, little doh-gies . . ."

(Style Note: Suggest the same offbeat, mock-serious administration we used in Adv.'s of GG I. Again, focus on GG's shrugging, genial, what-me-President? exterior as it masks tough, crusty, speak-up-sonny-no-need-to-shout Wise Geezer interior. Possible ad slogan: GIPPEROO'S BACK — UNEXPECT THE EXPECTED.)

On "It's your misfortune/And none of my own" everything is interrupted by an enormous explosion of propaganda. Women scream. The orchestra stops. NATO looks up from its braised celery. "What the — ?" Suddenly the rhetoric clears and the crowd of revelers parts for the dramatic slouch-shuffling entrance of Grom, Foreign Minister of the Evil Empire.

GG, typical grace under pressure, quips (from prepared text), "Who invited him?" There is nervous laughter, quick cutaways to Greer or Sammy shaking head in admiration, chuckling, "That Gipperoo — he's so cool." (Seriously, can we get Michael J.? Do we have other blax?)

Perfect Weinberger steps forward, offers to negotiate *mano à mano*. But GG restrains w/ a hand. (Reaction shots of Retton, George Will, ranking Republicans; CU unmistakable concern of our Nancy character.)

Grom delivers an ultimatum: cease development of the new Space-Based Particle Beam Boost-Phase Missile Smasherizer (SBPBBPMS), or the Evil Empire will tear up the Be Nice Treaty and eat Europe. "Go ahead!" defies Perfect. "And may you choke on it!" Thunderous applause from major defense contractors, prompting a GG grin. Insert an anxious Thatcher *sotto voce* to Kohl: "I hope Gipperoo knows what he's doing. . . ."

GROM: Your space weapon is destabilizing. How would you respond, Gipperoo Gung-Ho, if we of the Evil Empire were to be developing such a system?

GG (*from a position of strength*): Well, I suppose I'd just have to be patient, and wait for you to refine it. Then, when you'd brought it to a development where, a point of utmost technological, where you, because of a sophistication that, where you might have a workable system, guaranteeing ninety percent, because in boost-phase those, you know, missiles, I'd wait for you to *give* us that technology. Because *yes*. We do intend to give SBPBBPMS to you — for the safety of all our grandchildren. Whoever they are."

Great crowd response ("Viva Olé!" "Four more Grenadas!" etc.) as Spokesman Speakes' deft Q&A w/ reporters ("Wasn't that incoherent?" "No.") yields positive media slant. But Grom laughs and sneers, "Absurd! You will not even give us Apple computer! We are to be believing you would hand over state-of-art SBPBBPMS? Ha-ha-ha!"

Grom turns on heel, shuffle-slouches to door. Up EVIL EMPIRE HATE THEME. The crowd recoils. CU Grom: "Enjoy your second term, Gipperoo Gung-Ho — while you can!" He magically disappears in a cloud of limos, all thickly DPL-plated and impervious to parking tickets. Grim faces around the hall as pollsters rush to phones. Meanwhile, outside White House, the shady group debarks from its shady limos and approaches the front door. END ACT I.

Cut to inside White House. Emergency meeting called of Team Gung-Ho. Steadicam walk-through as Shultz character frowns w/ Spokesman Speakes, Regan figure confabs w/ Stockboy, etc. "Anybody seen Gipperoo?" asks Able Baker. All shake heads, decide to start meeting, get prelim biz over w/. Leave-It-to Deaver exits to ask GG's whereabouts of our Nancy character.

They sit around big table as Bush chairs. Regan, agitated, intros new problem. It turns out that, in order to fund development of SBPBBPMS and other DOD programs, his staff had to mount a treasure-hunting expedition to the Eighth Dimension.

REGAN *(w/ strained credibility)*: We had reason to believe there were substantial sums of money out there, in big canvas bags, that we could bring back to pay for all this.

BUSH: And?

REGAN: We were wrong. There's just a bunch of twig-people playing chess, and funny-colored lights.

STOCKBOY: Well, use them.

REGAN: We are. It's not working.

Baffled looks around the table. Cut to CU Shultz.

SHULTZ: What . . . uh . . . how . . . um . . . can you . . . funding . . . who . . . ?

REGAN: What does it mean? It means, gentlemen, that in approximately *(consults watch)* sixteen months, we will be attacked by Recessio, the Better-Offness Destroyer.

ABLE BAKER *(with a laugh)*: Hey, so what? By then Gipperoo'll —

Bush silently opens Pentagon-developed laser-enhanced cigar humidor. It plays tinkly music box song ("It's My Party and I'll Emerge as Its Front-Running Presidential Contender If I Want To").

BUSH *(worried; eye on '88)*: Sure, Gipperoo'll be in retirement. But some of us won't, darn it.

Music STING. Suppressed panic around table. Outside, through a window, we can see stern editorials being written. There is a sudden NOISE; all start and look wildly around. Stockboy blurts, "Hey, the Dow just fell . . . !"

BUSH: Darn it, Don, Gipperoo killed Recessio! I saw him!

REGAN *(shakes head)*: He didn't kill it. He put it to sleep.

BUSH: Well, then, darn it, why can't we put it to sleep again?

SPOKESMAN SPEAKES *(from prepared text)*: We're trying, guys, but —

ABLE BAKER *(standing, pointing)*: Look!

Cut to front page of media. Headline: WHERE'S GIPPEROO GUNG-HO? SEE RECESSIO BETTER-OFFNESS THREAT, SBPBBPMS TAB LINK.

Just then our Nancy character comes in w/ Leave-It-To Deaver. She's unperturbed, murmuring, "He must be here someplace." Points. "Oh, there he is!" All heads pull back, look down.

POV Team Gung-Ho: Gipperoo, in tuxedo, asleep under table.

OUR NANCY CHARACTER: Gipperoo? Dear? Honey?

GG stirs, looks up. Trademark grin, head shake, wave. Pan reactions of Team Gung-Ho — surprise, admiration. (Able Baker: That Gipperoo — he's so cool. . . .)

Cut to Gipperoo at head of table. All start to speak at once, but GG motions for silence.

GG *(presidentially)*: Wherever you go . . . *(Shrug)* There you are.

BUSH: Darn it — he's right!

TEAM GUNG-HO *(loyal, ideologically on-board, desperate)*: Let's do it!

Room erupts into well-coordinated p.r. blitz. But cut to White House, as shady men arrive at door. The light catches their faces — they are . . . the Junta. Hispano-Indian Catholic-But-Really-Pagan Music STING. END ACT II.

Rapid montage of full-scale preparation for nationwide live TV broadcast. Insert Shultz murmur to Council on Foreign Relations, "I hope this works." Speakes, from prepared text, opens first press conference in nine months with, "This will work. No one is cooler than Gipperoo Gung-Ho. This concludes the press conference. Thank you."

Cut to GG on TV screens around nation, world.

GG *(from prepared text; communicating greatly)*: My Fellow Gung-Hovians: no one wants peace more than we. But it must be a peace in which we, and not our enemies, prevail. That is why, tonight, I am asking our scientists and defense experts to cancel SBPBBPMS — not as a capitulation to the Evil Empire, but as a "down payment" on peace. Furthermore, I want you to tell Congress to use these funds to bribe the Monster Recessio, thus keeping him at bay, for the better-offness of all Americans, such as Bruce Springsteen, and Michael J., until at least the end of this movie. . . .

REPORTER: Will this really work?

STOCKBOY *(off the record)*: No.

Jump cut to inner foyer of White House. CU door. SFX: Knock knock!

ADMINISTRATION: Who's there?

VOICE OF THE JUNTA *(off screen)*: Nick!

CENTRAL INTELLIGENCE AGENCY: Nick who?

VOICE OF THE JUNTA *(o.s.)*: Nicaragua.

INTERNATIONAL MONETARY FUND *(after pause)*: Nicaragua who?

VOICE OF THE JUNTA *(o.s.)*: Tell Gipperoo Gung-Ho to back off, man. Nicaragua's got a right to eat three meals a day. That's the whole story of Central America, dig?

Cut to Oval Office. Perfect Weinberger barges in, interrupts champagne celebration of successful speech, shouts, "Nicaragua's going to dig a three-story hole and eat Central America!"

GG *(as our Nancy character prompts)*: I thought Cuba already ate it. . . .

PERFECT *(displaying aerial photos)*: They did. Nicaragua's going to eat what's left.

GG *(as flashbulbs pop, reporters smack foreheads, popularity index rises)*: Not if our Marines eat it first!

— and we pull back, troops mustering, boarding choppers, as allies applaud (insert Contadora shakily plopping Alka-Seltzer, slugging Scotch, etc.). Grom scowls, Dems shrug. I-can-walk-again miracle sequence as the Dow gets back on its feet. Spectacular Busby Berkeley fantasy water-ballet of Congress falling into line. GG and our Nancy character rise up in center of screen, in tux and gown, à la Fred-Ginger, Micky-Judy, etc., grinning, dispensing cheese. Up THEME ("You Make Me Feel Gung-Ho"). Insert CU vast majority of American people cheering, expressing unabashed patriotism, as GG gives trademark smile, head-shake, wave.

VAST MAJORITY OF AMERICAN PEOPLE: That Gipperoo — he's so cool. . . .

The End?

(Roll Credits, Debits.)

11:42 A.M.
_____

At about 11:42 the next morning, Vale phoned Helen.

They agreed to meet for lunch at a Mexican restaurant called Ramirez. Looking out from inside the glass-enclosed outdoor aquarium, Vale nibbled his chips and sipped his damn margarita.

"What is it all about?" he asked, after the usual introductory chitchat.

She was ten years older than Vale, the only woman humorist he knew. She published highly refined pieces, in which male or female narrators sincerely and briskly pursued absurd premises to their logical, earnest conclusions. Vale admired what he perceived as her asceticism. She hardly wrote — or, rather, she hardly published — anything else. She seemed to exist on five thousand dollars a year and lived in an apartment half the size of his. She never laughed politely if something wasn't funny, never pretended to be familiar with something if she wasn't. She had strong opinions about books and people, and no opinions at all about things she didn't care about.

It was as though she had decided that in order to be able to write only what she wanted, she had agreed to ruthlessly whittle away all superfluous affectation and unnecessary luxury — social as well as economic — from her life. It was she who embodied the Higher Seriousness of Humor. Vale had been stunned to discover she had a cat.

"What I mean is . . ." he began. He stopped and considered. He wasn't sure what he meant or why he'd called her. "What's the point of all this? Of the kind of writing that we do?"

"Is that what you mean? God."

"This is what I mean," he said suddenly. "What if — you know, Marx said, the means of production change the people who work with them — what if doing this work changes us? What if we're narrowing our perceptions until all we can see is the stupidity and self-delusion of the world? Because that's where we look for inspiration."

"I don't know . . ." she withdrew an inch and looked down.

Her lunch date had lost his mind and the entrée hadn't even come yet. "I don't know if I would call it inspiration, either."

"Whatever. You know what I mean. You ultimately see what you look for. Maybe we're too downbeat and serious. Maybe we're not playful. Maybe doing this kind of sharp, critical satire just makes us sharp and critical."

"Maybe we already are that way."

"Maybe." *She hadn't said the right thing yet, whatever it was.* He went on. "Everybody knows the world's imperfect. Why dwell on it? Why look for it?"

She said, "I don't know."

What kind of answer was that? How could she be unruffled and calm when Vale was having A Moment? "Plus, we write about people with real power, real weight in the world. And who are we? Gnats." *Vale drained his margarita. It was like limeade for robots — acrid and salty and vaguely corrosive. Nothing was working right today.* "Little leeches. Parasites on the hide of some huge hideous yak sloshing around the watering hole."

"I don't see it that way."

"We're like cops. Looking for word crimes, and lit crimes, and morality crimes. And it narrows our perceptions until all we can see is the — you know — the vast and multiform human panoply of . . . crap."

She laughed.

He smiled. "No, really," *he insisted.*

"I feel like writing these things makes my perception clearer," *she said, drawing on a cigarette.* "The only time I do my best thinking is when I'm writing. It's all the other times my perception is wrong."

Vale stopped, a salsa-laden chip in midair. "Well that's very interesting."

She took a sip of beer. "That's what Roth says. In one of those self-interviews he wrote, I think. He said, 'People say: You sit home all day at a typewriter. Don't you feel like you're missing something? Shouldn't you get out of the house and experience Life?' And he said that the time he feels most like himself, and most alive, is when he's writing."

Vale nodded. "And you don't think we're impotent, sniggering little nit-pickers?"

"I don't think I am."

"Touché." Then he said, "Make an interesting story, though."

"What?"

"Someone who writes but isn't suited to it. So it does change him."

She crushed out the cigarette as the waitress arrived with two mammoth plates. "I don't get it. Why does he do it, then?"

"Skip it," Vale said. He sometimes pondered ideas aloud in the presence of nonwriters; his audience was usually impressed, and it made him feel artistic. But not in front of her. "Tell me what you've been reading lately."

"Dick Francis. The horse-racing detective guy?" She made a face and shrugged. "I don't see what all the excitement's about."

Do-It-Yourself Whodunit

When my sister Liz told me that her husband Barney had sold the stores to that big national chain, I thought: good. Especially when Barney admitted to me that he knew they'd bought him out just to get him off the map. Not that I could imagine why they'd bother — Barney was hardly competition for those "home-improvement centers." When a store starts to call itself a "center," it usually means they've blown it up to the size of a bowling alley but kept the same number of help. Whereas Barney just had three normal hardware stores, each one the dimension of a regular neighborhood shop.

Still, they gave him good money — more than enough for him and Liz to live on for the rest of their lives, with a portion to leave to the kids, too. And I knew he had other items on his agenda.

"I've seen a lot of life," he told me the night we had them over to celebrate. "And I've got things to say about it."

Didn't I know it. I often thought that the main reason he went into the hardware business was not because he had a particular passion for linseed oil or duct tape, but to dispense advice. He loved helping people. He'd linger with a customer for twenty minutes, discussing the best way to hang a mirror, and end up selling maybe a four-dollar set of hooks. I admired that.

"What's your plan?" I asked him. "Set up a soap box in the park?"

"I'm going to write a book," he said.

Well, that wasn't as crazy as it sounded. Liz is a big reader, and many times had urged this or that favorite on him — she read mysteries almost exclusively — and I had a feeling that the ability a writer has to speak his mind appealed to Barney.

Liz kept us apprised of the developments. It seemed like Barney had been working those hardware stores — spending two days in each one per week, moving through the narrow, cluttered aisles, finding specialized little items the help couldn't find, talking to customers until they had to make up excuses to leave — exactly so he could sell them and get on to writing. He never once mentioned missing the stores, never went back to visit, or to hang around and look wistful and left out, the way men who retire often do. He bought a new electric typewriter, a carton of blank paper, and got to work. Two months later he called and said he'd finished his memoirs.

It was called *Fixing the World with Latex — and Love*. I wasn't crazy about the title, but then, they weren't my memoirs. I read it in one evening. Barney had managed to combine his whole life story — which was thirty years in the hardware business, remember — with his theories about society, caulking tips, endorsements for his favorite housepaint, and his plan for nuclear disarmament. "Things are really so simple," the book concludes. "We have the know-how, and we have the best tools and materials on the market. Now let's get to work!" It was one of the best books I had ever read.

I called him up and told him so the next day. "That book," I said, "made me want to march right into the kitchen and spackle that hairline above the stove."

"I'm glad to hear you say that, John," he said. I could hear him smile over the phone. "That's exactly my message." Then I suggested he let Liz go over it with a felt-tip pen to make some little changes, cross out some redundancies (there were some), correct the punctuation, and so forth — and he did. This was a selfless man when it came to writing, and just about the only happy man I knew when it came to living. Some people inquire about your life, and have lots of advice for everyone, but it doesn't stem from a desire to help. It stems from a desire to know more than you do, and make sure you know it. Barney Crandall, though, had things to say because he felt good and wanted to be useful. A valuable man.

Apparently, though, the big publishers thought otherwise. He sent his book out to twenty different companies, and eight months later it had been rejected by the whole contingent. He put up a chipper front about it, but I could tell it hurt. And there's no shame in that, either. You go have twenty different New York editors inform you they're not interested in your life story and pet theories, and see what shape your feelings are in.

But Barney spent maybe a day feeling bad. Then he sent it off to a place he told me *had* to publish it — Eastman House. When I asked how he could be so sure, he said, "Because I'm picking up the tab."

That showed how much I knew about publishing. I had assumed until that moment that being published was like a prize you won for writing something good. Oh, I knew the publishers hoped to make money on their books, but still. It finally got through to me, though, that a book was like any other piece of printed matter you could job out to order, like a pamphlet or a menu. I'm told such a company is known as a vanity press, which sounds to me like a big piece of cabinetmaker's equipment, but there you are.

Well, there was trouble. Once the books had been produced, the company just shipped them to Barney's house in a box, and that was that. He was distraught.

"I called Eastman House," he told me. "And I said, 'What about book stores? What about mass distribution? What about supermarkets?' And the fellow said, 'Sorry. Read the contract. All we do is print 'em. And now pardon me, I have another client to talk to.' Know what the other client wanted printed? A mail-order catalogue of lingerie for 'big, beautiful gals.' "

It was enough to throw even Barney off stride. A few weeks passed, and then one evening he phoned. "I just wanted to tell you two that I'm fine," he said. "In fact, I've gotten back to writing. I figured, what the hell. I enjoy it. And God knows I have the time."

"That's great," I said, happy for him. "What sort of thing you working on now?"

"A mystery."

It made all the sense in the world. Not only was that probably the main thing he had been reading for the last thirty years, but even I knew that mysteries are where a writer gets to show off the special knowledge he has acquired during his real career. I myself had read Margaret Truman's first book, set in Washington, D.C., and I thought: of course. She knows all about this venue, being who she is. Liz got on the phone later and said that she'd been keeping Barney supplied with books by Dick Francis, who was a racing jockey in England before he took to writing mysteries about — I found this a little hard to visualize — horse racing.

"What's Barney going to use as the setting for his mystery?" I asked Liz in jest.

She laughed. "What do you think?"

And so he did. His first one was called *The Case of the Cheap, Off-Brand Phillips-Head Screwdriver*, and it was a masterful piece of work. At least, I thought so, based on the typed-up manuscript he leant us. Here's the plot.

The president and editorial staff of a vanity press are found horribly murdered. The police are stumped. A man named Mr.

Campbell, who owns the local hardware store, is brought in to oversee the repairs to the damaged publishing company offices. While the police run around after the wrong scent, Mr. Campbell — using only his hardware expertise — figures out the killer's method, his motive, and finally his identity. (The murderer is "a jerk who sold catalogues of nighties for fat women." The way Barney reveals this is excellent, and includes a very interesting lecture by Mr. Campbell to the homicide department on the different kinds of sponge mops.)

I was thrilled. When I called up Barney to congratulate him, though, he sounded slightly subdued. I asked what he planned to do with it.

"Publish it myself," he said, a little preoccupied. "Not with Eastman, though. I'm thinking of starting my own company. Of course, distribution 'll be a bitch."

Now I admit I should have noted right then that something was amiss. You can hear things in people's tones of voice, never mind if they start saying "bitch" all of a sudden. But sometimes you just don't know that you know, and the moment passes. Afterwards, of course, I would realize that the moodiness I heard in him was highly uncharacteristic. At the time, though, I figured it was just a normal letdown, the kind everyone feels when they finish a big job.

The next book, *The Case of the Double-Locking Dead Bolt with the Lifetime Guarantee*, was — Liz informed me of this — a "locked room" problem. In this type of mystery, you have to figure out how the murder itself was committed, let alone who did it. I think that's a clever gimmick. And the way Barney handled it, the girls told me, was rather unusual. It was 180 pages long when he published it under his new company, Primer Press, and about four-fifths of it was a series of discussions between his Mr. Campbell, the philosophizing-hardware-store-owner-turned-amateur-sleuth, and his favorite customer, a curious and courteous woman named Mrs. Johnson (obviously modeled after my wife Ruth!). (Although she denies it.) Most of the conversations are about the different kinds of security equipment in Mr. Campbell's store.

" 'And what's that, Mr. Campbell?' Mrs. Johnson inquired.

"The hardwareman laughed mirthlessly. 'That is a cheapo brand of door lock,' he said in a contemptuous manner. 'Do not purchase it, Mrs. Johnson, because quite frankly it is crap.' "

The book is full of useful brand names (both pro and con), and has a series of excellent diagrams for installing a smoke alarm in your home. As for the mystery itself, that comes as a sort of dessert course after everything else. The whole crime story, with the introduction of the characters, the discovery of the body, the review of the possible suspects, the detection of the clues, the solution of the "locked room" problem, the climax, and the ending, take place in the last three pages.

Right near the end Barney says something (through Mr. Campbell, of course) that made me, for one, stop and mull it over. " 'Why did you need a dead body in order to have a mystery?' he wondered. 'Why did there have to be any crime in the world at all? Such violence was horrible to even think about! What a wonderful life this could be, if only people would repaint their living rooms regularly and love each other.' "

"Amen to that," I said quietly.

Next day, though, when I went over there to tell him of my admiration, we were sitting in the living room, just talking (I was talking; he was staring at a point somewhere between mid-air and the moon), when . . . well, when he suddenly aims this little crinkly white packet at me.

"John, you, uh . . . want one?" he says.

"I . . . ." And I looked again and ascertained correctly. "Since when do you smoke Camels, for God's sake?" I said. "I mean, since when do you smoke anything, period?"

He just muttered, "It's one of my vices. I smoke too much, I write too much, I live too much." Whatever that meant.

"Well no, thanks," I said.

This, too, was not like him. He had never smoked before. As he sat there, me rummaging around for small talk and him puffing into the atmosphere, I began to get a little irked. It occurred to me that this might be some sort of writerly affectation he was adopting, now that he was a published novelist. (Even if the one who published him was himself.) Then again, I told myself, he didn't light up with a grand flourish, or show off a cigarette case, or tap the damn things on the table like so many sophisticated types do. He just smoked. He didn't even seem to like it much. So what did I know. He was a writer, wasn't he?

Besides, it might have had some beneficial effect, because now the incredible part began. Writing mysteries turned out to be what Barney was born for because over the next three years he wrote seven others. And I have it on the authority of an expert (Liz) that every one is some interesting variation on the standard form.

One of my favorites is *The Case of the Criminally Overpriced Dustpan*. See what you think of this: A man dies painlessly (!) because, as Mr. Campbell discovers, he was complimented to death (!!). The killer, it turns out, is a brilliant but ruthless neurosurgeon. Mr. Campbell takes the doctor under his wing, convinces him to wallpaper his operating room to make it more soothing — and the doctor not only reforms completely, he brings the dead man back to life!

Of course, Ruth pointed out to me privately that there's a lot of violence in the background. (That, plus everybody in it smoked.) Mrs. Johnson has a chat with Mr. Campbell about masonry nails, goes outside, and is mugged. A teenage hoodlum steals the car of Sgt. McDuffy, the usual man from homicide. The kid then drives the car off on a joy ride and smashes it into a pet store, killing a window full of kittens and puppies. Mr. Campbell seems to grow more unhappy even as the murders grow less gruesome. And get this: the book ends with him drinking a lot of coffee.

That would be fairly insignificant if it were not for the fact that Barney himself was — or, until then, had been — strictly a one-cup-a-day man. The next time I saw him, though, he was drinking the stuff like water. Before lunch. With lunch. After lunch. And *black*. Not to mention the cigarettes. His posture was getting bad too; he looked like he was losing tone, like his skeletal system was slowly turning into India rubber. He slouched a lot. I thought: Barney is not a slouching man. Something's going on.

So maybe I wasn't all that stunned to discover that in the next book, *The Case of the Sandpaper*, Mr. Campbell starts to grow really sort of morose. Oh, he solves the mystery, all right — the whole problem and solution take a paragraph — but he spends the balance of the book brooding and feeling bad. "Mr. Campbell didn't know what to do," is how the book winds up. "Solve this crime, there would be another. What could he do about any of it? All he knew was hardware."

I'm afraid things got more grim after that.

We often go bowling, the four of us, but Barney had been canceling for three weeks running. So Liz urged me to draw him out and get him to go. Which I did, pulling teeth every inch of the way, finally hitting on the ruse of telling him his writing would go better if he got some exercise. He bought that, and we went.

We're at the Golden Lanes, tying on our shoes, looking forward to that relaxed, sociable feeling you get bowling — it's like going on a car trip, not much to do or many decisions to make — when all at once Barney stands up, frowns, bites his lip, puts his hands in his pockets, takes them out, and hits me with, "Think I'll go get a beer."

"You're kidding," was all I could manage to say.

"You want one?"

"Uh — no, Barn."

When he left Liz told us that Barney had gone way up from his usual one can of beer on Saturday. How about, say, a can a night. And two, three per day on weekends. Naturally his bowling went straight to hell. Instead of rolling the ball down there to knock over some pins, he gave it a sort of absent-minded, reluctant-minded push, like he'd been asked by someone at the other end of the lane — someone he didn't like — to send down the ball as a favor. I am aware that there are men (and women!) who drink much more than that, but for Barney to "imbibe" more than a can or two per week was almost the equivalent of his becoming an uncontrollable alcoholic.

Then came his next book, *The Case of the Various Kinds of Stain*.

Not much happens by way of "sleuthing" — Mr. Campbell teaches us how to paint a police station — but terrible things take place offstage. The killer's killer gets off on a technicality (we never learn who identified him, by the way). Death squads terrorize Ecuador (!) Sgt. McDuffy grows despondent and *commits suicide*. Mr. Campbell reacts to this by describing, in detail, the different kinds of masking tapes available on both the wholesale and retail "ends." They get a whole chapter.

Liz came over for lunch shortly after we'd received our copy of this one, and she was worried. "He's like a man who's lost his keys," she said.

I said, "Huh?"

"You know how when you can't find your keys, you get all frantic, and you look in the same place over and over, and you just can't let it go?" She straightened out her white cardigan sweater, as though by being personally tidy she could neaten up things at home. "Barney's like that. He spends all his time writing, or revising, or taking long walks with a notebook. Plus he drinks wine now. Red wine. Cheap red wine, if you must know. Those great big jugs that look like green watercooler bottles? Lord, his tongue is always purple now." She sighed. "I think he's trying to figure something out that doesn't have a solution."

"That's ironic," my wife Ruth said. It took me a second to get it. She can be very smart sometimes.

"Let me tell you, it's plenty other things besides that," was all Liz would comment.

Then he wrote *The Case of the Ugly Beige Extension Cord* — not the most pleasing title in the world, and frankly, not the most pleasing book, either. Mr. Campbell is invited to spend the weekend in a big country house with a strange array of characters. He summons everyone into the library, where he delivers a big tirade about storm windows. For some reason that is enough to convince a young man (whose father is "a big New York publisher") to confess to blackmail and murder.

The thing is, though, at no point does Barney ever tell

either Mr. Campbell or us that there has been a murder. No one is missing, let alone found dead. And no one is being blackmailed. Imagine you're having some friends over for dinner, and midway into the meal one of them suddenly stands up and cries, "All right! All right! Yes! I killed him!" You'd have to wonder about that. In fact, just about the only believable thing in this one is the final scene, where all the characters ask Mr. Campbell — who just stands there, mumbling about shellac — just what the hell is going on.

Barney delivered the next one himself. It was ten in the morning, and there was something a little off about him that I couldn't place.

"Brought this," he sort of muttered. We were in the living room — my wife Ruth had gone shopping — and I had him sit down. He handed me the book. *The Case of the Merchandise.*

"Kind of a halfhearted title, isn't it, Barn?" I said.

He shrugged, then looked away. He hadn't shaved, and had that slightly greasy look men get when they don't keep up with themselves. "I tried to, um . . ." His hand reached into his shirt pocket and brought out a pack of Camels. There was one left — a bent, ragged, pitiful-looking thing — and he stuck it in his mouth. "I'm experimenting with, um, some. Kind of a formal. Nonnarrative. I mean, nondidactic." His speech, of course, had by now totally deteriorated; for the last year he had gone around muttering through tight lips, cigarette or no, like some kind of jazz musician. "Anyway, nonsomething. The, uh, eruption of. Evil, I guess." He slapped at himself limply. At first I thought he was having some kind of epileptic seizure. Then I got it: matches. I went to the kitchen for some and he followed me in like a tired dog. "You . . . uh . . . you have any . . . ?"

"Coffee?" I said with a bit of sarcasm.

"Scotch?"

Well, I mean. I said, "Since when do you drink Scotch, for God's sake?"

"John," he said suddenly, and it was as though a flare had gone off inside him for a few seconds. "This writing . . . you can't just say what you think and blab away with your opinions. I see that now. I thought, mysteries. Fine. Hardware mysteries, it'll be fun. But you have to know evil, live with it, no, what am I saying, that's too strong. . . . Well, you have to look at evil in order to write about it, right? And where does it come from when you look at it?" (By now I was completely confused.) "From inside you! What's it doing there? How'd it get there? Writing mysteries — it's like being possessed by the devil!"

"Whoa," I said. "Hold the wire there —"

"Well, no. Not the devil. But by criminals. You can't write a mystery without being a criminal! Look at all the people I've killed! These others — how do they do it?"

"Who?" I said. I had no idea what he was going on about, but it was like talking to a man on a ledge. You'll say anything not to see him fall.

"The writers. Dick Francis. Agatha. P. D. James, Dorothy Sayers — a lot of women, John, what does that tell us? — Rex Stout. All of them. How do they live with all that evil?"

"It's not real," I said. "They make it up."

"No, that's the wrong answer. Never mind, it's not your fault." He waved fingers in front of his face like he was swatting away gnats. "Forget the Scotch. I just had one half an hour ago. Two, actually. That'll hold me. Anyway, there's the book. Hope you get something out of it. It's a failure, I think, but an interesting one." He stumbled out the back door, down the steps, and around the side of the house.

What could I do? I read the book.

Ten hardware distributors spend a weekend in a hunting lodge and discuss the declining quality of Czech wood screws. Mr. Campbell arrives (Why?), and warns them all about the careless use of Super Glue. One man, a Mr. Elkins (whose name in some sentences is Ellmann), says (quite reasonably, in my opinion) that such products have their uses. Various horror stories are recited about people who have had their fingers stuck to tables and their eyelids glued together. This goes on for 157 pages, until suddenly "a lunatic" bursts in and sprays the room with machine gun fire. Only Mr. Campbell escapes.

"Come on, Barney!" I said out loud when I got to the end. "That's very improbable!" I called him up. He sounded worse than when he'd left. He sounded haunted. Either that, or maybe he'd added another Scotch.

"I just read the merchandise book," I said.

"Oh?" was all he replied.

I let things remain silent for a few seconds, and then I said, "Don't you want to know what I think of it?"

"I know what you think of it. It's terrible."

"Well, now —"

"I know it is. It's all wrong." He sounded distracted. "Look, I have to go. I'll talk to you later. Regards to Ruthie."

The last book Barney wrote was entitled *The Case of the Professional Quality Ball Peen Hammer*. It had a kind of conclusive feel, even though not much happens. Mr. Campbell is there, all right, but it's as though he's now as vexed as Barney himself. Look at this: "He had told the police everything he knew. Yet they had learned nothing. If they wanted to drive regular nails into Sheetrock to hang their damn posters, he wasn't going to stop them. Let some other dumb bastard tell them about molly bolts."

Well, that "dumb bastard" part nearly made my eyes burn. It wasn't like Barney at all. Or maybe it was, by then, I don't know. Furthermore, Mr. Campbell does absolutely nothing in the book. The phone rings; he ignores it. Mrs. Johnson comes to the store and says she wants to build (get this) a sauna; he asks her to leave, and closes up shop. Sgt. McDuffy's replacement, Sgt. Kelly, arrives at Mr. Campbell's home. The hardwareman hides behind a sofa until the sergeant leaves.

It ends this way: "Of course, he could stop crusading. He could stop trying to make anything better. He could merely present the options of all the hammers he had in stock, and sell whatever tool the man selected. Was that so bad? To sell something to whoever wanted it, and let the world solve its own mysteries? What if that was all you *could* do, anyway?

"Mr. Campbell stood motionless, lost in thought. What if homes could be improved, but the people in them couldn't?"

I closed the book and, I have to admit, gave up. I just couldn't follow Barney into that writerish territory — I mean, I don't know what he meant by all that depressing, kind of self-pitying material at the end. I told my wife Ruth and she agreed, although she said she felt sorry for him.

Then, about two weeks after we got our copy of this last one, Liz called and asked if I wanted Barney's typewriter.

"How come?" I said. "Is he getting a word processor?"

She laughed at this. "No, John. In fact, he says he's giving up the writing. He claims he's said everything he has to say."

"That's not like Barney," I said. "Can I talk to him?"

"He's out. He's gone to the *bank*." Then she lowered her voice, as though confiding a secret. Who she was keeping it from I can't imagine, unless it was the cat. "Can you believe it? He's taking the rest of the money and opening a new store."

I was surprised, but said sure, I'd take the machine. And as I got to thinking about it, I began to get intrigued. Maybe I could write mysteries, too. After all, I've spent twenty-two years in the upholstery business. I've got a lot of stories I could tell.

11:44 A.M.

A few days later Michelle bestirred herself enough to tell Vale to phone Gary Dave.

"Can you transfer me right now?" he asked.

She sighed. "I — look, I don't know how to work this. Can't you just call him?"

Gary Dave also worked in the agency; Vale thought he mainly handled movies. Nothing fruitful could come of it — Gary probably wanted the name of an editor at a magazine — but Vale hung up and called back. Gary's polite, delightful secretary put him right through.

"Mister Vale," Gary Dave said. Vale had never met him,

*but over the phone he came across as mild and slightly superci-
lious, like a teaching assistant lording his little bit of power over
helpless undergraduates. In a voice so relaxed it needed crutches
for support, he murmured, "I have good news for you. How would
you like to go to L.A.?"*

"Why not?"

*"Let me tell you the specifics. Amy, your lovely agent, and
I, sent your material to Larry Mack at Galactic. They're looking
for someone to rewrite a comedy that Jack Dieffenbaker is going
to direct. And Larry liked the material and wants to take a
meeting. You go out next week, meet with Larry and Jack, come
up with a story, and then come back home and write some pages."*

"Sounds great . . ."

*Gary chuckled. "Larry really likes one of these articles of
yours. . . ." There was the sound of rustling paper. It was inconceivable that Vale's actual work was on his desk. It was done
for effect. "Something about a little camera, or something . . . ?"*

"Oh, yeah. Everybody likes that. Yeah, it's okay. . . ."

An Exclusive Offer to Readers of This Publication

Recent developments in microcomponent technology now permit us to make available an extraordinary precision device — the KL–1000. Weighing less than one ounce, it is no larger than a domestic olive, yet it performs all the photographic, data processing, and information-retrieval functions you yourself do — automatically.

The KL–1000 adjusts to available light, sets shutter speed and aperture, then calculates, displays, and prints out on plain paper tape the cube root of your social security number. This is photography made so automatic it leaves you completely "out of the picture." The KL–1000 not only flashes SAY CHEESE and STOP MOVING AROUND on its unique L.E.D. monitor screen, it also warns you that you're not taking enough photographs, advances the film after each exposure, then hot-wires your car to rush the completed roll to the drugstore for processing. Don't feel like capturing those personal moments of your life before forgetting them? Relax. It isn't up to you anymore.

A whole world of precision capability is out there, waiting to enter your home and your life with this fully integrated, so-much-more-than-a-camera device, so much more than a camera. Microfiche-and-chips technology makes it a computer, too — performing virtually all functions, including logarithms, in roman numerals. Its binaural jack accommodates two sets of featherweight headphones, so both you and a friend can roller-skate to Coast Guard channel-depth broadcasts. Its light-activated voice simulator tells you to balance the family budget, chart stocks and bonds, stop smoking, clean your room, and be considerate of others. You can talk back, too: the clip-on dynamic microphone instantly triggers a sustained, loud buzzing — enough to wake the soundest sleeper — if you say anything at all within a fifty-foot radius of the KL–1000.

Yet that is not all, because disc-and-data fineline crosshair-tronics has enabled us to program the KL–1000 to do *everything* — and more — automatically. Consider these exclusive features:

AT THE OFFICE

Thanks to minilaser technopathy, the KL–1000 not only copies any-sized document, it actually vaporizes the original's byline without a trace and substitutes your own name, sex, political affiliation, and yearly income. Its data-network-access function lets you be part of the grid, too, as it narrowcasts product inventory and inflow-outflow figures directly to your digital watch. The KL–1000A word-processing attachment assures perfection every time — misspelled words or computational errors are immediately obliterated by its built-in document shredder, which also shorts out all electrical power to the entire building and releases a semitoxic paralyzing gas. Just get it right the first time, and forget it!

WHILE TRAVELING

Optional carrystrap lets you wear it on your belt, or leave it in your room — the strap extends to a full half mile, and retains enough water in even the lightest drizzles to provide nooselike snugness and hamper torso circulation. Or remain in the room yourself; the unit travels freely on its own, and will simulate your signature on major purchases of clothing, art, and real estate without your even knowing. In every major foreign city, the KL–1000 does it all: orders gourmet meals for twenty while you struggle with the menu, loudly contradicts you in museums, and forwards your souvenir purchases to General Delivery, Lima, Peru. All you do is pay freight and handling. And you need never again worry about destroyed traveler's checks, canceled credit cards, and misplaced passports — the KL–1000 does all these, and more, while you sleep. In the morning, enjoy your own original compositions of up to twelve accordion-like notes in real music, "the international language." The KL–1000 will record and transcribe these melodies automatically, then engrave the notes onto an attractive brass pendant, which it will offer for sale to friends and strangers. Do not worry about accidentally switching off the unit, either, because you can't — not even deliberately.

AT HOME

Self-contained forty-eight-hour timer lets it tell itself when forty-eight hours have elapsed, after which timer resets itself automatically. All you do is hide in a closet. Later, use the microwave transponder attachment to receive hitherto unavailable signals from turkeys, roasts, and hams. When no one is home, it plays both eight-track and cassette recordings, switches lights and appliances on and off, and displays random words in Italian on its high-resolution screen. The KL–1000 wards off burglars all night long by announcing, in a voice mathematically similar to your own, "We're awake. . . . we're awake. . . ." Then, in the morning, it counts your pushups, uses all the hot water, and ignores you at the table. Coffee? Of course. There's even some for you. And don't worry about getting dressed — it gets dressed for everyone, then dials ten frequently called telephone numbers and leaves a short inspirational message in your name. All you do is stay undressed, watch, and go back to bed.

Advances in macrowaferonics enable the KL–1000 to use 3–D graphic simulation to transfer black-and-white computerized likenesses of you and your family to T-shirts, dogs, and frozen foods. Switch from audio to visual readout for its smoke-detection mode, and receive a hard-copy sheet reading SMOKE when your house burns down.

A device of state-of-the-art convenience, the KL–1000 has already projected your technological needs and, with funds transferred from your checking or savings account, has purchased itself. It has already expedited its own delivery.

Indeed, the KL–1000 is already in your home or office — over there, near that lamp. It is already on line, shredding potatoes and complaining about your posture, automatically. All you do is nothing. Just set it at HIGH and run away. You'll never have to do anything else for as long as it lives.

PART III

High Noonish

They flew Vale out first class. He enjoyed the free drinks, the shrimp cocktail, the china plates, and the big seat, but was unable to keep from thinking, *For this people pay six hundred dollars?* (The answer, of course, was, No. Their companies do.) The movie — free, naturally — was about brooding teenagers whom the world did not understand. Vale disdainfully refused the headphones, then spent the two hours while the movie ran watching the silent screen, mesmerized.

Vale had long ago conceded that movies were made principally for young people. He had no right to complain; when his generation had been young, everything had been made for them. Still, weren't the movies made when he was a youth better than

145

*the junk they put out now? To ask the question was to want to
talk about something else.*

*He had developed a rule of thumb for popular media based
on a theoretically typical American family of two parents, two
children, and a dog. It set forth, in a convenient, easy-to-mem-
orize way, the standards to be applied when producing any piece
of mass-market entertainment: novels had to be comprehensible
and appealing to the mother; movies had to be comprehensible
and appealing to the teenage son; television shows had to be
comprehensible and appealing to the nine-year-old daughter;
commercials had to be comprehensible and appealing to the dog.
As for the father, he watched sports.*

*But then, who was Vale to sneer? A South American novel
in his lap, he couldn't take his eyes off the damn movie. He had
to admit that the Image — any Image — exerted a hypnotic
pull on the mind. No wonder a tenth of the country couldn't
read. With so many pictures around, who had time to be liter-
ate?*

You could press your sacred copy of One Hundred Years of
Solitude *fervently into the grasp of passersby on the street from
now till doomsday; people would drop it as though their hand
had been shot by a gunslinger showing mercy and rush like
stampeding cattle to any appliance store where a color TV in the
window was showing the promo clip from* Romancing the Stone.
*What the hell, Vale thought. I would look, too. That's where the
world is. That's where we keep it — like milk in the refrigerator.
Up there, on the screen. In there, in the box.*

Magic Real Coffeeism

"Science has eliminated distance," Melquíades proclaimed. "In a short time, man will be able to see what is happening in any place in the world without leaving his own house."

Later, while viewing the outtakes, Juan Valdez was to remember the day his father had taught him to harvest coffee. Attired in the simple white trousers and shirt, with the red and white scarf and the broad-brimmed white hat, the elder Juan Valdez had demonstrated to the boy, whose name was also Juan Valdez, that vital task's unwavering methodicality. Only when each individual bean had reached its peak of ripeness and maturity would it be selected by hand, with a preternaturally precise exercise of discrimination and skill. In this way the tradition was passed on, from generation to generation, from Juan Valdez to Juan Valdez, assuring that all the coffee, foreordainedly harvested by all the Juan Valdezes, possessed a richness, aroma, and flavor to be found only in ONE HUNDRED PERCENT COLOMBIAN coffee. It was a process in which history itself would continue to mysteriously collude. All of the pickers — Juan Valdez, his father, his grandfather, and so on, in a timeless generational recession originating at the commencement of the lineage in a fierce and tragic commingling of Spanish and Indian blood — had, by some inexplicable vagary of cafeterian genetics unsusceptible to ordinary analysis, looked exactly alike. Each had displayed in the womb an expression of crinkle-eyed good humor. Each had been born smiling, with a thick, droopy, dark moustache. Inevitably, fatedly, each had been named Juan Valdez. Indeed, Juan Valdez himself had named his first two children Juan Valdez, and would have bestowed a similar appellation on his third, had not Juana, his wife, drawn his attention to the fact that the infant was a girl. Juan Valdez agreed to name her Juana, after her mother. But he was destined to think of her, and at times of lapsed attentiveness, to call her to her face, Juan Valdez.

At the beginning of the month that would climax in the termination of this obsessive nomenclatural tradition forever, Juan Valdez announced to his wife that the coffee was approaching its apex of ripeness, and ordered her to assemble the children. "Assemble them yourself," she replied. "I've been telling you for weeks — the kids have disappeared."

"But the men are coming," Juan Valdez said.

"Then let the men do the dances and help you pick," Juana muttered. "It won't kill them to do some honest work for a change."

Juan Valdez winced, as always simultaneously stung and impressed by his wife's audacious forthrightness. It was unthinkable to him that the men pick the beans. Their task, performed faithfully ever since he could remember, had been to observe Juan Valdez in his agronomical amassment. With their strange viewing equipment, they would follow him and the burro along the rows of trees, halting now and then to hasten to the town

square, where they would entreat the children to perform un-
seasonal folk dances in obsolete and inappropriate Indian cos-
tumes. These, too, they viewed through their apparatus. Now,
their immanent arrival made all the more inexplicable the children's disappearance, which Juan Valdez could account for in
only one way:

"Our children have been made invisible — by magic!"

It was an explanation to which he had daily recourse. He
believed passionately in the reality of magic, and invoked it to
explain whatever he did not understand. In this case, compelled
to surmise that his children had evanesced into thin air, he
concluded that they had been absorbed into the realm of the
spirits who lived among the trees, and who safeguarded the ex-
ceptionally aromatic flavorfulness of ONE HUNDRED PERCENT CO-
LOMBIAN coffee. He advanced this theory, with great assured-
ness, to his wife.

"You've gone completely nuts," she replied. "The kids have
run off somewhere. Somebody'll have to track them down."

So stunned was Juan Valdez by the undeniably compelling
wisdom of this pronouncement that he sat on a chair in the
kitchen, neither eating nor sleeping, for an entire hour. Finally,
with an air of titanic resolve, he announced his intention to
search for the children. "Good," his wife said. "Ask their friends
in the town. Maybe they know something."

Inspired by a sense of purpose augmented by a profound
anxiety, Juan Valdez decided to look first for Juan Valdez, the
eldest. A boy of surly temperament and sour moods, he had, at
that time, become a thorn in Juan Valdez's side — paying scant
attention to his father's instructions on how most efficaciously
to fondle and caress each precious slumbering bean, permitting
the burro to wander off self-indulgently through the orchards,
and whining in unending complaint about their lot in life. Using information gained from his son's friends in the town, Juan
Valdez rode a heaving, ancient bus to a small village in the
mountains near Natagaima. There he was met by a secretive
young man and conducted by Jeep into the hills. After a peril-

ous ride, through dense forest and along ill-maintained roads, they came upon a makeshift camp of tents and sleeping bags. It was in this verdant refuge of sylvan grandeur, among several dozen bellicose young men brandishing numerous rifles and pistols, that Juan Valdez found Juan Valdez.

In the interval since Juan Valdez had last seen him, the boy had undergone an indubitable metamorphosis. He was thinner, with a pronounced hardness of manner, welcoming his father with a private smile that contained no hint of youthful longing or adolescent melancholy. "So this is where you've run off to," Juan Valdez said. "On a big hunting trip with your friends, when you should be at home preparing to pick only the finest coffee beans in the world for ONE HUNDRED PERCENT CO-LOMBIAN coffee." Cradling his rifle in his arms like a baby, Juan Valdez replied, with the passionately rhythmic punctiliousness of articulation frequently characteristic of somber neophyte ideologues, that these men were his comrades. In Colombia, he explained, where in those days Juan Valdez awoke with the sun in the traditional way, to handpick only the richest coffee beans for the luxury breakfasts of Yanqui colonialist shitheads and their fat whore wives, it was time to rise up. Society had matured, and had attained its apex of readiness for the harvesting of that which had been sown by over one hundred years of capitalist imperialist economic exploitation. Caressing his weapon, Juan Valdez murmured the fervent hope that when he and these brave men descended from the hills and commenced their actions, he would be privileged, with this rifle, to pick off only the richest coffee owners, at their peak of unreadiness. Then, at last, life would mean something more than just the earning of a few lousy pesos harvesting beans until your back became petrified and the fingers turned into twigs, while the fat pig-owners drank champagne and went to the movies every night.

Juan Valdez, who in those days had never heard his son speak with such implacable vituperation, asked, "What are the movies?" His son answered that when they at last succeeded in kicking out the owners, he would take Juan Valdez to the movies to see for himself. "You're talking nonsense," Juan Valdez said. "Owners are owners, and pickers are pickers. The world is the world. The rest is magic."

"The world is what we make it," his son replied. "Not by using magic. By being realistic."

At that moment a bearded giant, wearing khaki fatigues and a beret, emerged from a tent, and seeing Juan Valdez in conference with Juan Valdez, said, "Eh. Pedrito. Come here." When the boy approached, the giant seized him by the shirt in a startlingly arbitrary cyclonic outburst and dragged him into the tent. Juan Valdez came out a few minutes later, the shirt torn.

"That was El Brazo," Juan Valdez said in a hushed tone revealing a paradoxical amalgamation of respect and annoyance. "He doesn't like it when strangers show up here. I told him you were okay."

"Who is this 'Pedrito'?" Juan Valdez asked.

The boy looked suddenly grave and very noble. "That is my revolutionary name."

Juan Valdez regarded his son's garment. The white T-shirt, its front rent in a single great tear where El Brazo had found a purchase for his impulsively admonitory grip, bore the likeness of a man Juan Valdez did not know, and some writing he was unable to read. Juan Valdez took off his own white cotton harvest shirt and thrust it into the boy's hand. "It gets cold out here at night," he said. "You must have a real shirt." The boy protested with such unrelenting vehemence that Juan Valdez was only able to persuade him to keep the harvest shirt by agreeing to wear his son's T-shirt in equal exchange. As he put it on he made one final attempt to convince Juan Valdez that the way in which coffee was grown and harvested was a part of nature, and that if he and his friends attempted to overturn it they would all be killed. To this Juan Valdez replied that they might be killed, but at least they would have died making sure the coffee finally *was* ONE HUNDRED FUCKING PERCENT COLOMBIAN. At least they would have helped to kick out the slave-driving vampire-owners, the sons-of-whores Yanqui cartel mongrels, and everyone else who believed a man could make a decent life for himself and his family out of nothing — by magic, picking one bag

per day, six bags per week, of the damned and cursed coffee
beans only when they had reached the peak of their eternally
despicable, loathsome, detestable, pestilential freshness.

Juan Valdez frowned. "You mean ripeness," he said. "It is
the crucial ripeness of the beans —"

"Freshness, ripeness — who cares!" the boy cried. "The
beans are a bunch of bastards and they can all go to hell!" Juan
Valdez had never before heard so blasphemous a slander of the
beans' patrimony. It would haunt him for years afterwards.

Juan Valdez told Juana that their oldest son had gone to
take part in a religious retreat in the hills near Natagaima, and
that he would be away for an indeterminate amount of time.
He did not mention the men with the guns, the diatribe about
the owners, or the fact that the boy had forsaken the traditional
name of Juan Valdez for "Pedrito."

"As long as he's eating, and not fasting like some of those
mystical nuts," was her only reply. "Meanwhile, you'd better
see if you can dig up Juan Valdez. The men sent a message
that they'll be here in a week."

After persistent inquiry, Juan Valdez was able to penetrate
the obstinate barrier of confidentiality erected by his other son's
friends, and in this way learned that Juan Valdez was living
with a group of bad men in a suburb of Bogotá. It was around
then that, four days later, after a journey by bus and on foot,
Juan Valdez arrived at their house, which, before its latter years
of neglectful dilapidation, had been a mansion of unsurpassed
magnificence. As he rang the doorbell, Juan Valdez concluded
that his son's residence in so splendorous a dwelling could only
be explained by the influence of a subtle and benign magic.
When a tall, thin man in a loose T-shirt and torn jeans opened
the door, Juan Valdez announced himself and asked if his son
were home. The man closed the door in his face. Juan Valdez
stood immobile and silent for five minutes, whereupon the door
opened once more, disclosing the figure of the second son of
Juan Valdez, the boy Juan Valdez. "Jeez, Pops, what you doing
here, man?" he said. A neurasthenic simulacrum of his former

self, Juan Valdez was thin and pale, displaying a highly strung
exacerbation of nervousness superimposed on a personality sus-
ceptible to a nostalgic melancholy mitigated only by a melan-
cholic nostalgia. Juan Valdez explained he had come to fetch
Juan Valdez for the harvest, adding, "The men are coming in
a week."

"The Man's coming?" the boy cried, his eyes wide and
evincing a feverish intensity. "Where — here? Shit." Juan Valdez seized his father's wrist and dragged him into the house,
which smelled of greasy foods, cologne, and certain chemicals
Juan Valdez could not identify. Juan Valdez said, "We gotta
tell Hector, man."

Juan Valdez escorted his puzzled, compliant father through
the mansion to the master dining room. The vast space was
occupied solely by a long mahogany banquet table, at one end
of which sat a stocky man in a white shirt and chinos. He was
in conference with two swarthy, muscular men, who eyed Juan
Valdez with contempt and Juan Valdez with suspicion. After
apologizing with a craven obsequiousness, Juan Valdez introduced Juan Valdez and announced that according to his father,
in a week the authorities were going to bust the ass of everyone
in the house. The ensuing uproar was galvanic. The two muscular men, with a quickness and agility belied by their considerable bulk, leapt toward Juan Valdez and pinioned him against
a wall. Despite the indignant protests of his son, they subjected
Juan Valdez to a violent and abusive search, jabbing and prod-
ding him over the length of his body as though firming up the
stuffing in a scarecrow. One of the thugs, in search of concealed
weapons, grasped Juan Valdez's trousers at the waist and tore
the garment to pieces. As Juan Valdez stood there, bereft of
dignity and slightly chilly in his thin cotton underwear, the stocky
man, whose name was Hector, demanded to know who he was
and for whom he was working. In reply to Juan Valdez's calm
repetition of his name and his patriarchal relationship to Juan
Valdez, Hector retorted that that was bullshit, that Juan Valdez
was not somebody's nice old father, whose life was dedicated to
rising early every day to handpick the world's richest and most

flavorful coffee beans at their most unutterably precise moment of perfection, but instead was obviously a gofer working for the scumbag Chucho, who had recently allied himself with some very crazy Italians based in Miami, who had managed to come down off their own shit long enough to figure out how to buy a new fleet of boats. Then, with a perfectly regulated and methodical fury that caused his face to turn red, he bade Juan Valdez inform Chucho that if Chucho thought he could scare Hector by sending an old-man flunky to threaten Hector with the cops, Chucho could go and perform on himself the identical love-act that Hector and all of his men had performed repeatedly on Chucho's mother, his sister, and also his grandmother.

After this virulent diatribe had at last subsided Juan Valdez said to his son, "What is he talking about? I don't know a man named Chucho. I haven't mentioned anything about cops."

"Come on, Pop," replied Juan Valdez, with an anxious glance at the smoldering Hector. "You just said the Man is coming here in a week."

"I said the men," Juan Valdez said. "The men who come to supervise the harvest. I came to bring you back."

The misunderstanding was quickly rectified. After directing toward Juan Valdez's son a look of bilious displeasure, Hector ordered his henchmen to produce a new pair of pants for Juan Valdez. But they emerged from a side room with a flat, blue piece of material that looked like cardboard. Juan Valdez regarded the stiff, rough square with bafflement, until Juan Valdez said, "Put it on, Pop," and, unfolding it into what resembled a pair of pants, helped Juan Valdez climb into it. The garment felt like wood. Juan Valdez chafed at the stiffness of the material, the awkwardness of the fit, and the disconcerting way in which the legs reached the floor, covering his feet. "You like, Pops?" Hector laughed. "Authentic Levis. American blue jeans. I got a hundred boxes in the next room, take all you want." Then Hector informed Juan Valdez that if he ever tired of working for peanuts, handpicking those crappy coffee beans Colombia dumped on the Yanqui market after keeping the decent crops for home consumption, he had an open invitation to work for him, supervising one of the crews of Indians in the Cordillera Oriental near Cocuy, where they were growing more coca than they could move in ten years, and where the cops were so deep in Hector's hip pocket that he used them to scratch his balls on command.

Juan Valdez declined. It was repellent to him that a grown man speak of his genitals with such unrepentent brazenness. Then he asked what coca was. Stifling an outburst of astonishment, Juan Valdez explained its botanical and agricultural characteristics, concluding with an inflamed exposition on its ability to stimulate the energies, elevate the spirit, and revive the self-esteem of those who inhaled its crystallized distillate. At this Juan Valdez nodded comprehendingly, and with open hands and a shrug of imperturbable nonchalance murmured:

"So it's just like coffee."

He begged his second son to abandon this unprecedented career and to return to the traditional life of picking coffee and performing unseasonable native folk dances in inappropriate Indian costume. The boy's demurral was unhesitating. "The coffee's okay for you, Pop," the boy said. "But forget me coming back. I do one run and make ten thousand pesos." Juan Valdez was stunned. That so vast a sum of wealth could be earned by cultivating a plant — this truly was the most powerful magic he had yet encountered. "In two months I do three, four runs, I got my nut," the boy elaborated mystically. "I dress real sharp and go to clubs every night. I got a color television and get all the American shows."

Juan Valdez asked, "What are shows?"

The boy sighed with put-upon surliness. "Skip it, Pop. The point is, you want me to come back and pick beans and eat yams? No way."

Many years later, and for several weeks afterward, Juan Valdez would remember what his wife said to him when he returned from Bogotá with the news of Juan Valdez's new profession and declared, "At least we still have Juana."

"That's what you think," was her reply. A letter from their daughter had arrived while Juan Valdez was away. The girl had established herself in Ibagué, in an apartment with two other young ladies her own age. She had secured the position of a secretary in an import-export firm. It was her intention to save her money and, someday, emigrate to the United States.

"She thinks everything is boring," Juana said, holding up a letter, which Juan Valdez could not read. "Me, you, coffee, Colombia — everything." His wife sighed and said, "Then the girl has the nerve to ask us send her some money for clothes."

Juan Valdez said, "We have no money. Send her this."

He handed his wife the red, black, and white scarf he customarily wore during the harvest. It pained him deeply to realize that his daughter, too, had rejected their family's traditional way of life. But he clung to the thin hope that the scarf might remind Juana of her parents, her home, and the beans. Juana took the shawl and wrapped it in brown paper, which she tied with lengths of rough twine. While she was doing so she happened to glance out the window. She turned to Juan Valdez and said, "The men are here."

He ran outside to meet them. As always, in those days, they arrived in two trucks, one carrying the men, the other transporting their equipment. The vehicles pulled to a stop in front of Juan Valdez's house and the three men debarked. The two who rarely spoke went wordlessly toward the other truck and began supervising the unloading of the equipment. The third, whom Juan Valdez had known for years simply as "Joe," waved a greeting. "Lookin' good, amigo," he said. Grinning, he made of his hand a gun and aimed it at the T-shirt on Juan Valdez's chest. "Springsteen, huh? The Boss! Stylish as hell. Nice jeans, too." He held out his hands toward Juana, his face growing suddenly grave and thoughtful. "Juana, Jesus Christ, I swear to God, you get younger and more gorgeous every year. What is it, the altitude? The goat's milk? Some kind of mountain yogurt you guys eat?" He took her unwilling hands as, silently and with unconcealed distaste, she endured his kiss on her cheek. He inquired if the secret to her irrepressible vitality were not the region's readily available supply of blow. Then he smiled, and with a nudge of insinuative conspiratoriality said, "Joke, hon. Hey, seriously, I know: not funny. Economics aside, it's bad news, snow. I've got colleagues back in the States — unbelievable. Monsters, they turn into, to stay high. I'm talking about a habit of, what? Four, five hundred? Dollars, babe. A *day*. Nasty. That's why I envy you guys. 'Cause you get the stuff for free, no, I'm kidding. You know me. I mean it's a situation of where I envy you for the whole natural, clean thing you have here. I swear to God, the more I'm in this business, the more I respect clean. Seriously. Where's the kids?"

Juan Valdez explained that only he would be available to pick the beans, to which Joe replied that it was no problem, they could do a bunch of one-shots and see what they got, provided that the donkey was still on the payroll and still remembered his blocking.

"That burro is smarter than most of the people here," replied Juana coolly.

"Hey, present company included, right? Juan, keep this gal, I love her." Joe clapped Juan Valdez on the back and said, "You get dressed while we set up in the field. Give us an hour. Take a siesta, hang out, whatever."

It was around then that, later, Juan Valdez walked with the burro out among the trees weighted down with the inexorably ripening beans. The men had established themselves in one of their customary spots, on a hillside affording a commanding view of an adjacent valley. One man held a small object with a glass dial that flashed in the sunlight. He read something on the dial, then returned to the oddly-shaped box on three legs, through which the men customarily viewed the harvest. Juan Valdez approached Joe and informed him that the beans were ready for him to commence picking. Joe, whose attention was occupied with the filling out of a form on a clipboard, did not look up, but merely nodded assent.

It was with a piercing melancholy and an unregulably lucid nostalgia, that Juan Valdez approached the first row of coffee trees. He had made such a trip hundreds of times in the past, always cognizant that his father, and grandfather, and their forebears had done the same. Now, for the first time, Juan Valdez was conscious of a terrible burden — the knowledge that he might be the last Juan Valdez to harvest this, the world's finest coffee. He touched the first bean on the first tree. It had not yet attained its peak of maturity. He decided to forego picking it, and to return to it twelve minutes later. He felt an adjacent bean, and was pleased to note its ripe resilience and firm fleshiness. He plucked it from the branch and dropped it into his shoulder bag.

"Wait for the slate, Juan," Joe said brusquely, then added a peremptory, "Hey. Hold it." With an impatient gesture toward Juan Valdez's clothes, he asked what the big idea was. To Juan Valdez's hapless look of confusion and puzzlement he demanded to know what the hell Juan Valdez thought he was doing, wandering through the trees in a torn Bruce Springsteen T-shirt and brand-new Levis, and that the hat was great, but what the hell happened to the big white pajamas and the native-looking serape, or whatever the Colombians called it. Juan Valdez explained that he had given his white shirt to his son, Juan Valdez, and his pants had been torn apart by the thuggish colleagues of his other son, Juan Valdez. As for the scarf, it was at that moment being taken by a neighbor to the post office, to be mailed to Juana in Ibagué. Joe acknowledged this information with a highly strung excitability, and after apologizing for permitting himself to become shamelessly and with an unforeseen rapidity bent totally out of shape, nonetheless insisted that without the white harvesting costume, the footage would not be worth diddly. Millions of Americans, he elucidated, wanted to see Juan Valdez in that white costume, which they had become accustomed to and which said everything the agency was trying to say, like: simple, peasant, care, happy, not poor, honesty, authentic, real and natural, close to the land, pride in picking, folkways, not torture, earthy, pure, not dirty, not corrupt, not communists, the personal touch, not slavery, not guerrillas, not military dictatorships with fat guys in pencil moustaches with their wife's cousin running the national cement company and getting kickbacks up the wazoo, not drugs, and not any of the other stuff that people in the States related to vis-à-vis South America and Central America and the whole current contemporary situation that was driving his client bananas.

Before Juan Valdez could ask what bananas had to do with coffee, Joe added that he had a very tight schedule because he had to be back in New York in three days to shoot some yuppedout models in suspenders in Central Park doing some kind of lawyers' picnic for a new diet mayonnaise. In reply to this perplexing nonsense Juan Valdez asked what Joe had meant by the millions of Americans wanting to see him in the harvest suit, adding that he had never been to America and could not imagine standing in a plaza large enough to hold so vast a quantity of people. At this, one of the two other men said whoops, and the other laughed. Joe answered never mind, that it was a Yanqui figure of speech, and reiterated his request for the white costume. Juan Valdez replied that he had other harvest shirts and trousers at home, although he was unable to understand why the men made so much over what he wore. Joe requested that Juan Valdez give him a break, and as the two men carried the equipment and followed, he escorted Juan Valdez back to the house. But Juan Valdez's other harvest clothing elicited from Joe a similar volcanic outburst of impatience, and the declaration that the color of these garments was too weird and psychedelic, and that they had to be white or everyone's ass was grass.

At her husband's silently pleading look Juana stifled her suspicions and mistrust of the men and volunteered to make a new suit of white clothes. Everyone breathed a sigh of relief. She produced a bolt of white cotton cloth, a pair of scissors, and her sewing basket, and was on the point of commencing, when Joe held up his hand. "You know what?" he said. "Let's look at some outtakes from last year, so you know what we're talking about."

"I already know," Juana said. "I made the clothes he wore last year, too."

"I know, Juana, but . . . humor me? I'm a gringo, right? You know what jerks we are. Ed, got that reel from last year?"

In response Ed declared that such a plan could be iffy, because they had never viewed prior footage in the presence of you-know-who. Joe silenced him and said to just do it. From the equipment truck Ed produced a strange boxlike machine with a dark window on its front, connected by plastic vines to a wall in the truck. He inserted a black rectangular object into a different machine and, after working many knobs and buttons on the various devices, the box with the dark window suddenly glowed to life. "Okay, Juana," Joe said. "Just give me the same all-white, and we're golden." At Joe's nod Ed pressed a stud on the machine.

At first Juan Valdez felt an impenetrable confusion: behind the window was a scene, like a painting, but in motion. A man in white trousers, hat, and shirt, and a colorful scarf, moved from coffee tree to coffee tree, accompanied by a burro, picking the beans and dropping them into a jute bag on his shoulder. Then, in a sickeningly lucid flash of insight and with a sudden swarming and irrevocable recognition that sent a hot vertigo flooding through him, Juan Valdez realized who the man was. He realized that the three men had done much more than merely observe, in a haphazard and lazy manner, the picking of the beans. They had somehow managed to capture him. He was there, in that box, displayed on that window. Juan Valdez reached out his hand, and touched the picture. It had no effect. Beneath his hand, the image of Juan Valdez smiled, inspected the beans, selected them for harvest, and dropped them into the bag. Juan Valdez had seen photographs, and he daily regarded himself in a mirror over the sink in his home. Yet this was neither a photograph nor a mirror. As for Juana, the pressure of her grip on his upper arm (for she, too, had been galvanized and rendered mute by the inexplicable and inconceivable phenomenon) served to remind him forcibly that it was no dream. Juan Valdez asked, with a demeanor of intimidated diffidence, how the device worked.

"Who the fuck knows," Joe answered, grinning. "Magic, huh, amigo?"

"This is the great invention of our time," Juan Valdez breathed.

"Here's the aerial sequence," Ed said. "When we used the chopper."

The picture suddenly changed, and it looked to Juan Valdez as though he were a crow in the air, beholding a plantation vaster than his ability to comprehend. The trees stretched for miles, carpeting every hill to its crest, reaching to the horizon in an uncountable numerousness. Creeping slowly across this undulating landscape was a host of ants. Then it was as though Juan Valdez had moved closer to the earth, for the image again changed, and the trees appeared larger. The ants were revealed to be men. There were hundreds of them, dressed in a variety of multicolored tatters. Juan Valdez had to stare at them for several seconds before discerning the meaning of their compellingly familiar gestures.

"They are stealing the beans!" he cried.

"No," Juana said. "They're picking."

It was true. As the viewpoint of the picture descended farther, Juan Valdez could see that this swarm of men, weary and bent and hastening from tree to tree, were picking the beans — not, as he did, with reverent exactitude and hyperdiscriminatingly precise care, but like animals, their hands like claws, sweeping into their heavily drooping burlap bags undifferentiated clusters of beans among which, to his mute horror, Juan Valdez saw some that almost certainly had not yet attained their peak of richness and flavor. Then the picture seemed to fly over that tumultuous landscape and stop above an isolated hill. Surrounded by the mountainous slopes on which the hundreds of ragged laborers swarmed over thousands of crowded coffee trees, was a single placid hillside, an island of calm amid a turbulent sea of vegetation and humanity. Its coffee trees were widely spaced, the paths between them broad and neatly grassed. Across it, at a leisurely pace, moved a single pristine white shape. It was the solitary figure of a man. Juan Valdez felt his heart knock against his rib cage as though he had been kicked by the burro, for he perceived that the man was incontestably himself, moving with insectile slowness among the trees. The contrast between his philosophical deliberation and the scrambling frenzy of the legions of other pickers struck him as monstrous.

"Who are those other people?" Juan Valdez asked in a quaking voice. "Why have I never seen them before?"

"Uh, nothing, they're just a bunch of guys," Joe said nervously. "We don't care about them. We're here to shoot you."

"Shoot me! Yes, shoot me!"

"Juan, easy. Don't flip out on me."

"Why are my children not in this box?"

"They're out of frame. This was the just-you shot. Juana, how about it?"

It was a revelation. To see, before one died, a depiction of one's true role, from the viewpoint of a bird while still reacting as a man — this, beyond all the other paltry events and phenomena of life, was truly magic. Yet it was awful, fatal, a magic that destroyed all other magic.

Juan Valdez turned away from the machines. He told Juana to never mind making the clothes. Then, in a voice of chastened defeat from which every vestige of hope had been irrevocably expunged, he asked the men to leave. He knew then that he would never again pick a single bean, regardless of its state of ripeness, flavor, or aroma.

At first, the men took this to be a joke. "Funny, very funny," Joe said nervously. "I mean, this is some kind of sly peon folk humor thing, right?" But as Juan Valdez persisted in his request that they leave, the men grew irate, the altercation culminating in Joe's heated declaration that Juan Valdez was not the only Juan Valdez in the book, that Juan Valdez would never work in this plantation again, and that the egos in this business were unbelievable. In reply Juan Valdez said calmly that he was finished forever with ONE HUNDRED PERCENT COLOMBIAN coffee. Later that day, after they left, Juan Valdez sat in a chair in his house and thought about the footage. He would remain in that chair, in the stiff blue jeans and the torn American T-shirt, for a long time.

11:48 A.M.

If fame was the religion of America, then Los Angeles was the Vatican. Vale had in one sense been summoned to serve; but he also viewed his visit as a deliberate act, in order to (or, at least, to try to) take advantage of Hollywood's mechanisms for addressing a wide audience. Magazines reached hundreds of thousands — movies, tens of millions. As a man would go to the town church on Sunday to address the collected populace, so Vale went, sort of, to L.A.

His first meeting began two hours late, at 11:48 one morning, in his duplex suite in a Beverly Hills hotel. Vale opened the door to a soft knock. "Hello, we're here," a man said. Beyond, in the corridor, a man and a woman were conversing. "You're the writer, aren't you. I'm Larry Mack, the producer of this thing." Mack was in his midforties: slim, tanned, with a dry, nasal manner suggesting the languorous fatalism of Jack Benny, as if he did not expect to be taken seriously, and did not care. "Let us come in and I'll introduce everybody. This is Jack Dieffenbaker, and Carla Cutler from the studio."

"Nice to meet you," Dieffenbaker said. It sounded like a challenge. He was also in his forties, dressed entirely in black, with the alert, slightly widened eyes of a man listening for danger. He was one of the most successful directors of commercials in the country, a feat all the more notable because he insisted on living in San Francisco rather than L.A. or New York. This was to be his first feature.

"Hi," said Carla Cutler. "Your samples were excellent." She was in her thirties, with the semipretty, chipmonkish face of a bank teller whom you would look at with mild interest while standing in line, and forget immediately after leaving. Vale thanked her.

The script which Vale was to rewrite was a fairly straightforward wild-and-zany physical comedy set in a hospital. The story, to the extent that there was one, concerned an intern who, because of his lifelong dedication to medicine, had remained a virgin. It was fiction.

After they had assembled in the small living room area, sitting in overstuffed chairs and on a couch around a low wooden coffee table, Vale brought out his notes. The problem, he said, was that the story had no connection to the real world. "What's the point of using a hospital," he explained, "if we're not going to exploit the real-life possibilities that everybody knows and fears?"

Dieffenbaker slammed his hand down on the table. "That is absolutely right," he declared. "Absolutely right!" He turned to Mack. "Hey, I like this guy! I like the way he thinks."

"You like his bent of mind," Carla Cutler said.

"I like the way he thinks! Because I'll tell you something: without reality, you've got nothing."

"So," Vale continued, encouraged. "I've jotted down some story lines we could incorporate." He shuffled through his notes. "Remember when the Shah of Iran was admitted to that hospital in New York? We do something like that: an Arab potentate admitted over big protests, pickets outside, cops and federal agents —"

"I love it!" Dieffenbaker cried, eyes wider still, smile huge. "So we have a scene where the hospital has been built wrong, and just before the Shah is admitted — it starts to collapse! It caves in! So the Secret Service is running around, 'Hmm, what's this? —' " He stopped and sensed a change in barometric pressure. Directing an intense stare at Vale, he said, "What? What's the problem?"

"Well," Vale said timidly. "How do you make it plausible that the building will collapse?"

"You just do it! You show the building shaking, and the floor buckling, and you do it. The audience will believe anything you tell them — as long as you're consistent."

"As long as you maintain a consistency," Carla Cutler said.

"No, Jack," Mack interceded. "I think he means — I mean correct me if I'm wrong, Noah — I think he means, isn't it very implausible that the hospital would start to cave in? And it is, in a way . . ."

"I don't CARE about what's plausible," the director said. "LIFE is implausible. I care about scenes that I can do some-

*thing with." Vale, not sure where things stood, was surprised to
see Dieffenbaker grin at him and say to Mack, "I think we're
going to be fine. Because you know what? I think we're thinking
on the same wavelength."*

"You're in sync with one another," Carla Cutler said.

*"I'll tell you what we are," Dieffenbaker insisted. "We're in
sync with one another."*

*"I hope so," Vale said earnestly. "I just want to get some
real-life concerns in here, so the comedy has a familiar background. The script as it stands is all virgin jokes and pratfalls.
There has to be a sane world for the comedy to have meaning."*

*"Exactly," the director said. Indicating Vale with his thumb,
Dieffenbaker turned to Mack and said, "You know what he has?
That man has instinct. And you ABSOLUTELY NEED that."*

"You need a feel for the material," Carla Cutler said.

"For everything! You need a feel for everything!"

*"No, you're right," she said. "You need a feel for every-
thing."*

*"Otherwise, what is it?" Dieffenbaker's voice got higher as
his argument reached its triumphant conclusion. "It's all shit!
You're fucked!" He sat back, face red, and smiled at her with
pride. "Do you know? Am I right?"*

*There was a silence as the air in the room slowly stopped
quivering. Finally, Larry Mack looked at his watch. "Well I'm
. . . hungry . . . I guess," he drawled. "Am I? I mean, I don't
have to be. Carla, are you hungry? Jack?"*

"I could eat something," Carla Cutler said.

*"We can go to that place on Beverly," Mack said. "That
salad place?"*

*"I don't . . . what's . . . ?" Dieffenbaker looked suddenly
bleary, as though his lecture had taken something out of him.
"What place is that, Lar . . . ?"*

*"Remember? I said, 'Here's a nice place to have a salad,'
and you said, 'Yeah, that looks nice —' "*

"OH! THAT! Yeah, sure."

"Or I don't know. Carla, do you have any preferences?"

"That sounds fine."

"I mean," Mack said. "Don't let me railroad everybody if, you know, if you're really going good here. I mean the food isn't important. Well, yes it is. But you know what I mean. We can send out for food if you're really . . . you know . . . cooking." He turned to Vale and addressed him as a colonial official would a native bearer in the bush. "What time do you have?"

"Almost twelve," Vale said.

"Then there you are."

They stood up, and the meeting dispersed as Carla Cutler called her office, Dieffenbaker called his secretary, and Mack called his wife. Vale stood around wondering what had taken place. Later, while the four of them walked to the restaurant, Carla Cutler said to Vale, "You know what you should do a piece on? Ice cream. All those fake ice creams. I can't stand that."

"Me neither," the director said. "If you're going to eat ice cream, eat it, for God's sake."

"Exactly."

"That's not a bad idea," Vale said politely.

We All Scream at Ice Cream

May we avail ourselves of this opportunity to acquaint you with the latest in our superb selection of gourmet desserts? Like the other items in our Creamytime Concepts line, the new one is comparable to the world's finest dairy-based frozen confections. Yet, it does not contain any ingredient that could conceivably or in any possible way even be construed as having anything remotely to do with actual ice cream per se. And they're delicious.

As a discerning type of person, you of course know that we are experiencing a frozen dairy- and nondairy-based renaissance. At its forefront are various rich, costly confections (supposedly made in Sweden, or some similar place) whose names, if you ask us, sound like the noise made by an individual dropping dead. Even we, who have expanded our refuse-hauling and chemical business into the ice cream substitute field, can't read them, frankly.

Plus, at a recent business lunch, one of our own vice-presidents overheard a man discussing those pseudo-Scandinavian dairy-based products in complimentary terms. Believing him to be choking on something, the vice-president rushed around the table and administered the Heimlich maneuver right to the man's stomach, and causing unfortunate damage to his nice suit, highly embarrassing the individual.

Yet, isn't life strange? Because for all their verbal power and negative downsides, these ice creams have set new standards in the marketplace. They have helped to elevate the frozen dessert from the innocent child's treat to the temptation of the world's most sophisticated, elegant gourmet. They have revived and advanced an ancient body of technique and lore that for so long has been almost like the quintessence of the ice creamer's art. Thanks to them it is now acceptable for adults to consume frozen desserts, "thank God."

What a cruel irony it is, however, that in so doing they have made the hitherto innocent words *ice cream* synonymous with the deadliest poison. You see, such dairy-based products are rich in heart-attacking cholesterol. In them one encounters, in abundance, the very sorts of so-called "refined" sugars similar to those found in the cheap candy bars eaten by certain mass murderers and other hoodlums. Their high butterfat content is anathema, not only to health-minded individuals watching their weight, but to their loved ones, who they would not want anything bad to happen to.

The question, then, forces itself into our brain: Can a person still eat an ice cream—like product?

This has been our obsession from the beginning, when Recychem Industries merged with Advantage Plus Marketing Consultants and gave birth to our company, Creamytime Concepts. Mr. Thomas Sherman, president of Creamytime, perhaps said it best: "Here is an important market no one has thought about. Any sensible person will refuse to eat ice cream because of the health angle. But he still desires a frozen dessert item. How can we be of service to that individual?"

Through careful research, utilizing space-age technology and the miracle of modern polymer chemistry, we have solved the problem and created a family of superb ice cream substitutes. They may be compared with any product on the market. Yet, they may be eaten with a clear conscience, without fear, and in public. All are delicious. None are ice cream.

Please peruse this list at your own personal convenience.

Your Grandmother's Icy Creme. Our first product, a nondairy "whitener"-based flash-frozen suspension. The juice of real wax fruit is distilled and pasteurized, then pressure trapped in luscious crystals of reusable Scotch ice. Comes in eight flavors. May require refrigeration after the initial break-in period of six months.

Yogolet-Ee-O. Developed to celebrate our merger with Apex Can and Gasket. Dense, creamy, smooth, and made entirely from yogurtlike substances, it stays fresh for years, and nitrogen-flushing assures that every pint is waterproof to ten atmospheres.

Le Chocolat Gourmaize. Our entry into the "chocoholic" market, made possible by an *exclusive* arrangement with Neb-Iowa Feed Co. Chocolatey, peanut buttery, and raspberryey ripples are threaded generously through a base made mainly of cocoa-processed corn cobs. We then take pure cane sugar, remove the unhealthful sugar, and use only the cane. Result: each serving has the fiber content of six pounds of ordinary, ho-hum bran flakes, with twice the crunch. These, truly, are luscious "empty calories" — without the calories.

Faux-Tutti. Last summer's craze along the Franco-Italian border, where the only language they know how to speak is quality. Our use of the new Dair-O-Mulch process makes it delicious. Our acquisition of Highland Pulp and Paper makes it possible.

It also makes possible our latest product.

This time we've eliminated not only the calories, the cholesterol, the sugar, the preservatives, the milk, the butterfat, the

egg yolks, the lactic acid, the lactose, the cream, and the ice —
we've even eliminated the dessert itself.

We call it *Conceptuoni*, and we think you will literally lose
your mind over the taste of it. It has all the texture, flavor,
fragrance, and mouth-watering creaminess of the finest dairy-
based products, but with one key difference: you see, it doesn't
exist. Not in any true physical form, anyway.

Conceptuoni is not a conventional ice cream, not a soft ice
cream, not a sherbet, not a *gelato*, not an ice milk. And it is
not a vegetable-based dessert, a tofu-based mix, a frozen yogurt,
a quiescently frozen confection, a granito, a kefir, a so-called
popsicle, a sorbet, a sorbetto, or a pudding. It's a little booklet
that you read, to yourself or out loud, whenever you crave the
ecstacy of a nice frozen treat. After dinner. In the afternoon.
Before retiring to bed. Whenever you wish an ice cream–like
experience without all the danger that comes from actual food.

Each *Conceptuoni* text — you may choose from seven flavors, with many more yet to go to press — describes, in sinfully
delicious verbiage, the most exquisitely sublime cold dessert
imaginable. Total calories: a stunning zero. Total reading time:
a convenient two minutes, on the average.

Here, at last, is the ultimate in ice cream–free living. With
proper maintenance, each *Conceptuoni* portion will remain forever as fresh as the day it was printed. Foreign language editions
will probably be available soon, for when you feel in a Continental gourmet mood. Or, with "a friend," experience exciting
new taste combinations by reading two selections simultaneously.

However you enjoy it, rest assured that *Conceptuoni*, like
all Creamytime products, is absolutely not ice cream and never
will be, period. And isn't that what's important?

11:50 A.M.

Things went less smoothly the next day.

"We have some great moments from yesterday," Vale lied. "But we need a skeleton — characters and plot."

"I . . . I don't know. . . ." Dieffenbaker was sitting back and grimacing at the ceiling, scratching his head. "I thought that bit with the hospital falling down was so, so fantastic. . . . Now I . . . I don't think it works. . . ."

"I do," Larry Mack said.

"Do you?" the director asked, brow furrowed with ferocious uncertainty. "You don't think it's too obvious?"

"Well," Mack said. "If done obviously, yes."

"But it could be valid if it isn't done obviously," Carla Cutler said. Vale noticed a magazine on her lap, at which she glanced from time to time.

Vale said, "So you're thinking maybe we'll have the hospital fall down subtly?" Mack caught his eye, but the producer's expression was unreadable. Vale felt obliged to soften what he'd said. "Like wing by wing?"

Dieffenbaker leaned forward. "I don't know if we should even have it fall down at all!"

"Why don't we table that for now," Vale said. "And talk about characters. See, I think if we took a satirical approach —"

"Oh, no."

It was like a thunderclap in the room. It had come from the director: Dieffenbaker's face was set in a mask of implacable resistance. "I don't do satire," he said. "That is NOT what I do." The silence was broken only by the slight crinkling sound of Carla Cutler turning a page in her magazine. "That is something COMPLETELY SEPARATE from what I do."

"It's not your style," she said, looking up briefly.

"Okay," Vale said a bit testily. "Fine —"

"But you know what we can do, Larry," he said smoothly to Mack. "We take our intern —"

"The one from the script?" Vale asked in fear.

"The one from the script. We take our intern, and suppose

he's kidnapped. Someone — boom. Or someone — he kidnaps someone — HE KIDNAPS THE SHAH!"

"Why?" Mack said dreamily.

"HOW THE FUCK DO I KNOW WHY? Just say. He kidnaps the Shah. And the Shah, he's, you know, 'This is most irregular, Doctor,' and he takes him . . . Well where would he take him?"

Mack murmured, "Where would who take who —"

"The intern. The Shah."

Carla Cutler looked up and said, "The Shah is an intern?"

"No, the, our intern. He takes him . . ." Dieffenbaker looked into space, musing. Suddenly he lost his concentration, stood up, and walked to the bathroom.

Vale, abandoned, sat back and doodled on his legal pad until the director returned. "Okay," he said as Dieffenbaker settled in. "Just let me run this by everyone and see what you think. Our intern — this is his first year. He's nervous, and afraid of the responsibility. So we set him up as hoping for a quiet year, with no crises or big decisions — and the Shah is brought in. The Shah's plane is forced to land near the city where our guy is —"

"I don't think this Shah thing works at ALL," Dieffenbaker said. "We're in some typical American hospital, and some SHAH is there? I mean, come on. Nobody will buy that. That's . . . that's beyond absurd. That's so absurd, it makes absurdity seem absurd. That's what I think."

"Then," Vale said dully, "what about the kidnap?"

"I have no problem with that. Larry, do you?"

"I have no problem with it, Jack."

"Carla, what about you?"

"If it works, it's fine."

"So," Dieffenbaker said, returning to Vale as though he had completed proving his case, "I'm not sure what you're doing with this." The man's face was crumpled into a grimace, as though he were staring into a blinding light. "You come out with this —it's a satire about the Shah of Iran? That's . . ." He sighed, suddenly weary. "I don't know! Maybe it's me! Maybe it's great."

"It's not — I mean, you take something like Doctor Strange-love —"

"This is completely different!"

"That's what I'm saying. . . ." Vale turned to Mack and semibegged. "Larry, what do you think? Where are we? What's going on?"

The producer was imperturbable. "I think we're having . . . ideas. Aren't we?"

"Yeah," Vale said. "But I have to go back in a few days —"

"Well whose fault is that?" Dieffenbaker challenged.

"What do you mean, 'fault'?" Vale's voice grew shriller. "I live in New York, okay?"

"You know," Mack murmured, "if you want to write mov-ies, you really have to live out here. I know you're a magazine writer, and all that. But if you're sincere —"

"Sincere about what?"

"About being a screenwriter. What do you use, a Selectric?"

Vale said, "A word processor."

"Oh." Mack's face fell. Somehow he was disappointed. "Well, I guess if you're busy . . . I have never used one of those things."

"They're great."

"Have you used one, Jack?"

Dieffenbaker's face looked suddenly sly and knowing. He nodded. "Let me tell you something, Larry. Those word proces-sors are fan-tastic. You know, I don't care what anybody says. These people who say 'It's too much technology, it's too compli-cated, it's inappropriate technology' — those people are full of SHIT."

Vale reached for the magazine that Carla had placed on the table. He could be imperious, too. He could withdraw, too. He could make a display of temperament, too. It was a glossy, slick home decorating magazine, percolating with chic art direc-tion and big photos. He read, "Eurostyle is the new way to say Contemporary." Vale thought: Hm.

"I wouldn't use one, Jack," Larry Mack said. "I'm sorry, that's how I feel." He looked at his watch. "So I guess it's time to eat something, isn't it."

Kidnapping with a Word Processor

I. INTRODUCTION

Read carefully. I am only going to say this once. I mean it.

If you want a more *efficient, productive,* and *convenient* way to conduct your "business," keep reading. You will be given an explanation and some instructions. Read it, and do what I tell you. Don't ask questions. Otherwise just forget it. Because it's no skin off my nose, all right? I'm Serious.

First: I know you. I know what you do. You are just like me, okay? I'm *nothing!* I'm *dirt!* But at least I know it. At least I admit it, okay? Do you? No. So who are you to talk. Right?

Fine. Calm down. I know that when you perpetrate a kidnap type of activity, you are faced with the headache of composing the ransom note. Let's stop bullshitting each other, shall

174

we? For once? Okay with you? There are only so many ways you can do this. You can call up the mark — but is that wise? Are you sure? To have your voice taped? And your line traced? Don't kid me. Come on. Or, you can handwrite a note. But is that wise? They ID your handwriting, and maybe you leave nice little prints THE SON OF A BITCHES. Because they can ID everything. I mean even the PAPER you write on. Are you familiar with watermark identification? No? Then shut the FUCK up. Because you don't know. Okay? It so happens that you do not know or have the knowledge, in this instance.

I'm Sorry. I did not mean to shout. But you shouldn't do things like that. Type things. Handwrite things. Are you fucking STUPID or what? I'm Sorry. Calm down.

Most likely you cut out words from magazines and news-papers. Oh, yes, I know all about that. I have done that myself. I have gotten ahold of magazines and had to read through them for the right words, inconveniencing myself over looking for an article with the word *location* or *nonsequentially numbered*. Yes, I have done it. And you know what? It SUCKS!

I'm Sorry. I get angry. In my emotions. I have an experi-ence of angriness when I happen to get pissed off, okay? Be-cause I'm not perfect like you, all right? Anyway, the magazines — I'm like you. I'm exactly like you. I'm a busy man. I'm very busy. You are busy, and I am very busy. With my schedule, as I'm sure you'll relate to. Tell me: who has time to read? Who has time to read *magazines* all day? I *hate* these magazines.

Well, okay. Fine. Just calm down. It's all over. You don't have to read any more magazines ever again. So just forget the magazines!

II. WHAT IT IS

What you do is, you get a computer. Don't tell me you don't know what one is. I do not want to hear that. I'm not stupid, okay? You're not stupid, and I'm not stupid. Hey, I at least have the common courtesy to respect your intelligence, all right? So how about some reciprocation? That's all. Some reciprocation of respect. Now. You get ahold of this computer, and you get a WRITE THIS DOWN. WRITE THIS DOWN AND DON'T FUCK IT UP. Yes, of course. You say, "Don't you have any respect for my intelligence?" I have respect for people's intelligence. Just please shut up. You purchase a "word processing program."

All that it is is, it's a little record that tells the computer what to do. And you know what? The computer does like it's told. And nobody gets hurt. And what you can do with it is, you can write basic form letters, for ransom notes, and print them up for whenever you do something.

You want a "for instance"? Fine. No problem. I am a reasonable person. I can give you a for instance.

III. A FOR INSTANCE

Let us say you snatch some rich woman's pet dog and you ask, oh, fifty thousand. What you do is, you have the computer. You get a word processing program, you put it in there, and you type on the keyboard, just like a typewriter. And you will come out with something like this:

> *Dear Mrs. X,*
>   *I have your dog. If you want to see him alive again, leave 50 thousand dollars in nonsequentially numbered small bills in the Ford Escort parked at the location of 5th and Main Wednesday night. No cops or I kill the dog, I Mean It.*

Now, isn't that simple so far? We have all written this sort of item at one time or another. Then what you do is, you store the note on another disk, and print it up on the printer you have to get, along with the computer. (It sounds like a lot of junk you have to buy but JUST DO IT. DO IT. Don't tell me about it, I don't want to know anything. Just do it.) Then you mail the note. Hey: Do It.

But you're an intelligent individual. You say to me, yes, of course, but in all truthfulness, do I need a fucking computer for that? No. You do not. But if you would just stop asking questions and *listen*. All right?

Now say you watch on the TV news a story about what has transpired. And you find out a couple things. First off, the dog's name is Cleopatra or some shit. Plus, the individual dog is a girl.

Now you are having some difficulty, my friend. If you want the note to be really effective, if you want that note to garner respect, you want it to be accurate and have all the important information. What if the mark says to her husband, "Hey. This guy's note is full of faulty information. So fuck him, honey, do not remit the cash or nothing to this individual. He's scum." So what do you do? No, no, you just shut UP. I'll tell you what you will do.

First off, what you will not do is, you will not find another big pile of magazines and hope there's an article on Cleopatra. Or maybe write a new note manually and take a chance on getting apprehended. No. No. No. *Wrong*.

With the word processor, you just retrieve the note from the disk you stored it on, which means hit a few keys and put it up on the screen. Then you may feel free to make all the changes you should happen to desire. You erase the words *your dog* and put in *Cleopatra*. You erase *him* and put *her*. You may even insert in a standard line that you keep on a disk, and make it nice and customized like, *This is your second note. Please remit the cash or I kill the dog Cleopatra*.

Is that clear? You may create a hundred basic notes and keep them on a disk. Then, you will always be ready with the correct ransom note.

Are you laughing? Do you think being modern is *funny?* Then go to Hell.

IV. JUST SHUT UP AND DO IT

What I can't stand is, people telling me I don't need this kind of fancy technology for my profession. You need it. You have to have it. Otherwise what are you? You're nothing. You're dirt. You're some low-life scumbag who can't even keep up with the world to do his job right. People like you have been screwing me over all my life, you son of a BITCH.

I'm Sorry. Won't you consider the advantages of word processing?

Make up your mind. Fast. I'm not going to write this article again.

11:52 A.M.
_____

Vale parked his rented car on a residential side street off Sunset and walked through enveloping heat down the hill toward the hotel. Mere existence was uncomfortable. The city had been overwhelmed by a Santa Ana condition: clear, unpolluted air baking in the desert had settled in the Los Angeles basin, creating the disturbing effect of being smothered by pristine transparency. You could see all the way to Santa Catalina as you slowly died of heat prostration.

In the lobby he asked directions to one of the bungalows, but stopped at the pool: the man he was to meet sat in a wooden rocking chair at a table under a Cinzano umbrella. He wore a white Lacoste shirt and white shorts, their brightness cut and muted by the shade. As Vale approached through the glare, the man scraped ash out of a curved pipe and tapped it into a glass ash tray.

"Like this setup?" he said, indicating his chair. "A little bit of Adirondack lodge out here under the palms."

"Very rustic. Pass the sour mash." Vale pulled up a white-grid patio chair and sat. "Nice to see you, Mart."

Mart had been one of the initial corps of editors — of the intellectual/political contingent — that made the humor magazine a success. In sentimental moments Vale almost considered himself a disciple of Mart's.

"You're out here for how long . . . ?" Mart asked, refilling the pipe from an unlabelled black pouch.

"Just a week. Taking — having — meetings about a rewrite for Galactic." Vale asked, "How long are you here for?"

"Three, four months. Whatever it takes. We're doing Switcharound Day for Columbia." He tamped the tobacco down, put the pipe in his mouth, and thumbed a lighter.

Vale nodded. It had been the one thing he had never understood about Mart. He had cowritten the magazine's first movie — a smash hit of historical proportions — and made a fortune on it. But rather than take advantage of that (as Vale was sure he would have) to pursue something serious — a serious comic novel, a serious stage comedy, a serious film comedy for grownups — he seemed content to putter around: contributing the odd humor piece to magazines, writing or rewriting the occasional commercial dreck movie. Vale was baffled. Maybe Mart was indeed working on some secret masterpiece of which Vale had no knowledge. Switcharound Day didn't sound like it.

"Didn't see you at Palermo's party," Mart said.

Vale said, "Oh. Well, I guess I wasn't invited, then."

Mart waved it off. Nothing was so important that it couldn't be minimized with wit. "The Little Chill. Everybody from the magazine reunited after, what, fifteen years?"

Jim Palermo was an art director whom Vale had worked with only sporadically. There was no particular reason for Vale to have been invited. But as he replied with good-natured chuckles to Mart's recounting of old enemies running into each other at the party, Vale inwardly died a thousand deaths. It was exactly the select squad of wise guys and humor commandos to which he took secret pride in belonging.

"I saw your piece in the Times Magazine," Mart said. "Very nice. Working on anything now?"

Vale smiled. "I came up with a title this morning, maybe it'll lead to something. 'Wifestyles of the Rich and Famous.' "

Mart sat back and rocked, puffing in absorbed meditation, nodding. Then he said, "Pun trap."

It had been a technical term at the magazine. "Maybe,"
Vale conceded.

"How about 'Knife Styles of the Rich and Famous.' People's
favorite silver patterns."

Vale said, laughing, " 'Lifeguards of the Rich and Fa-
mous.' "

It was the humorists' equivalent of ice-breaking small talk.
Vale sat back, a bit more at ease, as a couple in bathing suits
across the pool — a surly-looking rock musician and his carniv-
orous blond girl friend — muttered something to each other and
shared a nasty laugh.

"You're right," Vale said. "It is a pun trap. The thing to
do is get rid of the Life."

Mart nodded and murmured, "Get rid of Life, everything's
much easier." He looked at the smouldering pipe bowl and said,
"Hairstyles. 'Hairstyles of the Rich and Famous.' "

"Turnstiles," Vale said.

"Very nice."

" 'Turnstiles of the Rich and Famous.' "

Prose Styles of the Rich and Famous

In a hundred different tongues of a thousand different places; on the grandest of themes or the smallest of subjects; as intended for all of humanity throughout history or for an esoteric enclave existing ephemerally for an evanescent instant: these are the prose styles of the rich and famous. Come with us, on a whirlwind tour, as we taste of the achievements in leitmotif and language, content and concept, imagery and imagination, that have increased by an incalculable increment the collective culture and literary legacy of all mankind.

Throughout the grinding of our souls in the gears of the great Nighttime Institution, when our souls are pulverized and our flesh hangs down in tatters like a beggar's rags, we suffer too much and are too immersed in our own pain to rivet with pene-

*trating and far-seeing gaze those pale night executioners who tor-
ture us.*

These are the words of Aleksandr I. Solzhenitsyn, in his
epic and unforgettable account of the Soviet slave labor camps,
The Gulag Archipelago: a world-class style, for a world-class writer.
With its mesmerizing meter and inexorable industrial imagery,
this is a narration unafraid of the sound of its own voice. The
repetition of *souls* tolls like the bell that tolls for whom we must
never send to know. It tolls for thee, and we. And it tolls for
Solzhenitsyn, for whom that telltale toll would one day turn
into the tintinnabulating, tonic tocsin tinkle of cash registers
around the world, as this somber, sober, serious Soviet, this
emigré eminence on the edge of extinction, would live to see
his prose styled into blockbuster best-sellers from Walla Walla
to Baden Baden to Pago Pago. For Aleksandr Solzhenitsyn, coz-
ily ensconced in his fabulous, hyperexclusive New England
compound, it's Gulag moolah and Archipelago a-go-go, as readers
keep rushin' to the bookstores.

Meanwhile, a few hundred miles down America's Atlantic
seaboard, another sort of stylist explores his own perspective on
the human condition:

*Oh, the mandel bread was a much better idea. Homely,
tangible, and to the point of Victor Zuckerman's real life and a
Jewish family deathbed scene. But the oration on mandel bread
was Essie being Essie, and this, however foolish, was himself
being himself. Proceed, Nathan, to father the father.*

The singsong Yiddish tone, the underlying irony, the rue-
ful self-consciousness and self-conscious rue — the prose style,
unmistakably, of Philip Roth. In the Zuckerman books Roth
distilled the perceptions and preoccupations of a lifetime, a lifetime spent in the single-minded pursuit of art as only he —
progenitor of Portnoy, and the man who one day discovered
America saying hello to *Goodbye, Columbus* — could pursue it.

But no trivial pursuit, this; Hollywood was quick to beat a

path to his door, as Roth's smash novella became the hit film of the season, starring Richard Benjamin and introducing the ravishing Ali MacGraw as the pampered princess, Brenda Patimkin. Benjamin would go on to star in the movie version of *Portnoy's Complaint*, and although far less successful than its filmic forebear, this too would only add CASH to the COFFERS and RENOWN to the NAME of the already rich and famous Roth. The world now eagerly awaits whatever stylish prose Roth has next in store for his readers of both the Jewish and Gentile persuasion.

It seems impossible that there could be a prose style of a writer more rich and even conceivably more famous than Philip Roth. But the impossible becomes not only the possible, but the actual, in the presence of these world-famous sentences:

As France was caving in, people began at last to perceive that a main turn of mankind's destiny now hung on flying machines. . . . Massive bombings of cities from the air had, for some years after the First World War, been considered war's ultimate and unthinkable horror.

This could only be the prose style of Herman Wouk, storyteller extraordinaire. Who but the author of *The Winds of War* could capture in a single phrase the caving in of France, the hanging of destiny on flying machines, or the paradox of considering something unthinkable. THIS is prose as only the creator of *The Caine Mutiny* and *Marjorie Morningstar*, both made into fabulous Hollywood motion picture extravaganzas, can style it. Who but Wouk, whose output is exceeded only by his income, could have written, "The commander found Dr. Kirby, long legs sprawled, reading a German industrial journal and smoking a pipe, which, with black-rimmed glasses, much enhanced his professorial look." A pipe wearing black-rimmed glasses: THIS, truly, is a PROSE STYLE to make ROTH seem reticent and SOLZHENITSYN soul-less. All THIS, and ROYALTIES fit for a KING, make Herman Wouk the PREMIER PROSE STYLIST of the RICH AND FAMOUS THROUGH-

OUT THE WORLD, wherever FIRST-RATE means FIRST CLASS, and you can't spell LITERATURE without the L in LUXURY.

THE PREMIER, that is, EXCEPT FOR ONE.

A vision of a naked, giant, hairy body jumped onto the screen of her lids and she climaxed even before her husband was inside her.

YES, IT CAN BE NONE OTHER THAN THE IN-COMPARABLE HAROLD ROBBINS. WHETHER IN THE BLOCKBUSTING, BEST-SELLING *BETSY*, OR ANY OF HIS NUMEROUS OTHER NOVELISTIC TRIUMPHS, ROBBINS'S IS THE PROSE STYLE THAT HAS SET THE STANDARD FOR THE RICH, THE FAMOUS, AND THE FABULOUSLY SUCCESSFUL. KEEP YOUR LOQUA-CIOUS LUDLUMS AND YOUR CLANGOROUS KINGS, YOUR MONSTROUS MICHENERS AND YOUR COLOS-SAL CLAVELLS. WHETHER VACATIONING AT SUPER-FABULOUS SPAS AND SPOTS AROUND THE WORLD, OR WORKING IN ONE OF HIS MANY PALATIAL HOMES THROUGHOUT THE GLOBE, ROBBINS PERSONIFIES THE STYLISHNESS, THE PROSINESS, THE RICHNESS AND THE FAMOUSNESS THAT HAS MADE NOVEL WRITING SYNONYMOUS WITH GLAMOUR, GLITTER, AND GLORY. IT'S STRICTLY CAVIAR CONVERSATION AND CHAMPAGNE SHENANIGANS, SEVRUGA CERE-BRATION AND MOET MUSINGS, BELUGA BANTER AND PERRIER-JOUET POSTURINGS, WHENEVER ROBBINS SITS DOWN TO HIS GOLD-AND-PLATINUM OLIVETTI GATTOPARDO TYPEWRITER — ESTI-MATED CASH VALUE, TWO HUNDRED THIRTY-FIVE THOUSAND DOLLARS — TO CREATE ANOTHER NOVELISTIC EXTRAVAGANZA ABOUT THE LUSTS AND LOVES, THE TRIUMPHS AND TRAGEDIES, THE HEARTBREAK AND HEADACHES OF SOME OF THE MOST PRIVILEGED, PULCHRITUDINOUS, AND POW-

ERFUL PEOPLE EVER TO POPULATE THE PRINTED
PAGE. THE ACCOMMODATIONS ARE DELUXE, THE
WOMEN DELICIOUS, THE GOURMET MEALS DE-
LIGHTFUL, THE CLOTHING AND JEWELRY DIVINE,
FOR THIS MASTER MAGICIAN OF SENTENCES AND
SENTIMENT. HOW FITTING, THEN, TO LEAVE TO
HIM THE LAST WORD:

*Somehow she became confused, the man and the machine
they were one and the same and the strength was something else
she had never known before. And finally, when orgasm after orgasm had racked her body into a searing sheet of flame and she
could bear no more, she cried out to him in French.*

*"Take your pleasure with me! Take your pleasure with me!
Quick, before I die!"*

STYLISH PROSE, INDEED. AND NOW LET US
THANK YOU FOR TAKING YOUR PLEASURE WITH US.
HERE'S HOPING YOUR EVERY *MOT* IS *JUSTE*, YOUR
EVERY OPUS MAGNUM, UNTIL NEXT TIME ON PROSE
STYLES OF THE RICH AND FAMOUS.

11:54 A.M.

Mart said, "How about 'Pig Styes of the Rich and Famous'?"

*"Hey, wait a minute, that's it," Vale said. " 'Life Styes.'
There's something there."*

"Be my guest," Mart said, puffing.

"Mart, let me ask you something."

"Shoot."

*Vale heard his own nervousness in the formality of the re-
quest. He had known Mart for some years. But they were not
social friends; Vale's visit now was in fact a slight violation of
the customary script they usually enacted.*

That wasn't what worried him. He was more afraid of seem-ing naïve, unworldly, unsophisticated, uncool — exposed. Mart, reclining with pipe and rocker, the very image of Wisdom at Leisure, didn't help. A hot breeze drifted past, no different from the blast in the face when you open an oven to check on the progress of a roast. It rattled the low spiky palms around the pool. This was the West, and the West was desert. Out here, in this (aesthetically) lawless town, you were on your own.

"Why are you working on Switcharound Day?" *Vale said. After that it became easier.* "What about all that stuff you did in the seventies for the magazine? Don't you feel some kind of obligation to do something more substantial? I do. Am I nuts? Some kind of indictment, or J'Accuse, about the stupid country today? The government, the corporations, the military — and now Franklin Miller? It's unbelievable! Not because I'm heroic or noble. It's because I can't stand to have my intelligence in-sulted. That's all. That's my artistic motivation. It's all ego. Fine. Okay, maybe it's also psychologically easier for me. It's less of a burden on my inner circuits just to keep the same values I had in school. Or maybe I don't have the adult genes to be a hypocrite, which everybody assumes is inevitable and sort of okay once you pass thirty and own some property. Sure I want to own property. It's a nightmare! I don't even know what I'm saying. But you know what I mean. Look at what happens! Some old man says let's build a shield in outer space, and everybody says, 'Gee, that's a persuasive vision.' The weapons industry must have looked at each other that night and said, 'Jesus, nobody in their right minds is going to buy that.' They bought it! Congress bought it! Or, no, you're right: they pretend to buy it, to get the bucks. Star Wars to the weapons industry is like a wet dream that lasts ten years. Think of that. A decade-long wet dream. Ten years from now, after the funding is finally cut off, General Dynamics is going to wake up and reach for the phone and call up Martin-Marietta and say, 'Oh my god! That was fantastic!' Right? Se-riously. Old Pop says, 'We invaded Grenada, and by God we won, and now we're standing tall.' Grenada's like the size of this pool. And the next week everybody says, Hey, man, we're stand-*

ing tall. You know what the population of Nicaragua is? The same as San Francisco. The United States is at war with San Francisco! Forget, you know, 'self-determination,' and 'respect for sovereignty.' Seriously: why don't you write the kind of stuff you used to?"

"I don't care," Mart said.

It was uttered with such offhand frankness that it had the ring of a long-established philosophical position: I happen, for reasons we gentlemen agree are unfathomable and not subject to challenge, to be a Non-Carian. Vale could only bleat, "Really?"

"I don't care. And what's the point? The money sucks. The fame is narrow and worthless. The pieces get stale in six months. You put them in a book and it comes out a year later, and people say, 'Huh? Who? James Watt? Isn't he supposed to be dead or something?' Plus, look Noah, it's ten years later. I'm married and have a kid. Either I got tired of all that, or I got it out of my system, but I'm telling you: I don't care."

Vale said, "I know what you mean. I sort of don't care either." He stood up and sighed. "Until I see the news or read the paper. Then I get worried." He frowned. "Wish I had been at Palermo's party . . ." He held out his hand. "Anyway, when you're back in New York and you see everybody, I'd appreciate it if you didn't mention . . . this little psychotic episode just now."

"Don't worry," Mart said. He flicked up the flame on his lighter, and applied it to the tobacco. Once the pipe was lit, he put the lighter down and, puffing, shook Vale's hand. "They don't care either."

Dystopia Revisited

With 1984 now receding behind us, we find ourselves thinking, probably for the last time, of George Orwell's novel of the same name. Of course, we have thought about it before. I, for example, conceived the idea for this article back in November of 1984, but withheld writing it until January of 1985, in order to "play fair," and allow the year under consideration to expend itself. By the time you, dear Reader, are reading it, it will be even later. How time runs away from us! Orwell knew this, too, as he knew so much else. Yet, did he?

It is a question that will be much asked as 1984 ("The Year") slips from our grasp. Yet, before it fades too completely from memory, it may be instructive to ask ourselves just how many of George Orwell's predictions came true during the year whose number has become a household word.

I think it valid to make such an inquiry because Orwell,

certainly one of the best writers of his time, limned more than simply another sci-fi tale of a futuristic society, in which all the problems of life are supposedly solved, to make his contemporaries feel better. No, he was writing for us, too. Perhaps, in fact, he was writing more for us than for them! What if he was forced to write about 1984 because the audience of his own time, like the wife of a man who seeks an affair in the arms of another woman, "didn't understand him"? Perhaps, knowing that we would be alive in 1984, he was in effect signaling to us through the tunnel of Time, calling out desperately, "Alas! My contemporaries don't understand me back here! Oh you enlightened, much better readers of the future — help!" Then it was up to his terrific imagination to capture for us, as only the imaginations of the best writers are able to, the essence of our future times, by inventing something so completely fictional and "outrageous" that it told . . . the truth.

How was this possible? Because I think I may say that Orwell was, quite simply, one of the best writers we have ever had, although who "we" are is and remains ever elusive — the subject of fiction itself.

So enduring has this masterwork been that most of us, including myself, have not had to read it since high school. Yet it stays, both with us and myself. We remember, if not the exact line-by-line themes and imagery, certainly the most salient parts of the story, the principal characters, and some of the made-up words.

Has this dark, visionary tale proved accurate? Was George Orwell a true prophet, scorned in his own time and forced to use numbers as the titles for his books? Was 1984 the 1984 of 1984? Or was he simply an excellent writer? The answer, I think, is surprising.

For one thing, *soma*, the so-called wonder drug that banished care and made you feel that everything was just fine, is obviously cocaine. Of course, in Orwell's hellish society of the imagination, the drug was legal, whereas here, in so-called real life, it is not. Yet the media are replete with stories of the sky-rocketing popularity, and dangers, of this distillate of the hum-ble coca leaf of South America — so much so that, really, what's the difference? None, you will grant.

Furthermore, the worship of technology, which Orwell immortalized in the custom of having his people refer to dates as being either B.F. or A.F. (i.e., Before or After [Henry] Ford), can be seen in our present-day love affair with the computer. Indeed, it would not be too much to say that we find ourselves, in our own lives, thinking of dates in terms of B.I.B.M.E.T.H.C.M. and A.I.B.M.E.T.H.C.M. — Before and After I.B.M. Entered the Home Computer Market. How Orwell knew this was going to happen remains merely another mystery connected with his genius.

And what of HAL, the state-of-the-art computer whose obsession with control nearly wrecked everything? I suggest that "he" is analogous to the phone company. Nineteen eighty-four, we remember, will go down in history as the year in which AT&T broke up, wreaking havoc among all of us who had grown so dependent on that telephonic convenience. Machines, Orwell is telling us, become our masters, and we their slaves. How true!

To be sure, not all of the gloomy prognostications in the novel have come to pass. Orwell startled many (and angered more than a few) by predicting that poets would be outlawed from the "perfect" society of 1984. His exact reasons for this are obscure, and indeed, he was probably kidding. And what a fine joke it is. I laughed out loud when I read that section, something all too rare in contemporary fiction. Poets, after all, are the least offensive of writers, if for no other reason than their books are so short.

In any event, it does not matter whether he was predicting in earnest or in jest, since it is still legal to write poetry. Of course, one may argue that in effect it is "illegal," since society has crumbled so much, and Man is so uncultured, that it is virtually impossible to make a living as a poet. Yet, even though in a way this supports my thesis, I do not think that is what Orwell was referring to. No, he was warning us, in his typically hilarious way, about the death of art — which, luckily for all of us, is alive and well.

And he was astonishingly right about almost everything else. Who is Big Brother, if not our present-day anchor men on the network news? What are such phrases as "War Is Peace" and "Freedom Is Slavery" if not the precursors of such exercises in mind control as "Dodge Trucks Are Ram Tough" and "Coke Is It"? "But war *isn't* peace," one longs to cry. "And sometimes Coke *isn't* it." At such moments I am glad Orwell is no longer with us, thankful he is spared the torment of seeing his direst predictions come distressingly, inexorably true.

Harsh? Perhaps. Not only is it wrong to be glad someone is dead, but Orwell himself might have gone further, elaborating on his vision, or correcting and updating his predictions in a series of sequels. He might have written 1985, or 1984 II, or even a "prequel" along the lines of 1984: *The Early Months,* which would probably have actually been about the last eight or twelve weeks of 1983.

It is moot. We have only this one work to read, to remember, and to debate. Now that 1984 is literally over, we may inquire whether 1984 is literarily "over." I think the evidence shows conclusively that it is not. Man will be reading or remembering 1984 as long as he takes drugs, worships technology, and is enslaved by machines. It is, admittedly, a grim scenario. Yet we may be cheered by the knowledge that were George Orwell present, he could point to his masterwork of fictive prescience and nod, oh, so knowingly. To have the last laugh on society and be able to say, "I told you so" — such are the consolations of the highest art.

11:56 A.M.
_____

Vale returned to his room at 11:56 and lay down for a nap. That night, Vale confronted the problem of dinner.

He should have, he knew, leaped into the rented car and driven somewhere za-za and happening, struck intelligent poses in a banquette while facing the room, ordered anything and everything on the menu, and left in a haze of expensive intoxication. Or, he could have styled over to some bar or club and "picked up" a "woman."

But the room was so cozy, and the vast L.A. landscape so alien. Vale was as skilled at picking up women as he was at picking up barbells. And after his speech to Mart earlier, he felt depleted and foolish. So he took up the room service menu and cobbled together the most ridiculous thing he could think of: BOWL OF SHRIMP, $85, A NEW YORK–STYLE STEAK, $24.50, A PLATTER OF FRENCH-FRIED POTATOES, $3, SALAD A LA CAESAR, $6.00, CHATEAU DAUZAC MARGEAUX, $95, *and, since one always craves a bit of a sweet after beef,* TART OF SEASONAL FRUITS, $6.50.

The waiter brought the meal on a cart, and prepared the Caesar dressing while Vale watched. There was something obscene and surreal about it — Vale standing around in his bedroom watching some stranger in a uniform make his salad dressing — but he tipped the guy big and felt like a sport. Then he slipped into something comfortable, and sat down to this two-hundred-and-fifty-dollar steak dinner dressed in his underwear and the white bath robe that had come with the suite. He was looking forward to a showing of Some Like It Hot *on TV. He had seen the movie four times and watched it whenever he could.*

But he had misread the listing. Merrily dipping his astronomically priced shrimp in what was, after all, the usual ketchup and horseradish, Vale received as an almost physical blow the realization that instead of Some Like It Hot, *he was about to watch* S.O.B., *a satire he had never seen about the movie business. Nothing else was on, and dinner was served. He ate the excellent steak and watched.*

The movie was bad; in fact it was terrible. But didn't they

*deserve credit for at least trying to do something mean and biting
and for adults? Wasn't it refreshing to see a comedy with a point
of view? Shouldn't Vale applaud that such a film was made and
released at all? He drank the bottle of wine, got a bit tipsy, and
at that point had the misfortune to drop a french-fried potato off
its platter. It fell onto the white robe.*

*He picked up the french-fried potato. It had left a stain on
the snowy terry cloth. There was conceivably no reason for him
to attend to it. The robe wasn't his, and they'd send it through
the laundry tomorrow after he checked out. Still, he got up un-
steadily and lumbered into the fabulous bathroom. A speaker
connected to the TV had been installed under the twin sinks. He
rubbed at the stain with a damp wash cloth. Vale could hear
the pushy, pushy dialogue of the movie in the bathroom with
him, like a person receiving radio broadcasts in the fillings of his
teeth. His steak was out there getting cold. The movie was stupid. A portly Chicano man who looked like a South American
dictator had recently been in the room making Vale's own personal Caesar salad. Vale had ordered from the menu like a spoiled
brat and they had given him everything he'd asked for. Now he
was getting drunk in his deluxe accommodations, eating an ar-
bitrarily priced meal, repeating excuses he'd heard in other con-
texts about a movie he couldn't stand, and feeling guilty and
responsible for having dropped a french fry, thereby shattering
the perfection of the scene. This was Los Angeles.*

*Although he sometimes weakened, Vale disapproved of fan-
tasizing about money; doing so struck him as capitulation to E-
vil. But over the tart and coffee he dwelled on all that potential
scriptwriting dough. It worked an alchemical, transubstantiating
magic on Vale and the world around him.*

*The physical realm — the room, the chairs, the door he
closed — seemed to grow less dense; its customary affronts and
obstacles warmed and became pliable when daubed with the universal solvent of cash. At the same time Vale's abstract ego — a
normally elusive, inferred thing, like a ghost made visible only
by clouds of special steam — seemed to take on weight and bulk.
He could swagger with it through crowds, knock other egos out*

of the way, and move about the world with authority, impervious to challenge.

In other words, he thought, I can be like Jack Dieffenbaker.

Of course, he would never make that kind of money in his usual profession. Sometimes print humor was a drill that struck a gusher, but more often than not you came up with just about enough to lubricate the machinery to sink the next one. Those humorists that did hit it big dealt more with personal concerns: local history, the vagaries of daily life, household quirks, parental whimseys, and all the other fancies and fads and foibles and real-life, human things. Social or political issues were intellectual, but the mass readership went in for the emotional: the sweet, the cute, the so-true, the poignant, the heart-warming, the cockle-warming, the nice.

Of course, maybe Vale could change his style.

Lake Youbegone Days

I. FARM

You might think that most people in Lake Youbegone live on farms, but you'd be only half right. Lake Youbegone is, after all, a *town*, with stores and streets and municipal services. Still, we never think of ourselves as having "municipal" anything. You drive in here in your Datsun 280–Z and start talking about "municipal" and "civic" and "urban," folks know you for what you are. So you just keep on driving.

These days we're one farm less. Gene Berglund lost his — had his couple hundred acres auctioned off after being fore-closed on by a bank over in St. Cloud, the one the Jews are using to help destroy good Christian society in the five-county area. Gene took the foreclosure pretty hard but, like a lot of Lake Youbegonians, would rather eat nails than show it. Folks

195

who make their living off the land learn early that emotions are like the weather — you put up with them, wait for the bad to turn good, try to figure out how to cut your losses and who to blame things on. When I was growing up, Hoyt Krobknechter was the local champion of blame fixing. Once, when his smoke shed went up in flames, Hoyt accused Nikita Khrushchev of sending Russian agents to put him out of business and drive up the price of American bacon. Hoyt's daughter, Celia, sold a savory relish made from tomatoes that she crushed with her feet. I used to call her "Old Redfoot" until her brother, Earl, told me to stop calling his sister a Communist. He socked me in the shoulder. "Ow! Quit that!" It *hurt*.

Wednesday: Two days after the foreclosure. Bill Nyborg is riding his three-speed English racer down the dirt road that passes by Gene Berglund's farm. He's surprised to see a lot of activity: cars parked every which way on the grass in front of the house, men standing around outside. He pedals in to take a look.

Right away he recognizes Gene, standing in the center of the crowd, next to Hank Gunderson. Gene's in his usual over-alls and work boots, but Hank looks dressed like Sergeant Nick Fury in the comics Bill's mother yells at him about reading. Hank's jump suit of camouflage khaki, under his Trojan Seed Cap, might pass for stylish in some cities, but not here. No one in Lake Youbegone is a slave to fashion. About the only attach-ment you could describe as slavelike would be Ole Wittering's deep respect for the lemon meringue pie at the Piggyback Cafe.

"I would crawl over broken glass for this," he likes to say, shoveling in an extra-tall wedge — no small feat, considering how high Lucille piles the meringue. ("Like a beautiful snow-drift," she once described it. "That's the effect I aim for. I keep a photograph from the *National Geographic* Scotch-taped to the kitchen wall: a beautiful white snowdrift in the Alps or the An-des somewhere — no, it's the Himalayas. That's it. Because you can see those Chink mountain guides they have, standing around in the photo. Sherbets, they're called.")

Hank Gunderson's father started Gunderson's Reasonable

and Basically Trustworthy Garage, but ever since the Firestone
Service Center opened on Highway 52 Hank has had to scram-
ble to keep up the business. People are impressed by the Firestone diagnostic machines, whereas the closest Gunderson comes
to having diagnostic machines is the purple gumball dispenser
in the office. Hank's arm is around Gene's shoulder, although
Gene doesn't look too comforted by what's being said.

"You think it's an isolated case?" Hank demands. "You
think Gene's farm is the only one they want?" There are shrugs
from the audience on this. "Hell if it is. What about Deke
Lindborg's place over near Scheussler?"

"First Minny got that one," someone says. "No Jews on
their board."

"Of course not," Hank snaps back. "You think these banks
advertise who really runs 'em? You think the names on their
boards of directors mean diddly squat? Wake up. These Jews,
these niggers, these Communists — they sit home and see how
asleep all of us real Americans are, and they fall out of their
chairs laughing. And meanwhile old Gene here has to pack
up." Gene waves his hand around, as though to say, Leave me
out of this, but Hank's on a roll, and the crowd is getting interested. "You call that American?" Hank goes on. "When a
bank can just come in and take a man's farm away from him?
That ain't American. Know where they do that? Three guesses.
Russia."

This has its effect: all over the front yard comes the sound
of men thinking about something. These are mostly farmers and
mechanics and blue-collar types, so thinking is about as natural
a part of their job as playing the oboe. Finally someone asks,
"What can we do about it?" It makes Bill Nyborg turn his head
with a jerk in search of the source. Sure enough, it's his dad,
Nelson.

"You can join up with me and other true Americans who
are ready to fight to keep this country what it should be," Hank
says. "You can join the Colloquium."

Bill pedals away. Two years ago he sent away for a Complete Magician's Kit in the mail, but when it arrived it was so

pathetic — a little deck of cards, some disappearing balls that didn't work, a stick that was supposed to turn into a bouquet but didn't — that he went into a rage and strangled the cat.

"What's this?" his father asked.

"Dead cat."

"How'd it happen —?"

Magic, he thinks, but instead says: "Choked it."

"Oh."

Nothing happened. No punishment, lectures, nothing. He felt invincible. He had no need for magic ever again.

II. PHILOSOPHY

"All right. Before you touch a weapon, you have to know your enemy. The chart tells it all. Memorize it."

"Hank . . . ?"

"Top of the ladder's the International Monetary Fund. Owned by the Rockefellers and the Kennedys. Underneath is your Trilateral Commission, which consists of three branches: Wall Street, the country of Israel, and Motown Records."

"Hey, Hank, what's that black singer's name? Michael Johnson?"

"You here to learn about a threat to your freedom, Charlie, or tell jokes?"

"Come on, what is it?"

"Jackson. Michael Jackson."

"Right, Bill. So. What do Michael Jackson and Richard Pryor have in common?"

"Who's he?"

"You guys want to pay attention here —"

"That coon comedian. Answer: they both belong to the Ignited Negro College Fund —!"

"Who?"

"I don't get it."

"Aw, come on, you guys. You don't remember when they both set themselves on fire?"

"What the hell is he talking about? We come here to learn

about Communists or to talk about a couple of niggers setting themself on fire, for God's sake?"

"Never mind, forget it. Telling jokes to you bunch of small town ignoramuses's like pouring water down a rat hole."

"The Jews control the banks and the media. I mean that's so obvious it's not worth discussing. Then you got the blacks working for them, like a kind of army. That's why we need a white man's army."

"Hey, Hank, there's plenty of black guys in the U.S. Army. What about them?"

"Nyborg, if you were any dumber your wife'd need a license to walk you down the street."

"They're infiltrators. Just wait 'til the race war starts, and see whose side they're on."

"So they work for the Jews? And the Jews work for the Commies?"

"Frightening, isn't it?"

"My God, I had no idea."

Nels Nyborg had his doubts about joining Hank Gunderson's organization. For one thing, there was the name problem: Nels wasn't happy about belonging to a club called The Colloquium Invictus. Hank explained that first, it wasn't a "club," and second, the name had real significance. "It means an invincible gathering," Hank said.

"Then why not call it 'The Invincible Gathering'?" Nels asked.

The problem with that name, in Hank's mind, was the same as the problem with all the other ones he'd tried, like The Militia and Freedom's Guardians. Somehow each one ended up sounding like an insurance company. For a while he tried to invent one with deeper symbolic meaning, paying tribute to the land of the Founding Fathers, and reaffirming his and his followers' loyalty to the United States. So for two days he tried telling everyone his organization was to be called the New England Patriots. It sounded fine — in fact, there was something comfortable and familiar about it. Then Bill Hochstetter pulled him aside and reminded him that it was also the name of Boston's team in the National Football League.

Finally Hank sat down with a dictionary and came up with Colloquium Invictus. Nels was put off. All that Latin made it sound like Hank wanted everyone to get together and turn Catholic. Once Nels joined, though, he found himself amazed at Hank's insight and passionate commitment to freedom. Suddenly a lot of things that until then just hadn't made much sense started to fall into place. Like why so many people in show business were Jewish. And why he had never heard of a Negro physicist. ("Your African races are incapable of doing algebra," Hank explained. "It's all tied up in the genetics of their mind. They are unable to substitute letters for numbers, on account of the tendency they have not to be able to read. It's that simple.") When Hank announced to the membership of the Colloquium that it was time to assemble for field training, Nels was ready.

The "training camp" turned out to be about ten thinly wooded acres in a corner of Hank's brother's spread outside of Anoka. Hank told his men — about eight in all — to bring whatever rifles and handguns they owned, plus ammunition. Some of the men were duck hunters and brought rifles, but most didn't own a weapon. Rudy Tillman and Clarence Halvorsen, thinking that any kind of sporting gear would do, brought their fishing rods.

I wasn't present for what Hank described as the "field maneuvers," but I can imagine the sight: eight Lake Youbegone men, each the husband of a woman who's death on this sort of boys-only carrying on, running in a half-crouch through the brush, holding their rifles or handguns (or fishing rods) at chest height, dodging the enemy's bullets or flamethrowers or mind-corrupting pamphlets, or whatever they've been instructed by Hank to anticipate. Their faces are smeared with a dark brown paste Celia Gunderson whipped up in the kitchen — for camouflage purposes, although it's only about three in the afternoon so there's not much night for that darkened skin to blend into. On Hank's signal they immediately fall to their bellies. Hank calls this "the hit-the-dirt," but it's more a semantic conceit, really, since between the years of drinking Hamm's six-packs and restricting their physical recreation to golf, fishing, and occasionally (under protest) mowing the lawn, their bodies are such that it's more as though the dirt has hit them.

Frank Olson's rifle goes off when he falls. (No casualties.) Everybody looks winded and confused. You can practically hear Hank's thoughts: *If these men are the last bulwark of freedom and racial purity in white Christian America, we're doomed.*

Maybe he doesn't want to sap morale. Or maybe he really thinks they're underequipped. At any rate, what he says out loud is: "We need more armaments."

The following Friday, at exactly three o'clock in the afternoon, five men drive into Lake Youbegone in Hank's '80 Plymouth Horizon. They park along the curb in front of Dave's Lake Youbegone Friendly and Courteous Bank and Trust. The men are all dressed entirely in black, except for Clarence Halvorsen, whose wife put away his dark clothes for the summer. Clarence has on a light white cotton shirt and some checked golf pants his eldest, Anna, gave him for Christmas two years before. She now lives in Denver with two kids of her own and two from her husband Elliot's first marriage. Ask Clarence about the grandchildren and hear him laugh bitterly and snap back, "Which ones? Mine or the other guy's?"

Clarence has mixed feelings about Hank's cockamamie scheme for acquiring funds for arming the Colloquium Invictus. But while he wasn't surprised when Hochstetter and Magnesen dropped out, Clarence has always felt that loyalty was just about the most important human trait there is. Even a damn dog demonstrates loyalty. Besides, in for a penny, in for a pound. So here he is, standing lookout while the four others bluff their way into the bank, which has just closed to customers.

Not that Elliot is so bad. Obviously his first wife must have had something basically wrong with her, since the court awarded the father the children. But you have to feel sorry for Anna sometimes — having to finish raising some other woman's kids while she's got her hands full with her own. Clarence greets Louise Kramermann as she returns from lunch to the Fyne-Look Women's Store, and for the first time, as he watches her walk past, he wonders: Kramermann. Does her husband Albert perhaps have any Jewish blood in his past? Does she? Didn't they arrive here from Wisconsin a few years back? Aren't there a lot of Jews and niggers in Wisconsin?

Clarence's ruminations are interrupted by the sound of gunfire from inside the bank. A second later the door bursts open and Hank is running out, followed by Nels Nyborg and Frank Olson. "They got Rudy!" Frank yells.

Actually, Rudy had gotten sidetracked talking to Janet Hilverstram, whose folks used to own the Tase-tee Diner just outside of town, until they sold it to Don and Edna Spooner and moved to Arizona. Janet stayed behind. Why not? She had a good job at the bank, and at the time was going pretty steadily with Leon Krumhacker. Then one evening they'd caught the early show at the Deluxe Quad–5 movie complex in St. Cloud, and were driving back home, when Leon allowed his nondriving hand to explore the classified portion of Janet's anatomy. She announced her objections and gave him a slap.

"What's the problem?" he complained. "You thought it was great when Richard Gere just did it."

"You turn into Richard Gere, and we'll see," she answered. "Meanwhile keep your hands on the wheel."

Rudy knew of this incident from Janet herself. She told just about everybody in town, sometimes twice. It got so we had to ask ourselves: is she complaining about what did happen, or what didn't? He had just asked Janet about her parents when Hank yelled something about insurrection and Communist sympathizers, and hauled out his .38.

Rudy had enjoyed the benefit of the Colloquium field training course, but at that moment the sight of a naked firearm in the hand of a wild man like Hank Gunderson caused it to slip his mind. He executed a hit-the-dirt behind a desk. He heard some shots fired, some screams, and the next thing he knew there was Janet, on the floor beside him. She was quivering with fear, which was understandable, so as Hank led the other Colloquium members outside in a hail of gunfire — their own, since nobody in the bank had a weapon — Rudy took Janet in his arms. Then his hands started to stray — I guess Janet just had that effect on men. In the end he was able to accomplish what Leon Krumhacker wasn't. She either didn't notice or didn't mind.

III. REDEMPTION

The first time I realized that your ear was a hole in your head, I was leaning over toward Muriel Dintenfass at the church's Fourth of July picnic. We were sitting under the big dusty oak tree out behind the church, having just gorged ourselves on wieners and potato salad, and I was going to attempt to stick my tongue in Muriel's ear. I was homing in for the kill, when it struck me: *I'm inserting my tongue into a hole in this girl's head.* I pulled back and lost all concentration. Eight years later Muriel married Frank Olson. They'd raised two kids and had been husband and wife for fifteen years when Frank accompanied Hank Gunderson, Clarence Halvorsen, and Nels Nyborg out to the old Matern place for the big climactic shootout.

With them was Louise Kramermann. She had been passing by the bank when the Colloquium Invictus had shot its way out. Hank Gunderson had looked around wildly, spotted Louise, and in a second had dashed over, grabbed her arm, and dragged her to the car. "Let's GO!" he barked to Clarence, who was at the wheel.

"Where we going now, Hank?" Nels asked.

"Hey," Clarence said, starting the car. "What say we get on over to the Tap Room and get us a beer-and-a-bump."

Hank explained impatiently that they had just committed armed robbery, and possibly murder, and that even though it had been in the name of freedom and democracy, probably swinging over to the local bar for a round of drinks wasn't such a great idea. He told Clarence to drive west.

*   *   *

When I got there the FBI and the local police had the Matern place so completely surrounded with cars and SWAT team trucks and media vehicles from St. Cloud and the Cities, I thought: now *this* is news. Not the Colloquium holed up in that falling-down abandoned old farmhouse, but all this state-of-the-art hardware finally coming to Lake Youbegone, where our idea of modern technology is the Fry Baby presented by Garnet Crandall to his wife Ella for their anniversary last year.

Some shots came from the Matern house, the FBI and policemen ducked behind their cars, and I scuttled over to Walt Lambeaux, the county sheriff.

"What the hell you doing here," he demanded, his eyes on the house. "You think this is some human-foible type of event?"

He told me that one person had been killed and another wounded badly in the bank robbery, and that Hank Gunderson had more or less lost his mind. I said, How can you tell?, but he didn't think it was funny under the circumstances. That's a problem I've always had, growing up in Lake Youbegone: people here are big on "the time" for jokes and humor and such, which I guess is attributable to the fact that their economy revolves around farming, with its specific seasons for specific activities. It's death on joke telling, though. I once got off a good one at Ella Lundberg's funeral and next thing I knew Aunt Betty is poking me a good one in the ribs and hissing, "This is not the time!"

It sure wasn't the time for Louise Kramermann. We heard a few shots, and then after a silent period, a woman's screams — hers. Walt hustled over to consult with the SWAT commander. After a brief exchange the commander said, "Right. Let's take him." And then barked an order on his bullhorn. Three SWAT men in jump suits and science fiction headgear, who were taking cover behind a car, stood up and shot tear-gas canisters into the house as Louise kept screaming.

Walt's great-grandfather, Jacques Lambeaux, migrated down to Lake Youbegone from Canada, where he'd made a respect-

able living trapping beaver. There was a beaver pelt in the main
hallway of the Sons of Knute lodge, splayed open and sealed in
a glass frame, until Willie Bunsen mistook it for a flying possum
and swung a smoking stand at it during the Sons' New Year's
Eve party in 1966. His middle son, John, moved to Los Angeles
to become an actor. The most famous actor in Lake Youbegone
is Mr. Paul Denby, an English teacher at the high school, who
cast himself in the title role of our spring production, *Cyrano
de Bergerac*. French is the most popular second language taught
at the school, which means that about a dozen students take it.
A dozen is usually twelve, but if you go to Tollerud's Decent
Bakery and buy a dozen of Evangeline Tollerud's Norsk Butter
Cookies, Evvie will look the other way while she herself drops
in two more gratis. She's a Lutheran.

Some SWAT men in gas masks rush the house. Inside,
Clarence and Frank are lying dead, shot. So is Nels. Hank is in
a different room. He's sprawled across an old bed — just the
frame and naked rusty bedsprings. Louise is there too, cut up
pretty bad and out cold with shock.

When Louise was a girl, in Green Bay, she used to gaze
up at the constellations on clear evenings and feel duped. *They're
crazy. That's no swan. How do you get a woman in a chair out
of that?* The vast disparity between the supposed shapes of the
constellations, and their actual scattered, meager appearance,
struck her twelve-year-old girl's heart like a denial from God.
"Sorry, Louise. These heroes and animals and mythical beasts
up here — they're not for you."

Years later, after she and her husband Albert had moved
to Lake Youbegone, they were driving home one evening from
dinner at the Muellers, when Louise had a certain feeling. She
insisted Albert pull to the shoulder and stop. She got out, and
guided only by the cold blue light of the half moon she walked
through corn stubble out into the middle of a field. Thirty yards
out, she stopped and looked up.

"It was unbelievable," she wrote her daughter June the next
day. "The sky looked exactly the same. No hunters or scorpions

or water bearers — just the same old mess. If I'm due for any kind of deep, redeeming experience, I'm sure not going to get it living here."

Walt Lambeaux: "What gets me is, the stuff on the walls. Those words, written in, well, you know. Blood. Who wrote 'em? Hank, probably. What I want to know is, can't anybody in this town spell *Communist* right? Man kills his own troops and then himself — helluva way to run an army. Plus, what Hank did to that woman — it's a sick situation. But it's what I always say — start messing with politics and sooner or later somebody's gonna get their feelings hurt."

June lives in Sarasota, Florida. She last visited Lake Youbegone this past Thanksgiving with her husband Donald and the twins. "What a nice town," she said as they drove through. Who asked her?

11:58 A.M.

Larry Mack, Jack Dieffenbaker, and Carla Cutler arrived at 11:58 on what was scheduled to be Vale's last day in Los Angeles. "Sorry we're late," Mack drawled as they entered. "Something came up."

As they took their seats Vale noticed that Dieffenbaker looked at him from under sullen, hooded eyes, saying nothing. Carla Cutler seemed more abstracted and vacantly polite than ever. Vale asked if he should review the notes.

"You know what," Larry Mack said, in the tone of a man trying to beat back defeatism, but not all that hard. "I don't know if that'll help."

Vale said, "We have a structure problem."

"I'll tell you what we have," Dieffenbaker insisted. "We have a problem of STRUCTURE. Is the hospital falling down or isn't

it? Is the Shah in or out? Do we keep the nurse with the big tits or not?"

"What nurse with the big tits?" Vale asked.

Larry Mack said mildly, "We were discussing on the way over how it might be nice to have a nurse with big tits. Jack says it's a classic baggy-pants burlesque character, and I sort of agree with him."

"Yeah," Vale said. "But this isn't burlesque. Is it?"

"No, this isn't burlesque!" the director snarled, as though insulted. He gestured toward Vale and said to Mack, "I don't know where he's coming from, Larry. I — maybe it's me! Maybe I'M out of sync here."

Then Vale made his big mistake.

"Jack is great with moments," he heard himself say. "But this isn't a sixty-second commercial. It's a ninety-minute story. So before we can have any moments, we need a story, and an outline."

"WHAT?"

"I —"

"Don't talk to me about moments, Noah," Dieffenbaker snarled. "I know more about movies than you ever will. We are NOT in sync here, Larry. We are definitely NOT in sync."

"You're at cross-purposes," Carla Cutler said.

"Larry —" Vale pleaded.

Mack nodded and held up a hand. "There's no need for us to raise our voices. We can discuss this like grown-up people. Now Noah has a legitimate problem. But it's not just his problem. It's our problem. Because it's our movie. And the best way to deal with it, the thing for us to do, is this." *He got up from his chair and walked over to Vale.* "You, Noah, go back to New York. You write a first draft. You make it the way you think it should be. Jack, meanwhile —"

"Larry?" Carla Cutler said. "It's twelve-fifteen . . . ?"

"I'll be right there."

"You'll be right where?" Vale asked.

Mack, in a voice that said I-have-connived-and-I'm-not-

*ashamed, said, "We're meeting Murray Sammy for lunch up-
stairs."*

*"Now?" Vale laughed. "You came here to have a meeting
for fifteen minutes on your way to lunch?"*

*"I don't have to listen to this," Dieffenbaker hissed, as though
he were being abused. He stood and went to the phone.*

*Mack motioned for Vale to stand, then took him aside and
in low, confidential tones said, "Believe me, this is the best way.
Go back to New York. Send me what you write, and we'll take
it from there. I'll be in touch with Amy about everything."*

"So you're telling me to get out of town."

"For your own sake," Mack said.

It took Vale two months to write the screenplay.

*During this time Franklin Miller had been drawing nearer:
polls conducted in late August showed him six points ahead of
his competition, and the lead stretched to ten points by early
October. The script safely on its way to L.A., Vale turned his
attention to the presidential election, its front-running candi-
date, and the menace he foresaw for American society if the can-
didate won. He responded the only way he knew how: by writing
a devastating twelve-hundred-word article comparing Miller to a
six-pack of beer.*

Then, one morning, at 11:59, Larry Mack called.

*"Hello," he said. "Look, Noah, don't get excited. I just called
to tell you that I can't call you. Carla gave the script to Daniel
Tony, but he won't be back until tomorrow. I think he's somewhere in Europe. I know you're on pins and needles and I just
wanted to tell you what was going on. I can call you about it
after she talks to him and I talk to her."*

"When will that be?"

*"Oh God, I knew you'd ask me that . . . let's see. I have
a twelve-thirty lunch day after tomorrow. . . . Oh. I'm meeting
a writer in the morning. So I have to be in the office early.
Okay, let me call you day after tomorrow, around nine o'clock
in the morning. That's my time, of course. It would be around,
what? Noonish, your time."*

"I'll be here."

Vale hung up, snapping his fingers. Something was coming into focus. "Daniel Tony is coming back from Europe," he said. "Eurostyle is the new way to say Contemporary." He laughed. "Eurostyles of the rich and famous . . ."

That wasn't quite it, yet.

The Way We Live Today

(Excerpts, sans photographs, from
the latest issue)

HABITS AND HABITATS: Three Styes, Three Styles

Once upon a time houses were ho-hum, so-so. Design was a stalemate — sleek rad torture vied with dowdy trad plush. Interiors found success with excessive accessories — rinky-dinky bric-a-brac and ticky-tacky knickknacks got accolades from acolytes going gaga for frou-frou.

Now's different. Suddenly, style and comfort are lucky in love, not strange bedfellows. We're why: Everyone and his ex's a designer. Industry's keeping pace, as a host of new fabrics, furniture, and materials have arrived to fuel our obsession with pleasure, comfort, money, ourselves, and our marvelous, maddening, insatiable voracity for living.

Case in point: a trio of pigs. From disparate backgrounds come a spectrum of needs — and three distinctly different budgets. Result? Striking contrasts in look — and outlook — and a three-way mirror reflecting the way we live today.

EDUARDO PIG *(left)*, seen here with sow María and piglets Juanito, Elroy, Isabel, DeVan, and Carlos, is a security guard at a major office high-rise. "I don't know much about houses," he admits. "But you have to live somewhere."

DAVID SWINE AND JUDITH SOW-SWINE *(above)*, piggybacking piglets Jennifer and Max. He: "I took a few drawing courses at U.C.S.D. (University of California at Spam Diego), so I thought it would be fun to design our home myself." He's in marketing; she's a teacher.

THATCHER PORKER, JR., AND PATRICIA "PATSY" PORKER *(right)*, in front of their summer home, The Wallows. (Not shown: piglet Thatcher III, a boarding student at the Bacon Academy, Old Loyne, Connecticut.) "I don't have much use for 'style,' " declares heir to the Hog and Hog Distillery fortune. "Trends are fleeting. Quality endures."

A *Touch of the Tropics*

Straw walls say Polynesian Paradise, as Eduardo Pig's design for his family's one-room hut-style hut evokes images of island ease, lagoonside languor. Straw's natural texture lets this one does-all, shelters-all cabana breathe. Easily permeable walls let wind and weather go out with the same ease with which they entered. Neutral beige earth-tones set off a plucky mix of store-bought furniture (J.C. Pigpenney's, Sows-Roebuck), and street-found treasures. "You can pick up a lot of nice things people put out for the garbage," notes Eduardo, stating the case for scavenging. "Besides, new stuff is so expensive these days."

The sty also doubles as a social club/play den/guest room when Eduardo's two brothers, and their families, fly in from Puerco Rico to visit, chat, live, for three years. Are they crazy? Or lazy good-for-nada's? No, just unemployed: suddenly we've got more leisure, freedom, time to kill. Thus, this query: Did

Eduardo specify straw for its ease of construction, leaving lots more time to dance and sing and play?

"No," he corrects. "It's cheap."

PRIMAL DIRT becomes mud underfoot *(left)*, when rain enters through airy ceiling — this is back-to-nature at a down-to-earth price. Low-tech, high-touch straw wall doubles as perfect emergency fire fuel, or — as three-year-old DeVan discovers to her delight — a tasty, high-fiber snack.

OPEN HOUSE is more than a phrase. Front door is easily forced by the balmiest breeze — or by friends dropping in for dominos and *malta (above)*. Low upkeep, small initial cost, shrinking job market leave lots of time for both. But is home secure? "How the hell do I know," muses Eduardo, opening another bottle.

The Family That Sticks Together

"Sticks are easy to assemble and maintain," explains David Swine. "They left us time for maximizing our life-style." Sticks' economy was also a plus. "We spend all our income on ourselves," he notes. "We like to dance and sing and play." Both David and Judith are expecting promotions sometime soon, and have planned their home — and lives — accordingly.

In the Swines' rustic two-room sty, Scandinavian natural meets English country cottage. Walls and roof are interlaced sticks — braiding adds strength, pliability — while floors go under cover beneath textured, handsome twigs. Witty wicker furniture adds to the fabulous fibrousness. Construction's a snap, and so, sometimes, do the walls.

"We like to travel," Judith says. "And sometimes, when we take down the house to go somewhere, the walls break. David just makes another one."

Clearly, all's motion and change with this contemporary couple, and their house shows it. Call it one more sign that upward mobility is the poetry-in-motion of the eighties. Marking time's a thing of the past. Upbeat's the tempo for the way we live today — now's the heyday of rah rah, a holiday for hoo-hah and hot-cha ha-ha's.

ELEGANT FUN comes home to stay — until it goes out on the town, later — in roof detail (above). Peak, formed of hundreds of interlaced sticks, resembles multidigited alien hands clasped in prayer. Metaphor's serendipity: Neither David nor Judith are "conventionally" religious, although he's had "an experience with a deity."

THIS STY'S NO EYESORE, as front door (right) deftly doubles as back door. One entrance (all stick, natch) is energy efficient, too — no time's wasted trying to decide which door to use. What if dangers lurk out front? "What do we care?" David smiles. "We'll be in the Adirondacks, in our new truffle-hunting lodge." Judith, teacherly, adds a wistful, budget-conscious, "Someday."

Solid As a Rock

"Brick lasts forever," says Thatcher Porker, Jr., adding a waggish, "Not that I will."

Forget everything you know about Kierkegaard. Either/or gives way to neither/nor in Thatcher and Patricia Porker's recently completed three-room summer sty. Both straw and sticks — traditional materials for fair-weather second homes — were passed over in favor of safe-and-sound, so-old-it's-new brick. Thatcher commissioned architect Richard Mire and charged him to take his time.

"We were in no hurry to move in," explains Patsy. "At the time we broke ground, it was the start of the social season. We had a full calendar of charity dances, sings, and plays to attend."

Mire's brick-by-brick patience paid off: the three-box shape instantly appeals, piquing and peaking our insatiable appetite for geometry. Toura-loura-lourostyle is the new way to say contemporary, and says it loud and clear: Porker place evokes classic Irish pig pens, with a Retro-Deco-Bauho-Nouveau-Neo-Colonio-Brutalist twist. In sum, a monument to upward immobility, built like a brick smokehouse. The reason's simple: why be mobile, when you're already there?

> SAFETY FIRST is guiding motto of Porker sty *(above)*, as even front and rear doors are of brick. "The world being what it is," states sensible Patsy, "you never know when some maniac is going to come after you."

> TRADITIONAL ELEGANCE meets fizzy, whizzy fun, as Colonial cues — brick façade, shuttered windows *(left)* — sit cheek-by-jowl with hybrid details — part Post-Modern office, part modern post office: security grates over windows, panic-bar exit hardware on doors *(right)*.

CUISINE SCENE: Let's Go, Meats!

Suddenly we're fed up with hunger. Nouvelle, New American, Nuovo Cucina: baby corn in pomegranate sauce is fine, but what's for dinner? Squibs of squab and dabs of crab may avoid the fill for a power lunch, when our appetite's for work, and self-advancement's our just dessert. But Man (and, need we add, Woman?) cannot live by career alone. Something's needed for the inner self, when the phones are silent, the markets have closed, and that noise you hear isn't our state-of-the-art printer spewing data, but our stomach growling in earnest for a true gut rehab.

Today's hottest chefs are, audaciously, getting back to basics — meat and potatoes, rice and beans, macaroni and cheese — but with a difference: yesterday's not-so-hot frankfurter is in the dog house, replaced by an exuberant range of daring, vital meat dishes, substantial enough to make you forget that last, fussy, unfilling goat-cheese-and-chervil omelet, tasty enough to make you want to.

We followed Wolf, a free-lance predator and full-time meat connoisseur, on a recent prowl. "I got a hunch I know where I can get some good eats," this carnivore of animals confided enigmatically as we met him one morning. "Stick around."

Further queries elicited specifics. Industry insiders had tipped

Wolf off to a source of fresh meat — pork, to be precise. We nodded, impressed. Foodies in the eighties are enjoying pork's peak: now's swine are leaner, healthier, better educated, more affluent, and more successful than their forebears. From roasts to chops, whether broiled or pan fried or, as Wolf prefers, eaten "on the foot," today's pork is today's meat for today's meals for today's way we live today.

First stop was a small one-room made of straw. Wolf's insouciant knock on the somewhat flimsy door brought no response.

"Open the door and let me in!" he cried, offering us a conspiratorial wink.

But the reply was, surprisingly, wittily concise. "Not by the hair on my chinny-chin-chin!"

"Then I'll huff, and I'll puff, and I'll blow your house in!"

("Can you do that?" we asked, dazzled by this low-tech, hot-air, blow-hard strategy for instant demolition.)

("No problem," Wolf said. "The guy gambles, his wife gets sick, a kid goes on drugs — one way or another, I got 'em.")

PUFF CREAMS simple straw home *(left)*, as Wolf sends walls, roof flying. Such easy-to-build, low-budget structures have problems with weather — and with the way of the wolves of the world, as well.

PORCINE PANIC ensues as Eduardo Pig and family *(below)* escape — barely — with their lives. "Maybe the pigs in the next house will help us," Eduardo says hopefully. *¡Buena suerte!*

Wolf was undeterred. "Plenty of opportunities around," he leered. Our next stop was a handsome, countryish sty made of sticks. We arrived just in time to see the Eduardo Pigs turned away from the door.

"But Wolf is coming," María pleaded through the stick door.

"We feel really terrible about this." We recognized the voice of Judith Sow-Swine. "But we simply can't let you in. It's just not possible."

After Eduardo had herded his family away, Wolf approached the stick house and called, "Open the door and let me in!"

This time the reply was by plucky David: "Not by the hair on my chinny-chin-chin!"

"Then I'll huff, and I'll puff, and I'll blow your house in!"

("But they're sticks," we said. "It looks much stronger than straw. Can you really do it?")

("Simple," came the knowing answer. "The guy's company's getting squeezed from Japan, Korea, you name it. They scale back, next day, boom. He's on the street. Think he'll find a job like this one again? Check out the economy in five years. Dude'll be lucky to manage a McDonald's. Plus, she's a teacher — they don't make squat. 'Nuff said.")

A SHATTERING EXPERIENCE describes explosion of sticks (*above*) as gust sends sty flying. Wolf's remark about "scaring up something to eat" proves literal!

RUNNING HELPS reduce fatty fat, makes for leaner pork products. David Swine, wife, and piglets (*right*) show how.

Wolf knew a shortcut to our next destination, a squat brick sty. Not sheepish, he wasted no time.

"Open the door and let me in!"

"Not," came the measured tones, through the brick door, of Thatcher Porker, Jr., "by the hair on my chinny-chin-chin."

"Then I'll huff, and I'll puff, and I'll blow your house in!"

"Do whatever you like," Porker replied. "I, meanwhile, shall call my lawyer, my accountant, my broker, my investment manager, my banker, my congressman, my senator, my president, and the police."

Wolf took a deep breath and blew a mighty gust at the home. It had no effect. He tried twice more, to no avail.

("Can't touch this guy," he muttered, leading us away from the front door. "But that's the eighties. The rich got richer and the poor got screwed. Check out the numbers. Meanwhile I'm starved. What's that . . . ?")

It sounded like pigs — many of them, running in fear. We pointed down the road, to where Eduardo and family, and the Swines, approached. They spotted Wolf and scurried to the Porker house door. Thatcher opened it a crack and peered, unmoved, at them.

"Let us in! The Wolf is here!"

"Don't be absurd," came the airy reply.

"But we have no place to go!" Eduardo called.

"I'm sorry. This is my home, not yours."

"But — you can talk to *me*!" David Swine's voice cracked in near hysteria. "I'm not like these pigs. I'm like *you*! I listen to operas by Porcini! I read poetry by Swineburne! I own a litho by David Hamhockney! Goddamn it, I went to college!"

"Then you should have worked harder, or saved more," Thatcher Porker, Jr., said. "Or perhaps you should have gone to a different school. Or studied something more lucrative or practical. Or perhaps you should have married more wisely. Then again, you might have been more talented in your chosen field of endeavor. Or been more ambitious. Or more ruthless and less sentimental. Or perhaps . . ." (we heard him give a small piggy laugh) ". . . perhaps you should have had the good sense to have been born me. *I* did." He shut the door.

"Bingo," Wolf said. "Come on."

"DRESSING" IS A BUTCHER'S EUPHEMISM for slaughter and cutting up. We can see why one's necessary. But as the process is one of removal, a modest suggestion: why not call it *un*dressing? When asked, Eduardo Pig (*above*) replies with his final words: "I don't know. Hey, man, how come we're always the ones who get eaten alive?"

GOOD TASTE assumes dual meaning as Wolf feasts on David Swine and Judith Sow-Swine (*left*) last. (We declined the meal, despite its tempting freshness.) Her last thoughts: "This isn't fair." His: "Damn it, this isn't supposed to happen to pigs like us."

12:00 P.M.

It was twelve noon.

Vale was surprised at how placid he was about the whole thing. Miller, the rich, the poor, the country, the world, the future: after spending all of the previous day writing and revising a piece about the three pigs, Vale felt, at least for now, neutralized and at rest. Waiting for Larry Mack's call, he seized from the coffee table the guide to Ulysses and began reading. But he couldn't concentrate. The telephone remained provokingly silent. He skimmed.

The index caught his eye. Much of it was the customary listing of names and brief topics with page numbers — "parodies or imitations in Oxen of the Sun episode, 290". But the listings under key characters were outlines, with rhythmic, mesmerizing lists of subheads in a combination poetry and prayer: "BLOOM, LEOPOLD: his alias, 19, 37 . . . his character, 31 . . . his liking for melons, 127, 138 . . . examines his hat, 37 . . . feeds his cat, 137 . . . visits the library, 20, 210–212 . . . visits the lying-in hospital, 20, 289. . . ." Well, that's interesting, Vale thought. He picked up a pad and pen, and was writing a few things down when the phone rang.

"Hello, Noah," Larry Mack said. He sighed, suffering — the slight discomfort he now felt had been foisted on him by Vale. "I read the script. And Carla and Dan Tony read it. And if you want to know my reaction, I thought, 'This is a good script.' "

Vale stopped writing notes and said, "Really?"

"Yes, really. But it's not the movie I want to make."

"Ah."

"So . . . you know . . . thank you very much . . . I think you're a talented writer . . . and I'm sorry I'm a little late calling you back."

Vale looked at his watch. "Larry, Jesus, it's a quarter to two." Where had the two hours gone? "You said noon."

"No I didn't," he countered, a man used to being wrongly accused and accustomed to patient explanations of his inno-

cence. "I said noon-ish. Ish. Ish means, approximately. It means, not exactly. You know that."

"Yeah, but two hours later?"

"Well, what can you do? Look, I'm a terrible person. You know? Let's face it, I feed you to Jack Dieffenbaker and then we won't make your movie. I'm a terrible person."

"I forgive you, Larry."

"Thanks. By the way: you didn't tell me you wrote that eighties piece for That Damn Magazine. The one, you know — a couple for the eighties, and so on. I liked that. This morning I was looking through the folder Amy sent, I saw it and I said, 'Oh, I remember that piece. I liked that.' "

Vale said, "Why were you looking in the folder?"

"I was putting it in the file."

"The circular file?"

"The circular file, you know, you're very intelligent. I shouldn't tell you this but they don't like you at the studio now. They say you're a bad writer."

Vale laughed. "You mean, I'll never work in that town again, unless they need me."

"That's exactly right. Did I tell you that Jack quit the studio? He fired the agency, he fired the studio, and he went back to San Francisco. What the hell, the money's better in advertising anyway."

"He fired what agency?"

"Your agency. CPM. I hope you didn't think you got this job just on the basis of your work. My God, didn't you know he was Gary Dave's client?"

"No."

"Listen, I'll tell you something. Strictly entre nous? I don't think he'll ever make a feature. Jack. I think he's afraid to." He didn't pause for more than a second. "Anyway, what are you going to do now?"

"I don't know," Vale said. "I want some big change. But I'm beginning to think that maybe I really don't want a big change."

"Take a vacation. . . ." There was a long silence. "Hello?"

"I'm here." Such a thing had never occurred to Vale. "A vacation?"

"Why not? God knows you earned it. I mean, you know — to the extent that all this bullshit we do is really work. But with what we paid you, you can afford to go somewhere for two weeks. There's your big change that's not a big change. Go to Italy. You'll love it. I wish I could go with you."

"What about the election?"

"Listen, don't ask me about that. I never vote. They're always such creeps. Get an absentee ballot, you can be the last one counted. Or wait until it's over. Look, you want to improve your life or worry about politics?"

"A vacation." Vale said, "That's a good idea." He added, "Then I could come back and see what's next."

"Of course. That's what vacations are for. Send me a postcard. Just don't make it too clever. I can't stand clever postcards when people are on vacation and I'm not."

"Thanks, Larry."

"Okay. Good luck."

Vale hung up, and five days later was in a plane bound for Rome. The three pigs piece was on its way to Harvey Kramer, who might very well buy it, since Vale really liked this one this time. As for Vale himself, he was flying east — into the sunrise, toward a new day, and a new life, or at least a new time zone, at least for a couple weeks.

Decade of the Year

Now. In time for the eighties: a love story for the eighties starring a hero for the eighties and a sex symbol for the eighties in what just might be the first great American motion picture of the eighties.

He's a man for the eighties. She's a woman for the eighties. He drives a car for the eighties he bought with the profits accrued from an investment strategy for the eighties. She has the attitude, the career, and the two kids of a woman of the eighties — because she's a woman, and it's the eighties.

In their teens they experienced the sixties. In their twenties they made it in the seventies. And now they're in their thirties, because their thirties is their age for the eighties.

She's been a ten since her twenties. He's shot golf in the nineties since the sixties. Together they're to Jackson-Matthau in the seventies what Hepburn-Tracy were in the forties to Rogers-Astaire in the thirties — in the eighties. They're too young to remember the fifties but not too old to fall in love, commit murder, and break all the rules of life in the eighties.

He's surviving his own life as he lives it in the eighties, because he's a survivor. She's coping with living life as life is lived in the eighties, because she's a coper. Together they know that life in the eighties is nothing like what it was before the eighties — and the two of them are living it together in the eighties, because together they're a couple of livers.

Her hair color? A hair color for the eighties. And when she needs to get dressed, she wears the dressy sportswear specially created for life in the eighties. Sure, sometimes he gets a lousy headache. And when he wants fast relief from the tensions, pressures, and lousy headaches of living life in the eighties, he fights back with a one-man display of martial-arts fury designed for life in the fast, tense eighties. Not life in the less tense seventies. Not life in the even tenser nineties. Life *now*.

She's a Juliet for the eighties. (Her father, now in his eighties, was born in the nineties, and made millions in the twenties.) He's a Romeo for the eighties. (His mother, born in the twenties, died in the sixties — and left him thousands in fifties and hundreds.) Together they're Napoleon and Josephine for the eighties, in a motion picture for the eighties made by people mostly in their forties.

It's a film about their life — and our life — brought to life as only this director can bring it: a man *Time* has called "a Mike Nichols for the nineties" and *Newsweek* hails as "the Ashby–the Lester (the Wilder–the Cukor, 'the Lubitsch of the forties,' of the fifties — of the sixties) of the seventies — of the eighties."

It's a story for the eighties, about the eighties, in a film you will never forget until the nineties. Two people, born in the fifties and now in their thirties, finding life in the eighties as only they can find it. Now.

Coming next year.

Index

In the following revised index to *Thinthink: Let Mental Weight Loss Strip Your Mind to Its Bare Excellentials!*, page numbers are not accurate, nor does an entry's presence in the index necessarily correspond to its treatment or presence in the text. All quotations of Edward Abbott are excerpted from correspondence between Edward Abbott and Ilene Coltello. All quotations of Arthur Barger are transcribed, from memory, from conversations between Arthur Barger and Ilene Coltello, except where otherwise noted. All quotations of Ilene Coltello are transcribed, from memory, from conversations with her cat. The following abbreviations are used:

RAS   *Reductio Ad Superbum: The Doctor's Personality-Reduction Technique for Personal Maximization*, by Edward Abbott, Ph.D. (Springfield, MA.: Mapledale Press, 1985)

Th   *Thinthink: Let Mental Weight Loss Strip Your Mind to Its Bare*

Excellentials!, by Arthur Barger (New York: J. T. Cartwell Publishers, 1987)

OA   *Order, Alphabetical: Life, Times of an Indexer*, by Ilene Coltello (unpub.)

Abbott, Edward: training of (B.S., Boston Univ.; M.S., Boston Univ.; Ph.D. Psych., New York Univ.), 3; academic career of (Asst. Prof. Psych., Carnegie Tech., 1975–1979; Assoc. Prof. Psych., Carlsbad College, 1979–1982; Prof. Psych., Carlsberg Community College, 1982–1984), 4; professional frustration of ("The bitter truth is, [my love], that I entered the field of psychology just as all of America was leaving it. As my interest in personality structures and self-realization grew, the public's shifted to celebrities, elitism, and money."), 7

Academia: Abbott leaves, to write RAS, 12

Advance: Abbott uses all of, plus savings, while writing RAS, 13; Abbott requests additional, from publisher, predicting huge popular success of RAS, 16; Abbott denied further, by publisher, 21

Agent: Abbott takes job as editor at J. T. Cartwell during year's hiatus before publication of RAS, on advice of his, 22

Aggressive advertising campaign: Abbott blames poor sales of RAS on "incompetent" reviews and Mapledale's lack of an, 65; Abbott's efforts at providing, on talk shows, at book conventions, on radio call-in shows, in demeaning appearances at bookstores in malls, etc., 144

Alcohol: remaindering of RAS, and lack of paperback sale, as highlights of a year during which Abbott "cultivate[s] a taste for," 155

Art: indexing, to Ilene Coltello, after a twenty-two-year career as an indexer begun immediately after graduation from Saint Agnes's College, as an, 376

Assignment: Abbott's, to be editor of Th, 37; Abbott's, brings him into contact with Arthur Barger, 80; Abbott's, resulting in impressions of Barger and suspicions re Th, 166; Abbott's, which he refuses ("I told my fool of a boss, Davidson, that *Thinthink* was a patent theft of my own work, and I would have nothing to do with either the book, or the oaf who 'wrote' it."), 83; Abbott's, as insisted on by his employer, 188

Association: Abbott's, with Ilene Coltello, as ostensibly professional, i.e., an editor employing a free-lance indexer, 311

Attitude, Edward Abbott's: stubborn, re RAS ("A serious work of both

ment for so much as a cup of tea, 267; Edward Abbott's, to promote publication of OA, 499; Edward Abbott's, as lover, friend, gentleman, man, human being, 317

Firenze, Ristorante: Abbott and unknown brunette, described as being young enough to be his daughter, seen, by friend of Ilene Coltello, dining at, 86

Four Seasons, The: Abbott and unknown brunette, confirmed as being young enough to be his daughter, seen, by Ilene Coltello, lunching at, 666

Français, La: Abbott and unknown young brunette observed by Ilene Coltello, laughing in window of, 388

Franco's Pizza and Heroes: Abbott and unknown college-age brunette watched by Ilene Coltello, walking from apartment building to Sutton Place Theatre, viewing movie, then strolling arm-in-arm past, 348

Fyne-Tayst Deli, The: Abbott and unknown brunette teenager caught, by Ilene Coltello, receiving in doorway of unknown brunette's apartment, bagged midnight snack of sandwiches and drinks delivered from, 136

Galleys: of Th, including first version of index, impatience of Abbott to have Ilene Coltello sign off on, to permit next stage of publication ("I may have said any number of foolish things that evening, Ilene. Heaven knows I often do. But I had had a few at dinner — as had you. I simply can't be held responsible for everything I say — *or that is claimed I said* — when under the influence. I can't and I won't. Surely you know you have my utmost respect as an indexer, and as a lady. Now be a good girl and sign off on the galleys. We can't proceed with production without your signature. Cordially," etc.), 877 (*see also* Excerpt)

Hatred: Abbott's, of Barger, for his plagiarism of RAS, 663; Abbott's, of Ilene Coltello, apparently, as manifested by his cruel and abusive actions, 421; Barger's, of Abbott, Ilene Coltello, and anyone else less crass and vulgar than he, 956; Ilene Coltello's, of Abbott, for betrayal of her, 551; Ilene Coltello's, of herself, for her betrayal of indexing, 15 (INDEXER QUERY: IS PROPER USAGE "HATRED FOR"? IS THERE SUBSTANTIVE DIFFERENCE BETWEEN "HATRED" AND "HATE"?)

Humiliation: Abbott's, of Ilene Coltello ("Really, Ilene, so you let me

Maid, you pathetic old: refusal of Barger as consisting of vulgarisms, threats, and the characterization, 27 (*see also* Make)

Make: amends, as promised by Ilene Coltello, by explaining, over dinner, her collusion with Abbott to subvert Barger's book by sabotaging its Index, xxvi; roast beef, as promised by Ilene Coltello, for dinner, 26 (*see also* Malaprop, Mrs.)

Malaprop, Mrs.: Barger's wary, taunting acceptance of invitation ("What for? So you can go to bed with a clear consciousness?") as suggesting he is descended from, 25 (*see also* Manuscript)

Manuscript: visit by Edward Abbott to Ilene Coltello's apartment late one afternoon, at her urgent request to discuss Barger's, 24 (*see also* Mary, Bloody)

Mary, Bloody: Abbott's acceptance, during discussion of his refusal to assist Ilene Coltello in publishing OA, of a very strong, 23 (*see also* Mary, Bloody, another)

Mary, Bloody, another: Abbott's acceptance, during his rebuking of Ilene Coltello for supposing he could ever actually love her, of, 22 (*see also* Mary, Queen of Scots)

Mary, Queen of Scots: Abbott's inability, due to his state of inebriation by end of discussion, to distinguish between Mary Tyler Moore and, 21 (*see also* Matador)

Matador: slaying of Abbott with kitchen knife, by Ilene Coltello, as resembling actions and gestures of a, 20 (*see also* Mazurka)

Mazurka: appropriation of Abbott's keys from his trouser pocket necessitating the manipulation of his lifeless body as though he and Ilene Coltello were engaged, on the kitchen floor, in a horizontal, 19 (*see also* Meat store, gourmet)

Meat store, gourmet: disjointure, utilizing electric carving knife, of various component parts of Abbott's body, and their storage in series of waterproof cartons apportioned alphabetically (Arm; Foot; Head; Legs; etc.), performed with a neatness and dispatch worthy of a, 18 (*see also* Meeting)

Meeting: arrival that evening at Ilene Coltello's apartment of Arthur Barger for scheduled dinner, 17 (*see also* Menu)

Menu: presentation by Ilene Coltello of roast beef as main course of dinner (in response to Barger's gruff, "What's on the . . . ?"), 16 (*see also* Mephistopheles)

Mephistopheles: Abbott compared to, by Ilene Coltello, xv; confusion by Barger as to identity of ("I thought that was some form of mosquito"), 15 (*see also* Merv Griffin)

tion of cartons, by Ilene Coltello, after Barger's departure, 3 (*see also* Multitude)

Multitude: assembly of curious, outside apartment building, after arrival of police summoned by Ilene Coltello's report of "discovery" of dismembered body, 2 (*see also* Mumble)

Mumble: reply in form of, by Ilene Coltello, to police query re any known enemies of Edward Abbott ("Yes, one. *See* Barger, Arthur."), 1 (*see also* Murder)

Murder: (*See* Machiavelli, Niccolo)

New York Daily News: Headline in, as most concise announcement of Arthur Barger's arrest ("NAB HIT SCRIBE IN EDITOR AXE KILL"), 886

New York Post: Headline in, as most lurid announcement of Barger's indictment ("CASE OF THE HACKING HACK? SELF-HELP GURU 'HATED' CHOP VICTIM"), 377

New York Times: Headline in, as most restrained announcement of Barger's trial ("ON PUBLISHERS' ROW, A WHIFF OF SCANDAL ALLEGATIONS OF PLAGIARISM MARK OPENING OF BARGER TRIAL"), 854

Oath: testimony by Ilene Coltello given under, 776 (*See* Perjury)

Order, Alphabetical: Life, Times of an Indexer: merit of, as privileged glimpse into the fascinating and little-known world of indexing ("Accused I have been of missing themes or meanings of a book by focussing too narrowly on indexable categories — e.g., listing 'Foot,' 'Hide,' 'Trunk,' 'Tusk'; not listing 'Elephant.' To this charge, my plea? Guilty — with cause.") *See* indexers as jewelers — repairers, of watches — so intent on intricacies of mechanism they are oblivious of time of day. Only after painstaking dismantling, arranging of details, can we, I, pull back — *See* Forest, for the Trees; note Ramifications — of Overall Work, of index, of my actions. (Otherwise — how could indexing be?) (*see also* that it is even, perhaps, the indexer's job to ignore general meaning; subvert synthesis. Proper concerns, these are, of the contents tabler. The indexer 'deconstructs' the table of contents.) (*see also* this metaphor: a book as a personality, individual. Table of contents = childhood (basic categories established, implicit promise of their upcoming elaboration). Text itself = adulthood (specificity of content, realization and 'playing out' of potential). Index = se-